ACCLAIM FOR

High Stakes

"This is a well thought-out, layered historical, with evocative and vivid descriptions of life in the thriving, yet still lawless, nineteenth century Canadian town. *High Stakes* is a historical that can be enjoyed by both male and female readers ... a thoroughly enjoyable story and an incredibly accomplished first novel."

—*Jill MacKenzie, InD'Tale Magazine*

"The author does a number of things well in his debut novel ... an excellent job of capturing a time (1877), place, and society largely overlooked in the western genre ... The author also blends elements from several subgenres extremely well. The novel meets all the qualifications to bear the label "western historical romance" quite well ... (Men, by the way, can read this one without endangering their man cards. Did I mention the gunfights, knife fights, and fistfights?) ... *High Stakes* is a quick read. And it's fun. The ending, balanced on a thin line between expectation and surprise, shines."

—*Kathleen Rice Adams, Texan, voracious reader, professional journalist*

" ... a great writing style and an excellent plot ... For readers captivated by this turbulent period and allured by a story that tugs at the heartstrings, *High Stakes* is a must-read."

—*Norman K. Archer, Victoria, BC Historian*

High Stakes, in its first edition, made the finals for two distinct awards: Best First Western Novel of 2012 in the Western Fictioneers Peacemaker Awards, and again in the American Historical category of the 2014 RONE Awards

Publisher's Note: This is a work of fiction. Names, characters, places, and incidents are either a product of the author's imagination or are used fictitiously. Locales and public names are sometimes used for atmospheric purposes. Any resemblance to actual people, living or dead, or to businesses, companies, events, institutions, or locales is completely coincidental.

HIGH STAKES

Copyright © 2012 by **Chad Strong**

All Rights Reserved. Except as permitted under the U.S. Copyright Act of 1976, no part of this publication may be reproduced, distributed, or transmitted in any form or by any means, or stored in a database or retrieval system, without prior written permission of the publisher.

HunterCat Publishing
Ontario, Canada
www.chadstrongswriting.weebly.com

Musa Publishing Edition / May 2012
HunterCat Publishing Edition / February 2016
First Paperback Edition / February 2016
ISBN 978-0-9947350-0-3

Cover Art and Logo by Charlene Raddon of Cover-Ops:
www.cover-ops.blogspot.com
Playing Cards Section Break designed by Coreen Montagna
Book Layout © 2014 BookDesignTemplates.com

High Stakes

Chad Strong

For Cowboy Don
— Happy Trails!

Chad Strong
August 29, 2017

HunterCat Publishing

Ontario, Canada

Warning

This book contains adult language and scenes. This story is meant only for adults as defined by the laws of the country where you made your purchase. Store your books carefully where they cannot be accessed by younger readers.

This book is dedicated to my family, especially my wife, Christine, who jumped the broom with me undaunted by their cautions of the patience and fortitude required to live with a writer.

Thanks, Mom, for typing all my manuscripts in the early years. To you and Christine, both avid readers that you are, your feedback over the years has been invaluable.

And a special thank you to the folks at Musa Publishing who saw something worthy in High Stakes and worked with me to create a first edition to be proud of, and who stepped forward with assistance even after the closing of Musa's doors.

CHAPTER ONE

Curt Prescott led his horse down the worn, wooden gangplank and onto solid ground. The government docks at the foot of Wharf Street were bustling with merchants, seamen, laborers, and livestock. The late afternoon sun warmed the mud banks, infusing the air with the pungent odors of rotting seaweed and animal manure. Seagulls squawked raucously. Reeling above the harbor, they never tired of swooping to the ground to snatch whatever appeared edible, inevitably quarreling with each other over the tidbit.

Curt's gelding tossed his head and stamped a hoof. Curt stroked the buckskin's golden neck beneath his black mane. "Okay, Ace. I know you're as glad to be home as I am." He scanned the crowded area for a clear spot to stop and mount.

"Get on there, you!"

Curt spun toward the voice, for a split second thinking he was being given hell for holding someone up. But the herdsman's shout had been directed at a recalcitrant ox that was trying to avoid being loaded onto a small barge.

Locating a clear spot over by a stack of oak barrels, Curt tightened the cinch of his stock saddle — no little sissy pancake English saddle for him — and swung up. He rode up the dirt ramp that led to street level and turned northward along Wharf Street.

The waterfront had changed a lot since he'd been a boy scrounging for lost coins or bits of gold under the rickety stoops of ramshackle saloons. Since the gold rush of 1858, most of those old shacks had been gradually replaced by two- and three-story brick and stone buildings, many enhanced with decorative wrought iron detail.

The city of Victoria had come a long way from her roots as a Hudson's Bay Company trading post. Having weathered the growing pains of the Fraser River gold rush and its aftermath, she was now the largest settlement north of San Francisco and the capital city of the new province of British Columbia.

Curt rode along the street at a walk, reabsorbing the essences of home. Victoria, named in honor of the Queen, claimed to be "more British than the British," but nonetheless, it had seen a large influx of Americans, particularly during the gold rush years, and the fact was reflected in her architecture. The American-style streets with their long strips of side-by-side exposed storefronts could belong in any west coast town Curt had visited south of the border. But he had to admit, he thought the British colonial elements lent a quaintness and gentility to Victoria's streets that made them unique.

Now twenty-three years old, Curt had been born in the States himself, somewhere in the Washington Territory, though he had no recollection of his childhood before Victoria. When rumors of gold began, his mother had bought passage to Vancouver Island for herself and her only child in return for her favors to a gold seeker. Less than two weeks after arriving on the island, the gold seeker was gone, and Lillian Prescott was left to fend for herself and her young son in the muddy streets of their new city.

Curt often wondered if he had inherited his wanderlust from Lillian. For the last three years, he hadn't been able to resist the lure of the circuit of annual spring poker tournaments from Seattle to San Francisco. Yet, as driven as he felt each year to go, he was just as eager to return home once the last hand had been played. Victoria would always be home.

He turned right up Yates Street and rode the block to Government, the main street through town, but pulled to a startled halt at the crowded intersection. A parade of women marching southward blocked his crossing.

Two banners were strung across their ranks. The foremost one read: "Cast Out All Tarnished Doves and Gamblers!" The second one demanded: "Close Down All Dens of Iniquity!" The group of at least fifty women chanted the banners' words repeatedly. Some of their faces were familiar to Curt, but he had never seen their leader before. She was middle-aged, plump, and carried herself with a confidence the others lacked. They paused, filling the intersection like a herd of milling sheep, and shouted their demands at the Carlton Saloon, which occupied the entire northwest corner of Government and Yates and happened to be the saloon over which Curt kept a suite.

"What the hell?" Curt asked out loud. Were they targeting just the Carlton or each saloon in turn? The Carlton Saloon and Dance Hall was one of the better establishments in town. It was in no way one of the seedy places that Curt could see them wanting shut down.

One of the bouncers came out the front door and politely asked the women to move on. They ignored him and chanted even louder. He shouted his request over top of their voices, but they refused to budge or be silent.

So much for a peaceful homecoming, Curt thought. He reined his horse close to the boardwalk, trying to get by them. A bonneted young woman raised her frantic eyes to his and pointed directly at him.

"Cast out all devil-worshiping gamblers!" she cried.

How she could spot him as such, he questioned, dressed as he was in his travelling clothes and a reliable brown oilskin jacket and hat. He deliberately 'dressed down' for the road, both for comfort and serviceability as well as for safety from the unwanted attentions of highwaymen.

He tipped his hat to her. "I swear, miss, I've never worshiped the devil."

"Then, young man, he has you fooled, hasn't he?"

Curt had no reply to that. He tried to ride past her, but she stepped in front of his horse at every attempt.

"Excuse me, miss, but this is a public road."

She flung out her arms, startling Ace into throwing his head and trying to get away from her. She screeched again and again: "Cast out all devil-worshiping gamblers! Cast out all devil-worshiping gamblers!"

Her cries brought the attention of the whole group to her and Curt. They converged toward him like a mass of madwomen.

"Jesus!" Curt muttered and, instead of holding Ace in, let him spin and canter away, back toward the Inner Harbor. On reaching Wharf Street, Curt halted and looked over his shoulder. The women had not pursued him but were cheering themselves at having driven him off.

Raising his eyes to the clear blue sky, Curt said to the horse, "Well, I guess it's a nice evening for a ride in the country, Ace." Hopefully, by the time he'd taken a ride, the women would have moved on.

He reined northward and swung east along Johnson to skirt Chinatown, crossed Government above his former destination, and struck northward again on Douglas. Just beyond the city limits, the road passed through a high meadow of Garry oak trees. The site was home to a long-abandoned, whitewashed church which, only a few months before, had been in serious disrepair. Both the church and its cemetery on the opposite side of the road appeared to have received considerable attention since Curt had been gone. The church's roof no longer sagged, and the old moss-covered shingles had been replaced with new cedar shakes. A new sign declared the building "The Garry Oak Church of the People" and welcomed everyone to worship services and Sunday school with Pastor Richard Andrews. Curt couldn't recall what it had been named before. Most folks simply referred to it as the pauper's church, where the poor and unwanted were buried far from their polite society neighbors. The clapboard had a fresh coat of white paint, as did the little picket fence around the cemetery. The tangles of weeds and scrub had been cleared away, giving the place an open, approachable, feel. Curt could even see the low marker of the place where his mother had been laid to rest. The tall forest of cedars and Douglas fir surrounded the site with a sense of protectiveness.

Curt came to a halt in the deepening twilight. Mist was beginning to form in the open areas. It was late May, and the nights could still be cool. Despite the chill, Curt loved the mist, the way it cloaked him, made him feel safe. He drew a long, deep breath of the sweetly scented air. Scotch broom dotted the clearing along the road, and there was just enough light left for him to make out the deep yellow flowers sprinkled amongst the spiky, green stems.

The horse fidgeted.

"All right, Ace. Let's go." Beyond the edge of the forest, to the east of the churchyard, was a pathway, hidden at the bottom of the ravine. It would be dark soon, but Curt felt a pull to ride along it. He nudged the horse forward across the clearing and into the woods then down the gentle slope at a walk.

A creek gurgled at the bottom of the ravine, half-hidden from the top of the slope by tangles of blackberry brambles and bracken ferns. Once down on the path that followed its course, however, Curt was always impressed with a feeling of humility, of being not only dwarfed, but guarded and protected by the great trees that rose up and arched over the creek with their massive limbs. Long strands of grey-green witch's hair moss hung from the lower branches, and sword ferns colonized the brown earth beneath. It was almost completely dark in the shadows of the ravine, though enough light passed through the trees to show Curt his familiar path, to sparkle on the creek and shine on the wet rocks.

The path led him back to town, bringing him up on Johnson just east of Douglas. He took the roads the rest of the way to the livery stable on View Street, only a couple of blocks from the Carlton.

A lamp glowed above the big double doors of the livery stable, just bright enough for a man to see his way to the latch — or to be seen opening it. He let himself in, lit a lamp, and began to unsaddle his horse.

A few moments later, he heard booted feet trying to sneak quietly down the stairs along the outside wall. Then a shadow appeared in the doorway beneath the lamplight, the slim silhouette of a shotgun jutting out from a tall male body.

"Who's there? I got a gun, so best you mind."

Curt didn't even bother reaching for the Colt .45 strapped to his hip. But the fleeting thought reminded him that he was now back in Canada and that he had best remove the weapon before walking onto the city streets. "Hiya, Phil. It's me."

"Oh, young Mr. Prescott. How you doin'?" The muzzle of the shotgun dropped and the long, bowed legs shuffled towards him and into his light, revealing a middle-aged Negro in nothing but long underwear and untied, flopping boots. His back was stooped from too many years spent bent over a shovel.

"Just fine, Phil." Curt hoisted the saddle onto the nearest empty rack. "Expecting a horse thief?"

"Well, it's gettin' a tad late. Cain't be too careful."

"No, I suppose you can't."

"If'n I'd'a knowed it was you, I wouldn'a brought the gun."

"How's the missus and your boy?"

"Just fine, thank you." Phil leaned the shotgun in a corner and reached for Ace's bridle. "Here, lemme do that. You musta had a long trip."

"I sure did." Curt surrendered the reins. Unbuckling his holster, he stuffed his firearm into one of his saddlebags and slung them over his shoulder. In a pinch, he always had his concealed derringer and his boot knife. "Thanks, Phil," he said and started toward the door.

"My pleasure, Mr. Prescott. You have yerself a good evenin', now."

"You, too, Phil."

He paused barely a moment, just enough to cast a glance beyond the door, then stepped out into the night.

Walking westward toward Government Street, he noticed the clapboard building several doors down and across the street from the livery. It had been empty when he'd left a few months ago, but now it appeared to be in use as a saddlery. Things had certainly moved along while he'd been gone this year. When he reached the start of the boardwalk, he climbed the steps, and his boots were startlingly loud on the hard wood. This end of town was dead quiet at this time of night, but his senses were on guard just the same.

The Carlton Saloon and Dance Hall seemed to light the entire corner of the intersection by itself. Lamps blazed from the windows, and music from a decent orchestra rolled out through the open batwing doors. A few yards from the saloon, Curt halted while some drunk staggered out the doors and pitched face-first into the street. The fellow clambered to his feet and stumbled off, disappearing into the mist.

Curt took one step forward and halted again as another man emerged from the saloon. This one walked awkwardly as well, but that was because the shoulders of his coat were bunched up in the hands of Willie, the Carlton's owner and chief bartender.

"I asked ya nicely, preacher. Now I'm tellin' ya — stay outta my saloon! You ain't wanted here!"

"But, Mr. —." The preacher tried to turn around to face Willie, but his foot slipped off the edge of the front step, and he fell. Willie just let him go.

The preacher crumpled on the muddy street while men and dance hall girls pointed at him and laughed. Willie stared at him until he sat up and gingerly got to his feet. Then the bartender turned and marched back into his saloon.

The stocky preacher bent slowly and picked up his hat. He brushed the muck off it before replacing it on his grey head.

One of the men yelled, "Go on, get outta here!"

"Yeah!" added the girl on his arm. "We ain't buyin' what you're sellin'! But hey — if you wanna buy what we're sellin', now that's different!"

A fresh chorus of laughter rose above the music. The preacher gazed up at them, stiff with his pain, but said nothing.

Curt strode forward then, having waited long enough. "Show's over, gang." He cast a glance at the preacher, who met his eyes for a second before Curt angled for the door. The group's guffaws dropped to giggles, and one of them muttered to his buddy, "That's Curt Prescott. I told you about him." And the crowd moved back to let him pass.

Curt stepped over the threshold and scanned the room with his eyes. Though modest by big city standards, the Carlton was, in Curt's opinion, the best saloon in Victoria. It served good liquor, presented decent entertainment, and, tucked discreetly into a back room, offered all the games of chance a man could ask for: poker, faro, roulette, monte, dice, hazard, chuck-a-luck, and billiards. Even on a weeknight, most of the games were engaged with men who didn't care how poor their chances were of beating the house.

Curt strode directly to the bar though his eyes roved the room attentively. To his right, a dozen round dining tables were all in use by men, some with female companions supplied by the establishment. Beyond them was a small dance floor, sprinkled with sawdust and dotted with couples. Ensconced in an alcove centered before a raised stage, a small orchestra struck up a new tune.

Right on cue, a young blonde woman strode gracefully out onto the stage from the left wing. She wore a low-cut, off-the-shoulder dress of rich emerald satin. Every head turned to watch her, every hand laid down its cards. The raucous laughter, the clack of the roulette wheel, the roll of billiard balls — all stopped.

A big, open smile on her face, the woman known only as Delores spread her arms as if to embrace them all. Curt watched her through the haze of cigar and cigarette smoke as he moved toward the bar. She saw him and blew him a kiss. The other men turned their faces to follow the airborne caress. They did not appear surprised to see Curt Prescott on the receiving end.

She began to sing, and their faces returned to her voluptuous form. She had a legitimate voice, rich, smooth, and strong. Curt believed that, with the proper training, she could belong on the big stages of San Francisco, St. Louis, Toronto, and even New York. He had even offered to finance her venture, but she wouldn't go because he could never stay long in a big city. So here she remained, belting out bawdy lyrics to miners and lumberjacks in what places like New York would consider a common, small town saloon.

She leaned over the stage and, like a single animal, the men sucked in their breath and stared, hoping beyond hope that her ample breasts would spill forth from her stiff bodice. She straightened without mishap, pivoted, and wiggled her fanny at them, provoking a chorus of shouts and whistles. She finished her song, blew them a kiss, and glided off-stage. The entire house clapped, cheered, and whistled for several minutes before returning to their games.

From behind the bar, Willie approached Curt, a frothing mug of beer in his hand. He was short, thickset, and bald, save for a fringe of white hair from ear to ear. When he smiled, his ruddy cheeks popped out like two little crab apples. He set the full mug before Curt, who slid a coin over the polished bar top to him.

"Thanks, Willie."

"Glad you're back. God, I swear Del gets worse every time you go."

Curt's eyes flicked to the now empty stage, and an amused smile quirked his mouth before he lifted his beer to take a sip. "You can handle her."

"Me, yeah. But the girls are wearing pretty thin. She really gets wicked with them."

Willie Carlton was an ex-ship's cook who, despite his stature and one bad hip, could handle any sort of fracas man or woman cared to test him with. With only the barest education, he'd had the savvy to save his wages instead of blowing them on liquor and sport and then turned around and bought himself a saloon from which to sell the liquor and sport to others. Willie ran a tight ship — he took no guff from any man. Policing his own house the way he did, he was rarely raided by the city police, and if he was, he was always discreetly warned ahead of time. The games room would be shut down, locked up, and presented as a storage room for the inspection. The Carlton Saloon and Dance Hall passed every inspection and was noted as providing excellent fare and entertainment for local men and visitors alike.

Curt had never thought the name 'Willie' suited Carlton — William or even Bill Carlton would have been better. But somewhere the man had been tagged 'Willie,' and it had stuck.

Curt hadn't responded to the bartender's last statement, and a few seconds later, Willie drifted away. Curt sipped his beer through the froth, casting his eyes in habitual sweeps over the room, now and then focusing on the door when movement there caught his eye. At night, the large-paned windows along the front of the building reflected the interior and acted as a shield for those on the outside. Curt found a familiar comfort in the walnut wainscoting and the golden yellow upper walls. He dwelt on them briefly before turning his attention to the naughty positions of the naked women in the large painting behind the bar.

As he took another swallow of beer, Del rounded the corner of the bar to his left. She walked straight to him, a huge smile on her face. A young waitress darted out of her path, nearly spilling the drinks on her tray. Del's amber eyes glistened as she met Curt's, and she held out her arms to him.

"Curt, my lover, you're home!"

He enveloped her in a tight, warm hug, feeling her bosom press against his chest. She nestled her face into his shoulder.

"Curt, my Curt." She lifted her mouth to his firm, lingering kiss. "God, I missed you!" she cried as they drew back a bit. "Why do you gotta stay away so long?"

He eyed her without speaking while she stared up at his face. She ran her hands through his dark hair and sighed. "I know," she said, answering her own question. "I just hate it when you go."

As much as he loved her and understood how she needed him always close to her, her very neediness often strangled Curt. But he'd had his getaway and come back refreshed. "I won't be going anywhere for quite a while now."

She smiled, showing even teeth only slightly yellowed. "Good." She tipped her head back coquettishly. "So?"

He snaked his hand into one pouch of the saddlebags he'd set on the bar next to him and pulled out a thick fold of large denomination bills fastened with a silver clip. "And there's more tucked away safe."

Her amber eyes widened. He peeled out one hundred dollars and gave it to her. As always, she was delighted. She never seemed to get used to his gifts.

"Thank you, lover." She kissed the corner of his mouth and tucked the money snugly in her cleavage.

He watched it disappear between her silken swells and felt his loins stir.

"Anything else for me?" She batted her eyelashes at him and smiled demurely.

"Of course." He removed a small package from the same pouch and handed it to her.

Eagerly, she unwrapped the brown paper that hid it from her. She sucked in her breath when she saw it.

"Is it the one you wanted?" he asked.

"Yes! Oh, yes!" She held it up so it caught the light. It was a silver tussie-mussie in the shape of a cornucopia, with tiny dried flowers spilling from the mouth of it.

"Here, let me ..." He took it from her and deftly pinned it to her bodice. "When are you free?"

"Right now." She took his hand and started to lead him from the bar, but he held back.

"Just a second — I'm still thirsty." He picked up his mug to finish off his beer.

"Is that all you're thirsty for?" she asked. She took his beer from him with both hands and chugged down the remaining portion for him. Then she took his hand and led him up the crimson-carpeted staircase.

The entrance to their suite was a short distance down the hall, the first door on the left. Curt opened it with his key and locked it behind him once they'd entered.

It was dark, save for one wall lamp glowing softly in the doorway between the sitting room and the bedroom. He hooked his hat on the rack in the corner and retrieved his gun and holster from his saddlebags before following Del into the bedroom. He slung his gun belt over the bedpost and then turned his full attention to her.

She was eager for him and began undressing him with trembling hands. He removed his concealed weapons and placed them on top of his nightstand then spun her around and swiftly undid the fabric-covered buttons at the back of her dress. As the garment fell from her, she gasped and caught at the tussie-mussie, unpinned it and placed it on top of the bureau by the window.

He took both her hands in his and placed a kiss in each palm. She shivered, and he began to strip her of her lacy underclothes. She clung to him, holding on to his belt for support as he kissed her wherever he uncovered her flesh. With each kiss he inhaled the familiar scent of her, with each caress he found the places on her body that had always fascinated him. His arousal became more fierce as he allowed himself to revel in the sensations she stirred in him, and fleetingly he wondered why he ever felt the need for time away from this intoxicating woman.

"Three months," she gasped, "I've been waiting for you to touch me again. Don't make me wait even longer."

In seconds, he was out of his trousers, backing her towards the bed, and covering her with his lean, sinewy body.

Curt awoke when a stiff breeze blew in through the half-open window and pushed Del's tussie-mussie off the nightstand. It hit the floor with a clack. He eyed it momentarily then decided to get up. Judging by the brightness of the room, it had to be mid-morning.

Carefully, so as not to disturb her, he slipped out of bed and retrieved the tussie-mussie. It was undamaged. He walked past the alcove where their bathtub stood and placed it on her cream-colored dressing table. After pulling on his short underwear, he grabbed a chair from next to his bureau and set it down in front of the window.

Theirs was a corner suite, and this particular window faced south, giving him a good view of Yates and Government. A pair of etched glass doors opened off the east wall of the bedroom onto a railed balcony overlooking Government.

They had forgotten to close the velvet curtains last night. The bedroom was spacious and bright. In keeping with the rest of the suite, the lower thirds of the walls were covered in pure white wainscoting, the upper two-thirds painted in deep, natural colors. Curt's armchair and footstool and Del's chaise longue were upholstered in rich green velvet. A fireplace dominated the wall between the sitting room and the bedroom with a hearth opening on each side.

The floor beneath Curt's bare feet was cool, like the breeze lifting the sheers across the window. Familiar sounds of the city street below drifted in as well, along with an odd sound Curt couldn't quite place. He thought he heard chanting. He nearly dismissed it as a trick of the wind, but it steadily grew louder. He got to his feet, pulled on his trousers, and went out the doors to the balcony. He leaned over the railing to get a closer look. Below him, on the street, appeared the group of women from last night. Startled, he watched them a moment.

What the hell was going on?

As they passed out of view, he spun round and strode back into the bedroom, about to wake Del to ask her if she knew anything at all about the group. But she was sleeping so peacefully, he decided to let her be.

He made quick use of the water closet down the hall then washed and shaved at the basin in the alcove. The Carlton had been among the first to install indoor plumbing once water began to be pumped from Elk Lake a few years ago. Del awoke as he was patting his face dry. Stretching, she dragged herself from the comfort of the bed. She crossed the floor completely naked and kissed him good morning.

Hooking his hands around her hips, he asked, "Know anything about a group of women marching in the street?"

Her eyes flickered in surprise that he already knew. "Yeah. That's been goin' on about a month now." She brushed a strand of her flaxen hair off her face then laid her hand upon his chest and patted his crisp curls of dark hair. "Lemme get a cup o' coffee or two in me, and I'll tell you all about it."

CHAPTER TWO

After they'd both dressed, he took her to Earl's English Cafe, their favorite restaurant, only a couple of blocks from the Carlton.

Earl Stanbury himself greeted them as they walked through the door. A tiny, frail-looking man, he wore his black hair parted exactly down the center and greased back flat against his skull. Below his pinched nose, his mustache, too, was parted, combed, waxed, and tightly coiled.

"Ah, Mr. Prescott, Miss Delores! Your favorite table as usual." He ushered them to a table along the side where they could have as much privacy as was possible. Snapping his fingers, he called over a young waiter. "Bring the coffee pot, Aimes." Folding his hands together in front of him, he turned tiny black eyes on Curt and Del. "If he fails to please you, let me know, and I will fire him on the spot."

"Aimes has always done a superb job, Earl," Curt reminded him.

"Very good." Stanbury dropped away from their table and disappeared into the kitchen.

Del shuddered. "That guy always gives me the creeps. He's the only thing I don't like about this place."

Aimes appeared with the coffee pot and filled the rose-patterned cups. A tall, slender youth with big blue eyes and blond hair, he was only a couple of years younger than Curt and Del.

Curt looked up at him as he poured. "How are you today, Aimes?"

"Just fine, sir."

Del gave the boy a big smile. "You get handsomer every time I see you."

Aimes reddened and nearly lost the pot. He set it down on the edge of the table to take out his pad and paper for their order.

Del traced a finger briefly along his forearm. "How many pretty girls are after you this week?"

Aimes' hands began to shake, and he smiled nervously, unable to keep his eyes on her face. He looked to Curt for their order.

Curt was trying not to chuckle. "Let him do his job, Del. You're embarrassing him."

"I don't mean him no harm." She smiled up at the boy again. "I just want him to know we like him, that's all. With a boss like old Weasel-Face, he needs it."

Aimes swallowed and met her eyes at last. "Thank you, miss."

Curt ordered them a breakfast of boiled eggs, fried ham, biscuits, and fruit preserves, and Aimes left them for the kitchen. Del stirred cream and sugar into her coffee and took a long sip. Curt preferred his coffee black. He also liked to let it sit for about ten minutes before drinking it. He didn't want it cold, just warm enough to have a bit of a bite to it without scalding his mouth. He put his elbows on the tablecloth, linked his fingers together, and rested his chin on his thumbs.

"So what about this women's group?"

Del took another sip of coffee before answering. "Well, it all started just after the new preacher came to town."

"The new preacher?" Immediately he recalled the incident last night in front of the saloon.

"Pastor Andrews. He came over from New West, but rumor is he's really from back east somewheres. Trying to start some new, not-so-stiff kind of church, I think." Del sipped some more coffee. "So about six weeks ago, he shows up with his family. And that's when this Moral Action Committee shit started."

"That's what they call it?"

"Yep." She downed the last of her coffee just in time for Aimes, coming around with the pot again, to refill it. She flashed him a smile that flushed him red to his ears. He left when he saw Curt still hadn't touched his cup.

"These things never last long," Curt observed. "Any signs of it slowing down yet?"

"Nope."

Curt tested the heat in his cup by placing his fingertips lightly around it. He picked it up and took his first sip of the rich black liquid. Perfect.

Aimes came back with their meals, and they began to eat.

After a few moments, Curt said, "When we finish, I think I'll go have a talk with Dave Jenkins, see what he knows."

Del nodded approval and bit into her toast.

When they rose from the table, Curt left behind a twenty-five cent piece as he always did for the young waiter. The tip was half the price of one of their meals, but Curt felt the kid deserved it. He saw Del to the doors of the Carlton and walked downtown by himself. Above him, lazy white clouds drifted in an otherwise blue sky, but around him, the streets were busy with noon-hour traffic. His eyes habitually noted each person. Growing upon the streets, he had survived by keeping an eye on who was close by, who might try to harm him or steal from him or sic the law on him.

The police barracks and jail occupied the site of the original Fort Victoria in Bastion Square. Built of brick and stone, the building was two-story and fortress-like, with narrow, barred windows and parapets along each roofline. The main entrance was recessed between two single-story flanking sections that jutted forward to the street. Curt nodded politely to the two uniformed officers conversing next to one of the pillars in the doorway, strode past them, and let himself in. Peering over the reception counter, he spied the young constable with his feet up on his desk.

"Hiya, Dave."

"Howdy, there, Curt." Jenkins got up and came around the desk, his hand stuck out for a shake. Curt obliged him. Jenkins was twenty-two years old and in his second year as a constable with the Victoria Police Department.

He'd come to Victoria as a deputy, pursuing a pair of murderers with U.S. Marshal Frank Stone from Washington Territory. During the course of their business in Victoria, Stone had become infatuated and obsessed with Delores. He'd promised her he would find his men, take them back to Olympia, and return for her. He boasted he would take over the local police department and show them how to really tame a town. He ran roughshod over the local constabulary and terrorized even the mildest of ne'er-do-wells. Del was in love with Curt and not interested in the thirty-five-year-old Stone. She became more and more repulsed by the man the more he pursued her. While in the beginning, Stone had treated Curt with disdain, Curt's refusal to just go away had gradually infuriated the arrogant marshal. Stone found his two murderers hiding in an opium den in Chinatown and shot and killed them both, supposedly in self-defense. He instructed Deputy Jenkins to accompany the bodies back to Olympia so that he could remain and take care of some 'personal business'. His rantings so concerned the deputy that Jenkins was moved to warn Curt to beware of his life. The very next night, in a cold rage, Stone had drawn on Curt's back in Trounce Alley not far from the Carlton. Stone had missed. Curt hadn't, and Stone's body was shipped back to Washington Territory with the bodies of the two fugitives. Dave Jenkins decided to stay in Victoria.

Jenkins motioned to the wooden chair in front of his desk. "Have a seat. Want some coffee?"

The chair creaked as Curt set himself down in it. "No, thanks."

Jenkins returned to his wooden swivel chair behind the desk. He scratched his skull through straight, light brown hair then ran his fingers across his neat mustache. "How was your trip? The circuit still treatin' you good?"

"Fine."

"Great to hear." He spread his hands over his desk. "Is this a social visit?"

"I need some information, and I figure you're the one to give it to me," Curt said.

"Shoot."

"What's all this Moral Action horseshit? Anything to it?"

Jenkins smiled. "Naw, I don't figger there is. You know how these things come and go. Some old biddy gets an eyeful of a working girl, and it sets her blood to boilin' for a while. They always simmer down sooner or later."

Curt leaned back in the chair, propping his elbows on the arms and steepling his fingers before him. "Del tells me they've been meeting pretty regular for a solid month."

Jenkins waved his hand, dismissing the implication. "So far, that's all they done. They just sit around, workin' each other into a tizzy over the vice district 'til we haul in an 'undesirable' or two. I already told the boys'n' girls to lay low for a while. It's always worked before."

"I saw those old biddies marching down Government Street not two hours ago."

"If they was a troop of militia, I might sweat a drop or two over it. But they're a bunch of fat old cows. Nobody pays no mind to 'em."

Curt dropped his hands into his lap. "You're probably right."

"I am right."

Curt stood up. Jenkins followed suit, speaking as he rounded the desk. "But, listen, partner. Maybe you could go pay them boys up on Chatham a little visit. You know how fired up Fat Johnnie gets over stuff. If he sees you ain't a' lathered over it, he'll settle down. Just remind him to keep his girls to his own street. The rest'll follow his lead."

"Consider it done," Curt said, feeling satisfied with this course.

"Thanks a heap."

Curt turned his back to the constable and let himself out. He turned northward and walked along the harbor the six blocks to the red-light district. He paused near the narrow wooden Johnson Street Bridge. Across the harbor, the Lekwammen people went about their lives on the Songhees Reserve. Curt admittedly didn't know much about the native Indians, but they had never bothered him. He knew many of them held domestic jobs on this side of the bridge, while others sold fish and other goods to make a living. He found it just as irritating, though, that, like the blacks or the Chinese, they were utilized yet looked down upon by many whites. Like the British class system that was desperately trying to maintain its hold in Victoria, this was a prejudice he could never grasp.

He stepped off the boardwalk to cross Johnson. Wharf Street became Store Street, and it was like walking into another world. Warehouses lined the waterfront on his left, while Chinatown occupied the blocks on his right. Crazy, ramshackle wooden shacks, many perched precariously on stilts, lined the stream that flowed along Johnson and emptied into the harbor. They reminded Curt of the cheap saloons thrown up quickly during his boyhood. But many Chinese working men called these shacks home. Several brick buildings housing legitimate businesses had gone up as members of their community prospered, but most of Victoria's upper class saw only the gambling and opium dens and saw them as an embarrassing blemish upon their city. Yet Fan Tan Alley saw its share of elite gentlemen secretly indulging desires that were never admitted in polite society.

As Curt reached Herald and Chatham Streets, the painted, well-kept buildings of the business district fell away, replaced by dull, shoddy structures in near-ruin. This was no longer Chinatown. Every building was either a saloon or a bordello or both. There were no boardwalks. The inhabitants of this district rarely traveled the streets, as did the folks of the town proper, for they had nowhere to go. Whores lazed on the steps of their houses, roused into action only when a potential customer wandered within earshot. Their spangled outfits were as unkempt as their surroundings. Often, they wore only tattered nightdresses.

The men were no better. Dirty and shiftless, they hung around doorways and dark corners, drinking or drunk, some of them dopey on opium. None of them would ever leave here — that took ambition and money. Nor would the whores ever find a better life. There was no other work for them, and they were already outcasts, tainted by their own desperate acts. Financial independence was impossible — their customers had little more money than they did. What the women did earn paid their keep in the houses of their madams and bought the bare necessities of survival.

They watched him as he passed through their territory, but they did not solicit him. They knew better. Along the north side of Chatham Street, Curt stepped up to the doors of the Bull's Pride Bar.

Even at midday the place was dark. He looked in first, allowing his eyes to adjust to the dimness before stepping inside. It reeked of stale booze and tobacco and sweaty, filthy bodies. The walls and floors were bare, unfinished wood, and the tables and chairs were a jumble of unmatched pieces. The bar was a wide, warped plank atop a couple of empty beer kegs with split seams.

The denizens of the place fastened their rat-like eyes on Curt the minute he crossed the threshold. On his left, three of them sat hunched over a sorry excuse for a table. The one in the center clutched the liquor bottle possessively to his sunken chest. On Curt's right, two more hurried to escape his notice, scuttling, crab-like, to an even darker corner of the room.

Curt walked straight up to the bartender. The tall, pale, cadaverous man blinked at him with unbelievably large eyes.

"Is your boss at home?" Curt asked him.

It took the walking skeleton a moment to discover his voice. Then it was raspy, as though he rarely used it. "In the back."

Curt went to the door at the left of the bar. He rapped his knuckles on it twice then turned the latch and walked in.

A whore cowered on her knees before Fat Johnnie, who stood over her with one huge hand entangled in her curly hair, the other raised to strike. Her mouth was swollen and bleeding.

"What's goin' on, Johnnie?" Curt asked.

Fat Johnnie pushed the girl aside. She scrambled up so quickly she bumped into the heavy desk behind her. She cast only a single glance at Curt as she brushed past him and out of the cramped room.

Curt returned his eyes to Fat Johnnie, who smiled at him now with wet, flabby lips. Fat Johnnie's lips were always wet, which Curt found disgusting.

"Well, if it ain't the Boy King hisself, come to pay the common scum a royal visit." Fat Johnnie's voice held traces of the Cockney English accent he had been born with thirty years ago. He smoothed his ginger hair and scratched his mutton-chop whiskers where they joined his mustache. His cheeks flopped up and down as he spoke. His pale blue eyes were tiny dots in his fleshy face while his broad nose rose like a hillock in the middle.

"Knock it off, Johnnie." Curt leaned his backside on the edge of Fat Johnnie's cluttered desk so he could face him squarely. He folded his arms across his chest.

Grunting, Fat Johnnie settled his three-hundred-forty pound bulk on the loveseat behind him. "Nice suit. Bet that setcha back a bundle. Yer lucky yer such a scrawny little runt. If we was the same size, I'd kill ya for it."

Curt snorted, mildly amused. "Dave tells me you and the boys are sweatin' over these old biddies and their morality marches. He wants me to assure you that you can relax."

Fat Johnnie sucked a loud, wheezy breath, as though his nostrils, as wide as they were, weren't large enough to bring him the air he needed. "Yeah, well, that two-faced law dog ain't the one they wanna run outta town. He's been haulin' my girls in right'n' left. Finin''em like they was made o' money."

"He warned you to keep 'em to your side of town."

"Yeah, well, them poor angels can't make squat around here."

"The man's gotta do his job."

Fat Johnnie waved his hands on the ends of his stumpy arms. "Well, he's doin' it too fuckin' good! You go back there and tell him to ease the hell up, or we'll ease him into an early grave!"

Curt regarded the older man coolly, noting even in the poor light the carmine coloring his swollen cheeks. "Johnnie, consider something for a minute. Sure, you could get rid of

Jenkins pretty easy if you wanted to. But are you willing to take the risk of him being replaced with another Frank Stone?"

Fat Johnnie's eyes shifted away. He tugged at the bottom of his torn, brocaded vest and then at the stained ruffles below his string tie.

"I'll take that as a no. Then just cool down and let me handle it, all right?"

Fat Johnnie mumbled, "All right."

"Good." Curt rose off the desk and moved toward the door.

Fat Johnnie cleared his throat. "Still, maybe Jenkins don't care, but my gut tells me it's serious this time. If we sit on our asses 'n' let 'em get ahead of us, they just might run us out. And if they run us out, they run you out, too. Maybe you look better 'n us in them nice duds and that two-dollar haircut, but you're one of us, Prescott. Don't ever forget that."

His hand on the latch, Curt eyed him, considering taking offense to the way Johnnie had come close to threatening him. He decided to let it go. But he said, "And don't you forget just who it was that got rid of Stone. And who turned Jenkins around to our way of thinking. Stone was only here two months, and he was a bigger drain on you than Jenkins will ever be. If you don't pay up, Jenkins'll throw you in jail. But he won't hang you from a lamppost by your balls."

Fat Johnnie blanched, and Curt saw concession in his eyes. He twisted the latch and walked from the room.

Del must have been waiting and watching for him, for she waved to him from the balcony as he reached the corner below the Carlton. He waved back and walked into the saloon.

The afternoon had warmed considerably, and he wanted a beer before he went upstairs, so he headed straight for the bar. A waitress served him, a plump and buxom young thing he'd never seen before. She left the beer with him and smiled alluringly as she moved away. He nodded a polite thank you, despite the fact that he could nearly taste her overdosed perfume, and raised the mug to his lips.

She spun slowly around and came back toward him.

"Hey, honey. You're new in town, aintcha? Just passin' through?" she asked, stepping up really close.

"Nope."

"But I ain't never seen you before. I'd remember a good-lookin' fella like you." She snaked her tiny hands up his lapels and pulled herself up against him, a childlike, yet provocative, pout on her cherubic face. She patted her chopped-off brown hair with both hands and fluttered her eyelashes at him. She stretched hard to reach her fingers around his neck and rub her body against him. "I don't guess it matters, handsome. How'd you like to get to know this new-to-town girl? Special prices just for you. A nickel'll get you a look; two bits'll get you a feel. A half dollar'll get you in and a buck'll get you anything you want."

Despite her odd shape, she had a strange sensual allure. Her makeup and attitude made her seem like an old pro, but she couldn't have been more than nineteen or twenty years old. He said, "I haven't paid for it in years."

She pouted in earnest this time, her crimson lips jutting out from her face. Her hands slipped down inside his open jacket and traced the notched lapels of his vest then stole around his waist. "A man like you can afford," she pressed, "anything he wants."

"Yes, but like I said —." His ears caught the stride of high-heeled shoes as they reached the top of the stairs. He recognized

Del's walk. Her steps were muffled by the carpeted stairway behind him then clacked along the hardwood floor toward him.

"You brazen little bitch — get your greasy paws off him!" She grabbed the whore's arm and yanked it away from Curt. "Can't you tell he's mine?"

The whore stepped back and narrowed her eyes at Del. "Who says? I don't see your name on him anywhere."

Del's hand shot out and slapped the girl's face hard.

Curt caught Del's arm from winding back for a second blow. "That's enough, Del."

The stunned girl turned slowly back to look at them. There were tears welling in her eyes and a white imprint, edged in crimson, of Del's palm on her cheek.

"I say! Now beat it before I scratch your ugly little eyes out!" Del screeched.

The girl walked her fingers up Curt's vest. "I think it should be up to him, don't you?"

Del's eyes flickered uneasily to Curt's. He shrugged innocently then turned his eyes to the young girl. "The lady's right. I'm already spoken for."

Defeat darkened her face. She shot an evil look at Del. "Well, if you ever get tired of the old bitch, you just come look me up. The name's Mabel."

"You got it, Mabel."

She turned away but Curt touched her bare arm. "One second, Mabel."

Her eyes held a hopeful spark as she faced him once again. But they widened in fear as he stuffed his fingers deep into her cleavage and retrieved his gold watch.

"Guess it must've fallen out of my pocket," he said.

She tensed her body, as if expecting another blow. When it never came, she backed up then turned and waddled quickly away, disappearing into the kitchen behind the bar.

Curt regarded the stag engraved on the lid then tucked the watch back into his vest pocket and refastened the chain. When he raised his eyes to Del's, she was staring at him with relief in her moist eyes.

"You didn't actually think I'd go with her, did you?"

She shrugged. "I guess not."

He put his arm around her shoulders. "Hell, I probably got the clap just from lookin' at her."

That brought a chuckle from Del, and she hooked her arm under his jacket. He shared the rest of his beer with her then steered her up the stairs and into their suite. She let go of him to pull down the shades then faced him and began to undress.

He watched her without moving. One by one, her coverings hit the floor until at last they all lay in a heap about her feet. Her body was sculptured perfection. She held her head high, shaking loose her long tresses until they fell tantalizingly about her white shoulders. Her high, full breasts jutted out to him while her ribs tapered to a slender waist. From there she curved outward again over shapely hips and buttocks that flowed in turn into the long, sure legs of a dancer.

She came to him and began to undress him, planting soft kisses wherever she exposed his skin. He held himself in check, letting her arouse him as she chose. His weapons she laid carefully on the nightstand, but his clothes she let fall to his feet. He encircled her with his arms and drove his mouth hard against hers. She moaned and wound her arms up around his neck. He marked a trail of kisses down her throat, entwining his fingers in her hair until her knees gave way and he had to catch her before she fell.

Lifting her in his arms, he carried her to the bed and laid her gently down. Her arms locked around his neck and she kissed him ardently while he stretched out alongside her.

Caressing each other, they teased and enraptured until they could no longer bear the ache each aroused in the other. She clamped her arms around him, her nails digging like talons into his back, drawing blood. Time and place lost all meaning, and they burst over the threshold together.

CHAPTER THREE

They dozed together afterward, Curt on his back with Del molded against his left side. Her right leg coiled over his, and her head lay on his chest, cradled in the crook of his arm. Her skin was lily-white against his darker complexion.

Awakening, he absently stroked her hair. He knew why she'd wanted to make love so suddenly — the young prostitute. Orphaned at thirteen, Del had arrived in Victoria already a veteran prostitute when Curt met her at sixteen. He could only imagine what it had been like for her at that age to sell her body to men. But she was no whore anymore. For nearly seven years now, she'd belonged only to him. Still, the ravaging of her innocence had taken its toll, each past degradation etched deep into the lines of her face. Like Curt, she was only twenty-three, but ofttimes, especially when tired or stressed, she appeared closer to thirty-three.

The first moment he saw her she had struck him as special somehow — not only for her beauty or her talent, but also for something within her that tugged at a similar something within him. He became a regular customer and, within two weeks, convinced her that he could support her without the need for her to sell herself to other men. Already a skilled veteran himself at poker, it was easy to pay her more than she'd ever see if she spread her legs for every man in town, twenty-four hours a day.

And it was a lot healthier for both of them that way.

Since linking up with Del, Curt had bedded no more whores. She satisfied him like no other when he was home. When he was on the circuit, which was only a few months of each year, he preferred to focus strictly on the games themselves — at least, until they were over. Then he enjoyed the fun of seducing willing virgins like the daughter of the wealthy judge he'd bested at cards in Seattle. He suspected that Del knew he indulged in other women while he was away from Victoria, but she never asked him. If she ever did ask, he'd be straight with her, but it was not something they ever discussed.

Whatever thrill most men got from constant whoring around held no appeal for Curt — the dance hall girls were just too easy. But he held no inherent objections to prostitutes—indeed, his mother had been one. Lillian Prescott had started life as the daughter of a successful nurseryman and landscaper to the wealthy of Seattle. She'd grown up helping her mother in the family flower shop. At the age of twenty-two, she'd fallen in love with an army lieutenant. Her parents adored Roger until they discovered Lillian was pregnant. Her lieutenant was suddenly posted out before they could insist he marry her. Facing the shame and ruin of their family name and business, her parents packed her belongings and put her on a train to Portland and an understanding aunt, insisting she not return without a husband. But Lillian never went to Portland. Instead, she went looking for Roger. She never found him and in desperation found herself tossed into the life of an army camp laundress, following the troops from fort to fort from California to Puget Sound. She lost the baby she carried but later became pregnant with Curt. He had been born in a wagon somewhere in the Washington Territory. She had told him his father was an officer, but he'd always known she wasn't really sure. It was more likely the man was one of dozens of nameless, faceless enlisted men. They were far more accessible to the women than the officers.

She drifted up and down the coast during his first year. More than once they'd been forcibly removed from the rickety shacks and tents they'd called homes outside the forts. Finally giving up on Roger and unable to go home, Lillian became enamored with a gold seeker and his stories of the riches he would soon have. Perhaps he would be a suitable husband to present to her parents. She packed up her few belongings and her young son and accompanied the man aboard the ship to Vancouver Island. Victoria was young then and vibrant, and despite the fact that the gold seeker quickly deserted them, she was able to sell herself often enough to feed and clothe herself and her boy, until one day they found her body in an alley. She had been beaten to death. Her assailant was never identified. The local whores chipped in for a cheap pine box and a brief burial at the pauper's cemetery north of town. None of them would take in twelve-year-old Curt, though. They had enough difficulty keeping themselves fed and clothed. He began to hang around the saloons of the burgeoning town, doing odd jobs for a meal, scratching in the sawdust floors for lost bits of gold or coins.

He was not allowed to gamble in the square houses, but the crooked ones welcomed him and fleeced him with dispatch. Quickly he learned that most games were rigged in favor of the house, but five-card draw, he figured, a man could win or lose more by his own skill, with less reliance on luck, and he wasted no time in learning the game.

At first, he collected discarded decks and played straight games with other boys in the streets. Then he was lucky enough to catch the eye of the town's resident professional. Charlie Buttons dealt faro for the Golden Oak Tavern and Dance Hall and played poker on his own time. He succumbed to the boy's pleas to teach him all the skills of a real card player.

Curt had practiced for hours and hours. Charlie also taught him how to spot when others were cheating — all the false shuffles and cuts, how to bottom deal and deal seconds, and how to stack a deck right under his opponent's eyes. He instilled in

Curt a code of sorts. A good poker player won by his skill and lost with grace. Charlie considered deceptions and sleights of hand fair and part of the game only to counter a cheat and push him out. But cheating to win was contemptible and worthy of a bullet between the eyes.

When Curt reached sixteen, he was ready to play some serious cards. Quickly, he became known as the second best poker player in Victoria. When Buttons died in the fire that destroyed the Golden Oak, Curt became the town's king of the pasteboards. He was nineteen years old at the time.

He paid for his mentor's funeral and moved his base of operations to the brand new Carlton Saloon. His career flourished. When he got an itch in his feet, he saddled up and rode the mainland circuit as far south as San Francisco. The big towns were where he found and won the big pots. But the fancy cities could not hold him long. As soon as he'd made his money, he came back to the place he considered home.

Now, Del stirred beside him, her finger reaching up to scratch her nose, tickled by the hair on his chest. Her hand slid down the ventral strip of hair that ran down his belly and widened again around his navel. Then it became still, and she was deeply asleep once more.

Even with the curtains drawn, the light seemed intensely bright to Curt. His body had lain long enough — it wanted to be up and moving. Slipping out from under Del, he dressed silently. He tucked his Colt and gun belt into his saddlebags and went out the door.

The sun shone brilliantly, but his eyes were shaded by the brim of his navy blue dress Stetson. The streets were quiet. Only a few pedestrians were about, a few horses tethered outside stores, and one small wagon rattled past. Chattering away at each other, two middle-aged women were walking his way. Suddenly they saw him and shut their mouths. He stepped to the edge of the boardwalk, giving them room to pass. Pressing into each other like frightened sheep, they hugged the wall of the building until they were well past him. He did not turn around to watch them, but he could feel their eyes on his back.

Why they should be so afraid of him, he could never completely fathom. He had never harmed them. The only man he'd ever killed in Victoria — or anywhere, for that matter — had been Frank Stone, and that son-of-a-bitch had needed killing. He'd had his share of fistfights and drawn his gun occasionally, but in truth, eruptions of violence were rather rare in his life. He was respected enough to be left alone, and that was how he liked it.

Stepping off the end of the boardwalk, he figured that the town's bourgeois element did not understand his type, nor did they want to. He glanced eastward, toward the homes of the average folks. They liked their separateness and, as far as Curt was concerned, they could have it.

As he neared the livery, he recalled the new saddlery. The façade was painted a pale yellow with white trim, and the roof sported new shingles. The lettering in the big front window was brown, edged with yellow.

"Andrews Saddlery," it read, and on a shingle above the door was printed: "Richard 'Bud' Andrews, Proprietor. 38 Years in Fine Saddlery and Harness." A sign behind the glass in the door said "Closed."

Curt found that odd in the middle of a Saturday afternoon. He wondered if this was the same Andrews as the new preacher. He studied the saddlery while walking by, without pausing long enough to appear curious. He collected his horse from the livery and rode north up Douglas. Once outside the city limits, he paused to buckle on his sidearm. Although serious threats were rare around here, he'd been in enough scrapes to feel more comfortable with his weapon available, if only as a visual deterrent.

Behind him lay the town proper, with its buildings and clearings and human activity, but before him lay farmland and rolling hills and distant low mountains covered with evergreen trees. Although he could not see it from here, he knew all this was surrounded by ocean. He mused that one could conceivably live one's entire life on Vancouver Island and not even realize one was on an island.

Not far out of town, he crested the low hill that leveled out at the church site. In the brilliant sunshine, the fresh whitewash glared at him. He'd never set foot inside the church, not even as a boy. The service for his mother had been brief and held outside at her graveside.

The silence hit him suddenly. The clearing seemed completely separate from the town, insulated by the thick forest. He walked toward the gate in the tiny picket fence surrounding the cemetery. Growing amongst the young grass, tiny wildflowers of all colors competed for the nurturing rays of the sun. Curt bent and plucked a small handful before reaching for the gate latch. Broken off its top hinge for as long as he could remember, the gate now hung correctly and swung easily on its hinges.

Near the center of the site, he halted and looked down at her wooden marker. Plain and weathered, it bore only the briefest inscription:

Lillian Rebecca Prescott: Died 1866.

He squatted and laid the flowers on the green mound. Sighing heavily, he said nothing aloud. He just stared at her grave until his eyes lost focus. He wished he'd had more time with her. It had been so long he could no longer recall the exact details of her face. He remembered dark brown hair and eyes the same color and a missing left incisor. One of her customers had knocked it out for her. He remembered more clearly things she'd taught him, things about plants and flowers and how she'd brightened whenever she had a chance to speak of her true passion. She'd had so much more to give the world than her body, but it had seemed that her body was all the world had been interested in. If only he could have grown up faster and looked after her, so she wouldn't have had to do what she did to earn a living. He'd have given anything to make life better for her.

A twig cracked beneath a foot. He reacted instantly, instinctively. His hand found the walnut grip of his Colt .45 and pulled the weapon clear of its holster as he rose. His thumb cocked the hammer as he pivoted to face the intruder.

A stocky man in his mid-fifties froze just inside the gate. His grey eyes met Curt's with shock and a trace of fear in them. His hands held his felt hat at belt level. He was unarmed.

Curt tilted the Colt's muzzle aside, let the hammer down easy, and put it away. The man in the grey suit stepped forward hesitantly, and Curt recognized him as the preacher he'd seen Willie toss out of the Carlton.

"I'm sorry — I didn't mean to startle you."

"Forget it. My apologies for drawing on you."

"I should have realized you were deep in thought." The preacher stopped a couple of feet from Curt and held out a square, gnarly-knuckled hand. "My name is Bud Andrews. I'm the parson here."

Curt shook with him and was surprised at the strength in the shorter man's grip and at the calluses he felt on the hand. He looked into the man's face, noting the gay wrinkles around his eyes and the corners of his mouth. His grey hair was short, neat, and just beginning to thin on top.

"Curt Prescott." He watched for some sort of reaction to his name but if there was any, it was lost as the preacher lifted his head in reaction to a raven squawking as it flapped above them. The glance was brief, and the preacher's eyes came back to Curt's.

"I was just inside preparing my sermon for tomorrow when I noticed you out here. I wanted to introduce myself and to thank you for sparing me further humiliation the other night."

Curt shrugged, and his eyes sought the spiky tips of the evergreens on the hillside. "Forget it."

Bud shook his head. "I never forget a kindness." He paused briefly and then said, "I don't believe I've seen you in church at all."

"I've been away for some time."

"I see." The preacher looked down at the grave marker. "A relative of yours?"

"My mother."

"My condolences. I see she's been gone a long time now." He touched Curt's left arm with his open palm. "She's at peace now, son. But I sense that you are not."

Reflexively, Curt's arm drew tighter against his side, away from the touch. He had looked away when the preacher first reached out, but Andrews' words now made Curt's eyes whip back to his. The older man shifted uncomfortably under the intensity of Curt's probing gaze.

"Well, I just thought I would come and meet you. I won't intrude on you any longer." He stepped away then hesitated. "If you'd ever like to talk, I'm always available."

"Thanks, parson." Not that he was ever likely to take him up on it.

Still, the preacher did not go. He cleared his throat, looking back at Curt as if undecided about something. "I — I noticed that you're not wearing a wedding band. If you've got no one who cooks for you, perhaps you'd like to come to my home for dinner, as a small token of thanks. I assure you my wife is an excellent cook."

Curt's first impulse was to say no. But then, in a flash of inspiration, it occurred to him that this might be an excellent opportunity to learn more about the Moral Action Committee and to find out if it was a real threat or just another flash in the pan of righteousness. He met the preacher's eyes and nodded.

"Thank you, parson. I'm obliged."

A smile brightened the preacher's face. "Very good. Are you ready to go now?"

Nodding, Curt followed the preacher out of the cemetery.

CHAPTER FOUR

Pastor Andrews' home was a modest two-story, clapboard frame house on Timberline Avenue, which backed onto a deep, wooded ravine. The same ravine, Curt was certain, as the one that ran below the church. There was nothing extraordinary about the pastor's house — it was a classic example of ordinary. Apple green with spruce green trim, it seemed to blend in, as though it had grown from the earth like the trees. The front yard was small and relatively level and enclosed within a low white picket fence. The gate opened to a flat slate path to the front doorstep. The small lawn was healthy and trimmed, not choked out by last year's growth — Curt figured the preacher must be handy with garden tools.

Curt tethered his horse to the nearest hitching post and followed the preacher up the path. He noticed the daisies planted on either side of the front door. Still immature, the delicate white flowers waved with a gentle innocence atop their tall, slender stems. A memory nudged him. Innocence was, in fact, what they symbolized, if he remembered his mother's teachings correctly. He noted the neatly trimmed cedar hedges protecting the corners of the house. Cedars were strength. He smiled to himself as the memories and information flooded back to him after years of disuse.

The preacher opened the door and bid him enter first. The smell of roasting beef intrigued Curt's nostrils. He examined the small entry hall while the preacher followed him in and closed the door. A hat and coat rack stood at his left and a tall but narrow hall table on his right. The brown carpet beneath his feet was flecked with little fawn swirls and ran from the door all the way up the stairway straight in front of him.

The parson took Curt's hat and hung it next to his own on the rack. Then he cleared his throat and, as politely as he could, pointed to Curt's sidearm. "If you wouldn't mind ... I'm afraid my wife is uncomfortable around firearms. And I would prefer to know it is not at our dinner table."

"Certainly." Curt unbuckled it and held it out to him. "I tend to indulge myself in wearing it outside the city limits."

The parson drew his top lip between his teeth, deliberating. Then, without taking the weapon, he moved to the hall table and slid open the drawer. Curt took the cue and placed the rig inside.

Bud slid the drawer closed. "Thank you." He led the way into the parlor. "Please have a seat while I ask my wife to set another place for dinner."

Curt checked the lay of the room with a swift glance. A brick fireplace stood along the north wall, flanked on each side by a wooden chair with beige cushioned seats. A beige chesterfield faced the hearth, its back to the entry hall. A matching stuffed armchair had its back to the front window, and a mate faced it at the far end of the chesterfield. In between was a long, low coffee table. Different styles of parlor tables were set at advantageous places throughout the small room. Many of them were graced with a doily and little ornaments.

A dining table and chairs occupied the far end of the room. To the right of it was the doorway to the kitchen where the preacher had just gone. Curt could hear them talking. He caught only snatches of their hushed conversation. The wife did not sound pleased.

He shifted over and took the chair with its back to the front window, something he normally wouldn't do. But he doubted that any unforgiving sucker he'd fleeced in the past would come looking for him here. In any case, there was always the derringer in his vest pocket and the knife in his boot. What he wanted was a good view of the woman as she walked into the room.

While he waited for his host to return, he studied the small paintings on the plain, off-white walls. All the paintings were of scenery. One had grazing horses in it. Upon the mantle, a squat clock ticked softly. Compared to what he was used to, the home was drab, but it had a certain quaint charm that made him feel oddly at ease within its walls.

Bud Andrews, certain his guest was seated out of earshot, stepped up close to his wife and kissed her just above her right ear. She was chopping potatoes on the wooden countertop and barely glanced at him, so as not to take her eyes off what she was doing with the knife.

"Is your sermon prepared for tomorrow?" she asked.

"Yes." He watched her a minute while he chose his words. "Sarah, I've brought a guest for dinner."

She stopped chopping and raised her eyes to look straight into his. "Who is it? Do I know him?"

"No, but you know *of* him."

A trace of impatience flickered in her hazel eyes.

Bud pressed a hand on her arm, as if to steady her. "Now, Sarah, it's very important you don't get upset."

"Why should I get upset?"

He winced at the rising sharpness in her voice and glanced toward the doorway to the parlor. "Because the young man is Curt Prescott."

Her mouth opened wide, and he knew she was about to shriek. Quickly, he covered her thin lips with the palm of his hand, praying she would keep silent long enough for him to explain.

"Don't fly off the handle now, just listen." Tentatively, he removed his hand, ready to put it back the instant she opened her mouth again. Clearly, she was struggling to contain herself.

"I met him in the cemetery on my way home. I've heard his description so many times I thought it might be him before he even told me his name. And I saw that he was kneeling before Lillian Prescott's grave. He's the one I told you about who aided me at the saloon. I don't think he knows that I realize who he is." He paused to collect his next words. "Of all the undesirables in this town, I've heard Curt Prescott is the most prominent. He's so young, so successful, and yet apparently so untouchable by the law and by other criminals that he is the greatest attraction to sinful living our young people see." He had to stop and draw a breath after his long statement. He was glad Sarah was waiting for him to finish, even though her arms were crossed below her bosom and her jaw closed tight. "If we can lead him away from his sins, perhaps the others will follow."

Sarah's jaw began to work as she determined to speak quietly. "You brought him into this house? Our house? *My house?*"

He nodded.

"How could you bring filth like him into our home and dirty it so?"

Although he knew what she meant, he said, "I assure you his clothing is quite clean."

She flinched, as though about to snap back at him for that.

"Sarah, you do understand what I'm trying to do here, don't you?"

Reluctantly, she nodded.

"Please go along with me. If he knows that we know who he is, he'll catch on to our efforts, and we'll lose him. Promise me you'll follow me in this."

He waited, his heart pounding in his chest, while she deliberated. Finally, she nodded.

"Thank you," he said, squeezing her arm. "Now come meet him."

Curt looked up as the parson returned to the parlor with his wife. She was plump and stood just as tall as her husband. Her brown hair had streaks of grey running through it and was wound into a tight bun at the back of her head. Her loose-fitting beige blouse was done up tightly at her throat and tucked snugly into the waistband of her brown wool skirt.

Curt stood up, his eyes on her face. By the rigid way she carried herself, he was certain she was the one who had led the march.

"Mr. Prescott, I'd like you to meet my wife, Sarah. Sarah, our guest, Mr. Curt Prescott."

Curt flashed her his best smile and stepped closer. "It's a pleasure to meet you, Mrs. Andrews."

There had been a definite wariness in her eyes, but it faded under his brilliant smile. She lifted her hand, and he clasped it gently and briefly.

"Thank you for welcoming me into your lovely home."

A tight smile cracked her stern features, but her eyelids fluttered. "You are quite welcome, Mr. Prescott." She smoothed the loose hairs at the back of her neck with the hand he had touched. "Please make yourself at home."

"Thank you."

"Bud, have you offered our guest some refreshment?"

"Not yet, dear."

"Well! Is that any way to treat a guest? There is some apple cider in the pantry."

Bud moved to fetch it, but she overtook him and brushed by him. "No, no — I'll get it. You entertain Mr. Prescott."

Bud stared after her then rubbed a hand down his face from his eyes to his chin. Curt got the impression Bud was astonished at her. No doubt the woman was a shrew. Curt would lay odds she normally ran this household like a drill sergeant. But he had just charmed her stripes off, and her female vanity had taken over. She would now be the dutiful wife while Curt was present in their home.

The preacher collected himself, turned back to Curt, and bade him sit. He took the chair against the wall between Curt and the fireplace. A moment later Sarah returned with two glasses of cider. When Curt thanked her, she smiled gaily and left them for the kitchen.

Curt sipped the cool cider, forming a question carefully in his mind before asking it. "Sir, if I might ask ...? What brought you to Victoria?"

"Well, largely a fascination with the western frontier and a concern for the spiritual well-being of its people."

"You consider Victoria still a frontier?"

Smiling almost apologetically, Bud pushed his hands against his knees and straightened his spine. "It's very different from Upper Canada — or should I say Ontario. It's been ten years since confederation, but I still think in the old terms." He chuckled at himself. "But there's no shortage of preachers there. I was originally called to New Westminster, and we arrived late last summer, but then this came up ..."

"So you've come where you're most needed," Curt remarked.

"Yes." A light sparked in the quiet grey eyes. "Victoria is the largest settlement on the west coast north of San Francisco. There's much to be done here."

At that moment, the front door opened, and a young woman bounded through. "Oh, Dad! I'm sorry I'm late. Is Mother upset?" She had an armful of books and paper, which she unloaded onto the hall table.

Both Curt and Bud stood. Free at last of her bundles, the girl turned into the parlor, smiling at her father. Then her eyes fell on Curt, and she halted as though struck.

Her innocent prettiness was the first thing about her that captured his attention. Then, as he ran his eyes over her petite form, he discovered further details of feminine perfection. Her gentle curves were to him wasted, hidden beneath a loose-fitting white blouse and brown skirt. She had long, honey-brown hair run through with streaks of gold. Feathery bangs fell over her forehead from a center part, and the hair from her temples was drawn back and tied in a ponytail at the back of her head, where it hung loose with the rest of her hair. Her oval face was delicately boned, her nose small and pert, her lips full but firm. Her eyes were the green of young spring leaves.

"Mary, this is Mr. Curt Prescott. He's our guest this evening. Mr. Prescott, my daughter, Mary."

Her father's voice reached the girl and appeared to jar her aware. She stepped hesitantly into the parlor and held out her hand. "How do you do, Mr. Prescott?"

"Very pleased to meet you, Miss Andrews." Curt clasped her hand barely longer than he had her mother's but flashed her the same smile.

He looked directly into her eyes, and she looked back. Her gaze lacked any suggestion of brazenness. Instead, there was a timidity she tried to hide.

Her mother bustled from the kitchen, wiping her hands on a towel. "It's about time you got home! I've had to do it all myself." Suddenly, Sarah's eyes caught Curt's. She shut her mouth and pursed her thin lips as she collected herself, presumably to correct the impression she was making on their guest. "Mary, would you please come help me in the kitchen?"

"Yes, Mother." Mary tore her eyes away from Curt's and hurried after her mother.

As they reseated themselves, Bud said, "Please excuse my daughter. She's young and a bit too impulsive for a girl. But her heart is in the right place. Those books she was toting are schoolbooks — she assists the teacher with the children on Fridays, and on Saturdays, they clean the building before Sunday church."

"Commendable," Curt remarked.

"Yes, we're very proud of her."

Curt looked around with a curious expression. "Anymore of your children going to jump out and surprise us?"

Bud chuckled. "No. We had a son, Miles. Mary's twin brother. He was a lieutenant in the Royal Navy. He was lost at sea during a horrible storm."

Curt saw moisture brim in the older man's eyes. "I'm sorry."

Bud cleared his throat and collected himself. "Thank you. Miles was the main reason we chose to come out west. To be closer, so he might visit us when he was on leave." His head dipped as he struggled to hold back the emotion. "But he was lost before we even arrived. We didn't find out until we reached New Westminster."

"That must have been very hard. Sounds like you're a close family."

Bud nodded.

The women began putting dinner on the table and shortly called them to it. The family bowed their heads while the parson said a short, simple grace. Curt watched them in silence.

As they began to fill their plates, Bud said, "You haven't told us what it is you do, Mr. Prescott."

Curt disliked lying and hesitated. Ultimately, these people were the enemy. They would destroy his life if he let them. He knew he'd get nowhere with this family with the full, unadulterated truth. "I have a number of business interests scattered throughout the Pacific Northwest. Once a year I travel to keep abreast of them all. That's where I've been the last few months."

"I see."

Sarah shook a spoonful of mashed potatoes onto her plate. "What kind of businesses are they, Mr. Prescott?"

"The details would probably bore you."

"Nonsense. Especially when a boy — a young man — makes such a success of himself so early in life."

Curt ignored her veiled insult and prompting. He asked the preacher, "Is that your new saddlery near the livery?"

"Why, yes."

"Forgive me if I seem ignorant, but I didn't think men of the cloth were allowed to make money."

An understanding smile dimpled Bud's cheeks. "One of those misinterpretations of scripture," he said. "It's one thing to lust after money and material wealth and another to provide for one's family. The Lord wants us to have full, abundant, comfortable lives — he just doesn't want us to put the pursuit of that comfort before Him." He paused, looking to see if Curt was interested. Curt folded his hands above his plate to let the preacher talk.

"If I didn't work outside the church, my family would suffer. We would have to live off the charity of others. We'd become a burden on the community, not a help. And goodness knows what would happen then, to all of us."

"I see your point."

"My work provides a necessary service. Besides, I seem to think better when I'm working with my hands. I believe inspiration often comes best when one is otherwise occupied."

"You might be right."

Bud smiled and resumed eating. Curt glanced over at Mary and found her watching him. He smiled at her — just a friendly smile, but she blushed and looked away.

"My father was a saddler in Scotland and his father before him, and so on," Bud volunteered. "If you'd like to, I'd be pleased if you'd drop by the shop sometime, and I'll show you around."

Inclining his head, Curt said, "I'll do that. Thank you."

After dinner, the men retired to the parlor with cups of tea while the women cleaned up. When Bud's wife and daughter joined them, they took what Curt felt certain were their habitual places. Both of them sat on the chesterfield, Sarah at the far end and Mary at the end nearest Curt. He watched Mary smooth her skirt and make certain it covered her ankles to her laced black shoes.

Curt shifted his attention to Sarah. "If I might ask, Mrs. Andrews, are you the one I saw leading a march down Government Street this morning?"

She straightened her shoulders and lifted her chin. "Why, yes."

He cocked his head to one side. "What was it all about?"

At first, she seemed surprised at the question then apparently remembered that he'd said he'd been away. She smoothed her skirt over her round knees. "We call ourselves the Moral Action Committee of Victoria. After seeing the deplorable state of affairs in this town, I took it upon myself to organize the women into a force to be reckoned with. We will stand for unrighteous behavior no longer."

"Why specifically tarnished doves and gamblers?"

"Because they are the most visible forms of vice and corruption. They lead decent men astray and steal their souls as well as their money. They spread diseases into our homes so that the innocent suffer. Our children see them on the streets and hear their foul blasphemy. We don't want them growing up thinking these things are part of a God-fearing life. And it seems that, wherever these evildoers are, they attract more of the same. Have you seen the filth of Chatham Street? And of Humboldt? Why, one cannot even approach the bridge to one's own parliament buildings without being accosted by rogues and vagabonds! They are as much a blemish on this city as the reeking, garbage-strewn mud flats below that very bridge. We will not allow it to contaminate us."

Curt raised his eyebrows. "You've dealt yourself into a pretty steep game. You're not afraid that the odds maybe against you?"

"When God is for us, who can be against us?"

He had no answer for that. He looked from her to Bud then to Mary. "Were you in the march, Miss Andrews?"

Her head jerked as she looked at him, as though startled that he should actually speak to her. She shook her head. "Um, no, Mr. Prescott, I wasn't."

"You don't agree with your mother's campaign?"

Sarah sniffed. "Of course she does."

Mary looked at her mother, then at her father, and then finally at Curt once again. She locked her fingers together in her lap. "I believe that something must be done. But I don't believe that running these people out of town is the answer."

Curt saw Sarah toss her eyes at the ceiling but didn't let his smile get too wide. "What do you think is the answer?"

Mary drew her top lip between her teeth and stared at her father. He inclined his head as if to urge her on. She switched her gaze back to Curt. "I think we should do something to help them. The women especially. The poor things seem so desperate — I can't imagine they'd choose to live life the way they do."

Curt watched her closely. Color had risen in her cheeks, and while her eyes flitted to and from his, she completely avoided looking at her mother. A glance at Sarah showed him why. Her mother's eyes were daggers, stabbing at her from the other end of the couch. Sarah's thin lips were pressed together so tightly they were a mottled white. Her hands clamped around each other in her lap, as if each had to hold the other from taking her daughter by the scruff of her neck and marching her to her room. Curt imagined Sarah would lock her daughter up until Mary saw things her way.

"What would you do?" he asked Mary.

"Well, perhaps a collection could be taken up. Perhaps if the families that have the means would each take even one of them in —"

"Bite your tongue!" shrieked Sarah, unable to contain herself any longer. "You would have the decent families of this town sully their homes with those — those — harlots!"

"But, Mother —"

"How can you even entertain such thoughts? I suppose you would even have us bring one into our home!"

Bud winced, but he kept silent.

Mary's voice lost some of its volume but not its conviction. "Yes."

"Certainly *not* while I'm alive!"

Mary sank against the back of the chesterfield, and her eyes dropped to her hands. Curt looked from them to Bud, who had in no way attempted to interfere. His suspicion that it was Sarah who wore the trousers in this family began to solidify.

But Mary's attitude was unique among the townsfolk here. If they did not show outright hostility toward the prostitutes, they displayed a distant tolerance. As long as the whores didn't bother them, they wouldn't bother the whores. They preferred to pretend they did not exist, that there was no problem. Which was good in some ways, bad in others. While it meant the prostitutes were not harassed, it also meant that they were not helped.

"Where do you stand on this issue, Mr. Prescott?"

He looked up at Sarah, who impatiently awaited an answer. He moved his eyes to Mary's downcast face as he responded. "No disrespect intended toward you, Mrs. Andrews, but I agree with your daughter. There has to be a positive, constructive way to deal with the problem."

Mary's head lifted, and she gazed at Curt with astonishment and admiration. Her mother gasped.

"As I mentioned earlier, I travel quite a bit, and everywhere I go, it's the same. There is no place for these women as they are. You kick them out, they'll only settle in another town just like this one and probably get kicked out again. You'd just be dumping your problems on someone else, not solving anything."

Bud spoke for the first time in several minutes. "You're talking about rehabilitation."

Curt poked the air with his index finger. "Exactly."

Bud leaned forward, focusing all his attention on Curt. "How would you go about it?"

Mary tried to stay abreast of the conversation as their guest began to explain his ideas. As much as she wanted to hear them, she was so excited over having been heard that she lost track of his words. No one, with the exception of her father, had ever really wanted to know what she thought.

She watched him as he spoke to her father. His stunning good looks made her suck in her breath every time she looked at him. She'd seen handsome men before, but he possessed something beyond handsomeness. It was something from within him, emanating from him, pulsing and charging the very air around him.

He spoke with a confidence that assured her he knew exactly what he was talking about. She believed he must have done some extensive research. That showed he was committed, not merely trying to impress anyone.

He was well dressed, but conservatively so. He was probably well-off but did not make a show of it. She noticed his hands were clean, even under the manicured fingernails. His fingers were long and obviously agile, as opposed to her father's, which were short and thick. Big veins tracked across the broad backs of his hands, which were sprinkled with spiky dark hairs.

As if of their own accord, her eyes sought out his left hand and discovered the lack of a wedding band. What felt like a jolt of lightning struck her as she suddenly became aware of the direction of her thoughts. The man had been in their home not three hours, and she was mesmerized by him.

Curt was aware of Mary's scrutiny of him, although he carefully appeared not to be. He had finished talking and was listening now to her father's point of view. Sarah broke in on them with a scoffing laugh.

"Honestly, Bud — you don't expect the law to do anything about them, do you? The law in this town is a farce!" She squared her shoulders to Curt. "Do you know what the officer said to me when I asked him what the police force was going to do about all this vice? He said: 'This town is a navy port, ma'am. The lads need entertainment when they come ashore.' I couldn't believe it — just couldn't believe it!"

Curt set his face in a grim expression, holding back the grin that wanted to spread across it. "Mrs. Andrews, does your committee have any set plans as to how it's going to accomplish its goals?"

Self-importance filled her face now that she was once again the center of attention. It was obvious to Curt that she hated to be anything less.

"We are trying to have the town council hear our grievances and then act upon them. So far, they have avoided us like the plague, but we will persist until we are heard."

"I'm sure you will." He looked up at the mantle clock. It was nearly eight. He gripped the arms of the chair. "I'm sorry — I didn't realize the time. I have to be going."

He rose, and the others followed suit. He said good-bye to the women in the parlor, being sure to compliment Sarah once again on her cooking. Bud saw him to the door. Checking over his shoulder first, Bud slid open the drawer and allowed Curt to retrieve his firearm. Then they shook hands.

"Thank you for coming over," he preacher said. "You have some very interesting points of view. You'll have my wife thinking for days."

Curt smiled. "Thank you for the invitation. I'm glad I took you up on it." He reached for the doorknob.

"Please feel welcome to come calling anytime."

"Thanks. I just might." He opened the door and stepped out.

He walked out to the road and led Ace down the block in the deepening hues of evening, reflecting on what he'd learned tonight. At the present moment, the Committee was nothing more than a nuisance. He would give it time to either die out or flare up before taking any action. There was no point in creating a problem where there was none.

But in the meantime, he could begin to stack the deck in his favor. He would wind himself around the lives of this family and, card by card, deal himself into their trust. Should the need arise, he would destroy them from the inside. How many of those old biddies would follow Sarah Andrews once they learned that her daughter was sleeping with the enemy?

CHAPTER FIVE

The Carlton was filled to bursting with customers as Curt pressed his way through the doors. Del was belting out a song above the din — only half the room had stopped to watch her tonight. He shouldered his way to the bar and ordered a shot of rum.

Willie approached him, walking with his odd rolling gait as though he were still shipboard in rough seas.

"Business is good tonight, eh, Willie?" Curt remarked, tossing a coin on the bar top.

The bartender nodded as he poured him a shot. He left the bottle and took the money. Curt picked up the little glass and tossed back the liquor, enjoying the sear of it down to his belly. He scanned the room, knowing it wouldn't be long before some sheep came willingly to be sheared.

For now, Curt chose the only empty table in the place, one right at the edge of the dance floor where he could enjoy an unobstructed view of Del.

Del watched him while she strutted about the stage, her view repeatedly interrupted by couples dancing on the floor between them. All the women dancing were paid for the service. Not all of them also bedded their male partners, but most of them would to turn an extra buck. She was glad she didn't have to do that anymore.

As the swift tempo of the lurid song she sang dropped and changed into a slow love song, she curbed her wriggling and stood at center-stage. Her eyes fixed on Curt, she crooned the song for him. She didn't mind that he remained engrossed in the game — the quick glance and reserved smile he gave her were enough to let her know he was listening.

The couples below her coarsely waltzed to the music. Not one of them could dance like her Curt. When Curt danced with her, it was to her as if they were making love on their feet. His movements were sure, smooth, and rhythmic, though in bed they often lost the restraint he showed on the dance floor.

She smiled to herself as she remembered how many of the women below her had tried to catch Curt and even steal him away from her. They hadn't stood a chance. He was her man. He had rescued her from a doomed lifestyle and made her his queen.

She almost faltered in her refrain as a big, tall man stumbled onto the floor. From the corner of her eye, he'd looked like Frank Stone, but a direct look revealed him to be only a lumberjack. She'd never seen him before, but that meant little — new hands were always coming in to replace the crewmen lost on the job. This 'jack was drunk and dancing with only a whiskey bottle. He stomped around, pitting and splintering the dance floor with the pointed metal calks studded into the soles of his boots. She glanced around for Willie, who would surely throw him out for wearing those boots in here. Oblivious to the damage he was causing, the lumberjack whirled carelessly, bumping into the couples as though he wasn't even aware of them.

His haunting resemblance to the late marshal was enough to stir angry memories in Del. Memories of how, even though she'd already belonged to Curt at the time, Stone had tried to make her his. The bastard had even tried to rape her when she'd repeatedly refused him. Only Curt had saved her from that horror.

She finished her song and curtsied at the edge of the stage. The lumberjack whirled close by her at that very moment. His eyes met hers, and before she could react, he had reached up and plucked her off the stage.

He swung her to her feet, dropping the whiskey, oblivious to the couple that stumbled over the rolling, spewing bottle. He tried to dance the new tune with Del. She struggled with brewing outrage, but his iron grip was unbreakable. He had pulled her too close for her to knee him in the balls. Her silver derringer was in her reticule — which she'd left upstairs.

As he twirled with her about the floor, she saw Curt on his feet and about to intervene. But at that second, an idea struck her, and she smiled at him, inclining her head with a wink for him to wait. He hesitated then sat back down.

She turned her face up to her captor and smiled sweetly. "What's your name, honey?"

It took him a second to focus on her, and then finally he said, "Wesley Keegan. My friends call me Wes." He squeezed her so tight the old Colt Navy revolver jammed into his belt gored into her ribs just below her breasts. "You call me Wes, little darlin'."

"Wes is a handsome name," she said. "It suits you." He was ugly enough to stop a hitch of six runaway mules. "I'll bet you're American," she said, "and that you're new here. Otherwise you wouldn't be wearing that six-shooter."

"A man's got a right to be armed, wherever he is. Ain't no sissy Canada Bobbies gonna scare me none. Hell, I ain't never seen a one of 'em even carry a gun." He smiled, revealing yellow-brown teeth and breath that nearly made her retch.

"They do when they need to," she told him then returned to pouring on her charm. "You're a fine dancer, Wes. I think I like you. But you see, we have a little problem."

"What problem? I don't see no problem, sweet thing."

"I'm only tellin' you this 'cause I think you're nice, and I don't want to see you get hurt." She pressed her lips tightly together, trying not to laugh. "See, I belong to that man over there, and he don't like me dancin' with other men."

Keegan followed her gaze to Curt, who stared back at him darkly. "What — that little pipsqueak? Hell, I'd take him apart with one hand. Want me to, little darlin'?"

Del feigned greater concern. "He's too good a shot — you'd never get near him."

He squinted at Curt. "He a gambler?"

"Yep."

"Then he probably gots more on him than I can see."

"Yep. He's got a boot knife." She wouldn't tell him everything, certainly not about the derringer.

"Well, I got me a knife, too."

Del followed his hairy paw to the shaft of the biggest knife she had ever seen. Sheathed in leather at his left side, the length of the blade had to be ten inches. The broad handle was overlaid with shiny blue abalone.

"I took me that off'n a gambler in 'Frisco who tried to cheat me. 'Course, I gutted him with it for good measure."

A fleeting fear rippled through Del before she feigned approval. Keegan had loosened his grip enough for her to slide her hand up his arm. She pointed to the knife when they were in a position for Curt to see it. The gambler nodded to her that he had.

"You still gotta get close to him," she insisted. "It'd be better if you could sneak off a shot." It would be better for him to be at closer range for Curt's derringer.

He grinned devilishly. "You want me to, darlin'?"

She nodded.

His attitude became suddenly wary. "What'd be in it for me? You gonna be grateful to me?"

She smiled and slid her hand down to squeeze his crotch through his pants. The lumberjack grinned and chuckled.

"Bet that's a bigger piece o' meat than you get from him. Darlin', I'd purt near split you in half."

She cooed and rubbed up against him.

That convinced him. Nearly dragging her to within twenty feet of Curt's table, Keegan pushed her away from him and pulled out his gun. The dancing couples gasped in shock and fell away from him.

Del stepped back a few paces to watch Curt. She loved to see him move. The lumberjack had already drawn. In one smooth, lightning-swift arc of his arm, Curt's hand snaked into his vest and drew the derringer clear. Cocking the hammer with his thumb, he rose from the table, turning his body squarely to Keegan's, and fired. The .41 caliber bullet pocked into Keegan's right bicep. The lumberjack's pistol clattered to the floor without ever having been fired. His body twisted sideways, and he clutched at his arm with a roar of pain.

Then there was no sound but the slip of Curt's weapon back into his vest. The silence was broken seconds later by Del's laughter. She held her stomach and pointed at the astounded lumberjack.

"You stupid ass! You stupid fuckin' ass!"

He stared at her as she laughed, finally catching on that he'd been suckered. His huge jaw set hard, and his face colored as red as the blood splotching his shirtsleeve.

Del walked up to him. As she reached him, her laughter stopped abruptly. She hauled off and smacked him across the face with a crack that made everyone flinch. "Don't you ever touch me again!" she told him, her voice venomous. "Nobody touches Curt Prescott's woman! Nobody!" With that, she spun away from him and strode to Curt. She pressed close to him, kissing the corner of his mouth. He smiled at her and gave her a squeeze.

Willie, who had run out to the bar room from the kitchen when he heard the shot, now rolled over to the lumberjack. He took him by his good arm and dragged him toward the door. Keegan was too stunned to resist, although he easily could have. Willie shoved him at the door and pointed down the street.

"The doc's that away."

Keegan gaped back into the room. "He tried to kill me! Why don't somebody get the law?"

Willie shook his head. "Mister, you really are a stupid ass. If Curt Prescott had wanted to kill you, you wouldn't be on your way to the doc's — I'd be sending for the undertaker. Now get out! And don't ever come back in here with them bloody boots on, or I'll shoot you myself!" The rotund little man shoved the giant in the kidneys, forcing him out into the street to a chorus of laughter from the houseful of patrons.

As soon as the lumberjack was gone, Curt was besieged by men wanting to take him on in a game of poker. Curt obliged them, leading the way to the games room. Del got a drink from the bar then returned to stand at his shoulder and watch the game until her next set.

At closing time, they met at the bar and climbed the stairs to their suite together. As they closed the door behind them, Curt let out a chuckle.

"I trust you thoroughly enjoyed that little game?"

"I sure did — the bastard. That'll teach him a lesson."

"And everybody else who doesn't already know better."

Del walked into the bedroom and started getting out of her clothes. After shedding her dress, she made a face as one of the hooks to her corset got stuck on some threads. Curt stepped up to help her.

"Thanks, lover."

Once she was clear, he squatted at the corner of the bedroom rug. He lifted it and tossed it back, exposing a floor safe. He spun the combination and lifted the lid.

She glanced at him over her shoulder. "How much did you win tonight?"

"Just over a hundred bucks."

"Not bad."

He stacked most of the money from his wallet and pockets neatly into the safe. He reserved some to work with.

"You gotta have close to two hundred thousand in there," Del said, slipping on a peach silk dressing gown. "I seen a lotta gamblers in my time, darlin',and you're the only one I know who can hang onto his money." She smiled, adding as an afterthought, "And we still live damn good." Lifting her shoeless foot to her chair, she unsnapped her stockings from her garter belt and began to roll them down.

His mind drifting to the past, Curt muttered, "Things might not always be this good." He closed up the safe and dropped the blue carpet over it before standing.

"Oh, they will. You're the best. We'll always be set up fine." She gazed at him as he turned to face her.

He took a long, appreciative look at her legs. Stepping closer, he stroked the inside of her raised thigh. Then he brushed her hands away from her stocking and slowly rolled it down himself.

In the morning, they took brunch in the empty saloon as Earl's was closed on Sundays. The Carlton always had a morning spread of cold meats and cheeses, scrambled and boiled eggs, breads and pastries, and fruits and vegetables laid out along the far end of the bar. While they ate, Curt outlined his plan for Del on how he would gain the Andrews' trust in order to destroy the committee. She thought it was a good plan, with one exception.

"I just don't like the idea of you bein' seen around town with — with — what's-her-name?"

"Mary." He sipped his coffee and set it down on the dark walnut tabletop.

"How plain," she remarked with a sniff. "I'll bet she's as boring as her name. And a virgin too, right?"

"Of course. But that's what'll make it sting so bad."

She nodded once and looked down at her scrambled eggs. She pushed them around her plate with her fork.

Curt reached across and covered her hand with his. "Del, nobody's gonna know I'm seeing her until the very last second. The Andrews don't know who I am, but nearly everybody else in town does. If anybody sees us together before the right time it'd blow everything. As it is, I've gotta risk they don't drop my name to the wrong person."

She raised her eyes to his, and a small smile curved the corners of her mouth.

He squeezed her hand. "So don't worry. Nobody's gonna start thinking I've lost interest in my queen of hearts."

Her smile widened, and her teeth showed brightly between her red lips. "I love you."

"I know." He lifted his hand and stroked her rouged cheek. She leaned her face into his palm and sighed contentedly.

Shortly after noon on Monday, he left Del at the Carlton after brunching at Earl's and headed for Andrews' Saddlery. A tiny bell tinkled above his head as he entered. The pungent smell of leather rushed into his nostrils.

Neatly displayed on long racks to his left were a dozen saddles of various styles, most brand new but some secondhand. Hanging from wooden pegs on the wall behind them were bridles to match each one. Two small windows broke the monotony of the long wall. Beyond the second window and up to a sales counter at the back of the room, the wall was filled with halters, breast collars, and all sorts of miscellaneous horse gear. From the wall on his right hung a couple of driving harnesses. Curt wandered down the open aisle toward the counter. Further down were shelves of saddle soap, neat's-foot oil, assorted buckles and snaps, and other goods. A doorway opened in the right-hand wall directly opposite the counter.

Bud appeared in this doorway, wiping his hands on a rag which he then stuffed into the pocket of his denim apron. When he saw Curt, his face brightened. Smiling warmly, he extended his hand. "Mr. Prescott — I'm so glad you came by."

Curt shook with him. "Afternoon, sir. Nice place you have here."

"Thank you. I must admit I hadn't expected you so soon."

"I was free, so I thought it was as good a time as any."

Bud placed his hand on Curt's back. Steeling himself, Curt allowed it there. "Would you like to see the shop — where I do the actual work?"

"Yes."

Pleasure was obvious on Bud's face as he steered Curt through the doorway. The back room was rougher in appearance than the front. It smelled of wet leather and dyes. But it was spacious and well laid out, providing ample room to move about from bench to bench. Each workbench had its own set of tools, kept handy on a hook or in an appropriate box or drawer. Bud led him around to each station, briefly explaining what he did at each one, what function each tool performed.

A large, square, metal tub caught Curt's attention. It was half-full of water, kept lukewarm by a burner underneath. He tapped it with his fingers.

"What's this for?"

Bud stepped closer, apparently glad Curt had asked him a question. "To soften the leather. You see, when the leather is wet, it can be shaped easily into any form I choose. Then I just let it dry, and it keeps its new shape. Otherwise it would be quite a lot of trouble in the tight spots."

"I see. But I thought it wasn't good to get leather that wet?"

"I oil it well afterward, and the flexibility comes back." Bud chuckled. "You may think it's a strange comparison, but I like to think of soaking it in the water as a baptism of sorts. It prepares it to accept its new life on a saddle tree, just as baptism prepares a man to accept a life shaped by Jesus Christ."

Glancing away, Curt prepared himself to withstand the upcoming sermon. As he suspected, the parson had more to say.

"Then, as we regularly clean and oil a saddle, we keep it supple and strong. When we ask Christ's forgiveness and believe that He sustains us, Our Savior cleanses us and nurtures us through even the most arid times of our lives. Without the oil, leather dries up, cracks, and becomes weak. Without Christ, the same thing happens to a man's soul."

Curt saw in Bud's eyes that he truly believed all he had said. But it meant nothing to Curt. Less than nothing. He looked away from the preacher's face, swinging his eyes over the shop once more. "Pretty interesting."

"I didn't see you in church yesterday."

Curt drew a deep breath. "To tell you the truth, parson, I've never been much of a church-goer. No offense intended to you."

"None taken. But you might find our church a little different. It's my personal belief that rigid rituals for the sake of rigid rituals more often block our access to God than facilitate it. I prefer a more relaxed, open atmosphere where people can ask questions and explore their relationship with spirit rather than have some dogma forced upon them."

"I see." Curt toyed with a long leather lace hanging from a nail in the post next to him.

"Ultimately, our relationship with God is a personal one, and I find private prayer very rewarding."

"Can't say as I've ever done any real praying." Curt wandered over to a bench and picked up a metal tool to examine.

"Prayer is simply conversation with spirit. While you certainly may if you wish, you don't need to fold your hands and kneel in a gilded pew to connect with God. You can be standing alone in the middle of the wilderness, and if you speak to Him with sincerity in your heart, you are praying."

"Hmm." Curt put down the tool and picked up a small hammer.

"My son, I would never force anything on anyone, but it does concern me that you appear to have no regard for your own —"

The bell jingled out front. Bud said, "Excuse me," and walked out to meet the newcomer. Once through the doorway he said, "Ah, Sarah."

"I have Mary scrubbing floors today," Curt heard her say. "So I brought you your lunch instead."

"Thank you, dear. Mr. Prescott is here — dropped by for a visit."

Curt took that as a cue and stepped into the store. He took off his hat for Sarah's sake.

"Why, how nice," she said with a smile too tight to be genuine. "It's lovely to see you again, Mr. Prescott."

"And you, too, Mrs. Andrews." He noticed the small wicker basket on her arm, covered with a red- and white-checkered cloth.

"If I had known you were coming I would have made more." She walked up and set the basket on the counter.

"Thank you, but it's just as well — I've already eaten."

Bud asked him, "So you won't mind if I partake?"

"No, go right ahead."

Bud settled himself on the tall stool behind the counter and folded back the cloth. He picked out half a sandwich and began to munch on it.

Sarah turned her plump body to face Curt. "Will we ever see you at our home again, Mr. Prescott?"

He threw her a charming smile. "Anytime you'd care to invite me, I'll be there."

She very nearly giggled. "Would tomorrow night be all right with you?"

"Tomorrow night would be just fine."

She smiled and looked over at her husband. "Wonderful! Did you hear that, Bud? He'll join us for dinner tomorrow evening."

Bud nodded. "Mary will be so pleased."

Curt caught the startled look Sarah shot her husband.

"Truly," she said after some hesitation. "She couldn't stop talking about him all evening."

Curt sensed that was an exaggeration, but it was still enlightening. They were wasting no time matchmaking, which suited him just fine. It made his job that much easier. He had figured the preacher would've been far more subtle, far more cautious. Which was strange, in a way — Sarah was the rigid one. Bud, at least so far, appeared as easy-going as an old dog on a hot summer day.

Curt bowed his head to Sarah, then to Bud, and confirmed his arrival at their home the following evening at five. Setting his hat back on his head, he turned and walked out of the saddlery.

CHAPTER SIX

Bud opened the front door at Curt's knock the next evening. Without waiting to be asked, Curt removed his gun belt, which he'd deliberately worn, and tucked it in the hall table drawer. Bud smiled and invited him to sit in the parlor. The preacher picked up on their conversation at the saddlery from the day before. Curt sat quietly, listened politely, and tried not to appear too bored.

Curt didn't see Mary until she and her mother began setting the table. They exchanged a greeting just before sitting down to eat. She seemed even more nervous than she had the other night, her eyes darting to and from his face, her hands unsure of what to do with their utensils. He wondered if her mother had told her of the matchmaking plans. He wondered how Mary felt about that. There was no anger or resentment in her face — she probably liked the idea as well. He smiled at her. She dropped her fork.

After dinner, they had their tea in the parlor again. Curt entertained them with small talk and was always alert to whatever they volunteered to him. As the clock chimed eight, Sarah offered more tea and rose to fetch it. Mary got up to help, but her mother waved her down. A moment after Sarah left the room she summoned her husband. He excused himself and went into the kitchen.

Aware that they'd been deliberately left alone and doubly aware that two pair of ears would keep close tabs on them from the kitchen, Curt contemplated his next words while he settled his eyes on Mary. She was studying her hands in her lap. He shifted in his chair, enough to make her look at him out of reflex. She smiled politely and moved her eyes off to one of the pictures on the wall.

"You're not talking very much this evening, Miss Andrews," Curt said, breaking the silence.

Startled, she struggled for her voice. "I — I suppose I haven't got much to say."

"I don't believe you. One look in your pretty green eyes was enough for me to see an intelligent young woman with a mind full of things to say."

His compliment caught her off guard, and crimson flooded her cheeks.

"And you're modest, too. I like that. Vain women make me ill."

She dipped her head forward, as if trying to hide from him. He noticed a particularly wide strip of gold in her hair, running from her left temple, curling over her ear, and blending into the long hair resting softly on her shoulders.

"Your parents seem to want us to get to know each other better. How do you feel about that?"

She flinched then tried to cover it by tucking her hair behind her ear even though it didn't need tucking.

When she didn't answer, Curt said, "I can't speak for you, of course, but I would welcome the chance to know you, Miss Andrews. I believe we have some common interests." He paused, letting her think briefly on that. "But of course, if you're not interested, we should inform your parents at once, so there'll be no misunderstandings."

She bit on her bottom lip. He remained silent.

After a long moment, she said softly, "Perhaps ... if we went very slowly ..."

He could see she was trying to maintain the correct degree of propriety while letting him know she was, indeed, interested. He smiled. He had given her the choice, and she had made it.

Clasping her hands tightly in her lap, Mary tried to stop trembling. She just could not believe that this charming young man was the rogue her parents made him out to be. She had been shocked when they revealed his identity to her after he'd left the other evening, and even though she understood her father's reasoning, she was uncomfortable with pretending she didn't know what kind of man Curt Prescott was.

What shocked her even more was that she felt no revulsion toward him when she knew she ought to. He was the embodiment of sin, at least according to her mother, and should be shunned.

But she much preferred her father's approach. Shunning him could not change the man. It was necessary to accept him as he was into their lives and hopefully, by example, show him the way.

If he could be changed, it would be a boost, too, to her father's spirits. He had come west so full of optimism, hoping so hard to make a difference in the lives of the people here that it had crushed him when he had failed to reach those who most needed reaching. He had been laughed out of every saloon and sporting establishment in town.

But it had not even been three months. She had pointed that out to him — and the very fact of his growing new congregation. It seemed to make him feel a little better, but still she could tell he felt a failure. The faithful didn't need him as much as the lost. If he could turn Curt Prescott away from sin and onto a righteous path, he would feel like he had accomplished something.

Straightening her spine, she privately vowed to shake off this paralyzing case of nerves that had struck her since Curt Prescott came into their home this night. She would do everything she could to help her father win Curt over to God.

The Carlton was quiet when Curt walked through the doors later that night. It was Del's night off. He checked the saloon with a brief glance to see if she was having a drink with the other girls. She was not.

He strode up the stairs and found the door locked. He twisted his key in the lock and went in. The lamp between the sitting room and bedroom was up full, its light intense in the doorway, but fading to dark shadows along the far walls.

"Curt, darlin'— is that you?"

"You bet!" He tossed his hat on the rack and followed her voice to the alcove off the bedroom. She was submerged to the shoulders in the white claw-footed tub, her flaxen hair already washed and half-dry, piled atop her head. A few strands hung down, wet and dark. The alcove was lit softly with another lamp.

"Little late for a bath, ain't it?"

She shook her head. He walked across the floor and sat on the edge of the tub near her feet. She pressed her feet against the end of the tub, raising her shoulders out of the water until her breasts appeared to float on the surface. He admired them, feeling himself stir. He could never get enough of her.

"How was your dinner?" she asked.

"Good."

"Are they eating out of your hand yet?"

"Damn close. Mama and Papa Andrews have already got me figured as husband material for their little girl."

Del's eyes widened, and her mouth dropped open. "I didn't think them religious types moved that fast."

He cocked an eyebrow. "From what I've picked up, the old bitch's been trying to get her married since before they left back east. She's nineteen years old."

"Practically an old maid. And never even been kissed, I'll bet."

"I'd back that bet any day of the week."

Del chuckled, squeezing the large sponge in her hand. Then she looked him over with a sultry smile. "When was the last time you had a for-real bath?"

He turned thoughtful eyes to the ceiling. "Couple days ago."

"Then I think it's time you had another one." She flicked the water at him.

He raised his hand to block the splash. "Hey — you're gettin' my clothes all wet."

"So take 'em off, stud. I want you in this tub with me. Pronto."

Grinning, he stood up and shucked his clothes without delay. Facing her, he stepped into the tub. She ran her fingers over his lean and supple sinews then grabbed his stiffening prick.

"That's a good boy."

The second he was seated their mouths came together, rough, demanding, and hungry.

He had no idea what time it was when a loud knocking jarred him out of a peaceful sleep. Someone was hammering at the door.

"Goddamnit." He extricated himself from Del, who clung to him still half asleep on the bed. The pounding continued while he pulled on his pants. He grabbed the Colt from its holster and cocked the hammer as he approached the door.

This better be good, he thought as he stepped to the side of the door. Without a sound, he unlocked it and threw it open.

A boy of about twelve in tattered overalls looked up at him. It was Fat Johnnie's messenger boy. Curt eased the hammer down and lowered the Colt. He checked his annoyance.

"Hi, there, Mickey. What's the problem?"

"The boss is in jail, Mr. Prescott. And some girls. He wants ya to come down 'n' get him sprung."

"Why can't he just bail himself out?"

"Constable Jenkins won't let him."

That was strange. Lay enough money in Dave Jenkins' hand, and he'd spring the devil himself. It warranted a looking into. Curt sighed. "Okay. I'll be down there in a bit."

The boy nodded and was off down the hall toward the open window near the back stairs. Curt closed the door.

Del was sitting up as he walked back into the bedroom and started dressing.

"That fat sonovabitch. Sets himself up a whoremaster and then can't even look after his business. How the hell did I ever get elected nursemaid for these crybabies?"

"'Cause you shot Frank Stone, that's how."

"Yeah, well, he and I had our own disagreement."

Del smiled softly. "And I'm grateful you won."

He met her eyes and returned her smile.

"But you did everybody a favor, all the same. Nobody else woulda dared."

Curt chuckled wryly. "The asshole came lookin' for me. I merely obliged him." He buckled on the Colt and pressed his hat on his head. "I'll be back as soon as I can."

"I'll be waitin'."

He went out the door and down the back stairs. The alley was dark and empty. On Government Street, he lit himself a thin cigar and smoked it as he walked. A few windows of the police barracks glowed softly with lamplight. He let himself in to find Dave Jenkins waiting for him at the front counter.

"Curt — I been expectin' you."

"What gives, Dave?"

With a glance at the night clerk and a jerk of his head, Jenkins led Curt back to the holding cells. The second they saw him, Fat Johnnie and the three prostitutes rose from the bunks they sat on and nodded at each other.

Jenkins scratched at his stringy hair. "Ol' Johnnie here — " he cocked his thumb at the fat man " — decided to break some real important bones tonight."

Fat Johnnie charged the cell bars and shook them. "How the hell was I supposed to know they was somebodies?" His hair looked orange against the burgundy suit he was wearing.

Jenkins continued with barely a glance at Johnnie. "Seems Johnnie's gals here were takin' a stroll around the Amulet Hotel and picked up three well-heeled customers. Took 'em back to Johnnie's joint for the fun 'n' games and got more'n they bargained for."

"Just look at 'em!" Johnnie yelled.

Curt eyed the women closely. All three of them had black eyes, swollen lips, and several ugly bruises elsewhere on their sparsely-clad bodies.

"I hadda go in there and bust 'em up! Nobody smacks my girls around! Nobody but me, anyhow!"

"The sharp edge is, though," Jenkins told Curt, "that them three boys is kin to that Judge Laird across the pond in New Westminster. You know, the one makin' headlines in The Colonist about being chums with old Hangin' Judge Begbie, and together they're gonna clean up B.C."

"I read that, too, but I think it's a load of crap. Just Laird looking for attention."

Jenkins shrugged. "Maybe. Anyways, these boys made sure I knowed they got political connections. They said if I didn't lock this bunch up, they'd make sure their uncle hears about it. They could take my job, Curt."

"I see." Curt considered the situation carefully. "How long do these boys plan on staying in town?"

"Considerin' they shouldn'a oughta hit them gals, I asked 'em to leave on the first ship out tomorrow mornin'. And I'll see that they do."

Fat Johnnie spat on the floor in disgust. "Sure — them pretty boys get off easy, and us victims get locked up! Some justice!"

Jenkins scowled at him. "I'd say two broken arms, three broken noses, and a few lost teeth is fair payment."

"Fuck you!"

Curt stepped up to the bars. "Jenkins did the right thing here, Johnnie. After all, your girls were uptown. If they hadn't been, it's likely none of this would have happened. These boys could cause us all a lot of grief. I think you ought to spend the night here, and Jenkins'll let you go once the boys are gone. It's the best thing all around."

Fat Johnnie's face turned livid with rage. "Whose side are you on? You're outta your mind! I ain't stayin' here all night!"

Curt casually took out his watch and read the time. "It's ten after three, Johnnie. You've only gotta stay half a night."

"God damn you, Prescott — you're supposed to help me, not leave me in here!"

Curt cocked an eyebrow at him. "You fucked up, Johnnie. Take the consequences like a man. Maybe next time you'll keep your girls to your own end of town."

He turned away from Fat Johnnie, said goodnight to Jenkins, and walked out the door.

CHAPTER SEVEN

Thursday evening, shortly after the supper hour, Curt took the liberty of presenting himself at the Andrews' front door. Bud's face brightened with surprise.

Curt took off his hat. "Evening, parson. I hope I'm not intruding."

"No, never. Come in, come in! We were just wondering when we would see you again."

Curt smiled as he tucked away his gun belt. "Be careful — you might find it hard to get rid of me if you're always so hospitable."

Chuckling, Bud showed him into the parlor. Both Mary and Sarah had been crocheting doilies. Already having set them down, they rose to greet him. Sarah overflowed with sickly sweetness, fussing over Curt as though he were her newborn son. Mary said hello and hung back, out of her mother's way, but her eyes glowed with warmth when she looked at him.

When finally Sarah had eased off and they'd all sat down, Curt directed his attention to her.

"I'd planned to attend your committee meeting last night," he lied. "But I got tied up. Would you mind filling me in on the results?"

Straightening her spine with self-importance, Sarah smiled. "Certainly. The town council at last attended, and they have our grievances now in writing. They have promised to look into each matter very carefully and to see that something is done."

"Can you be more specific?"

"They will have a meeting with certain constables to make clear the laws on —," pausing, she cleared her throat deliberately, "— prostitution and gambling in this town. Laws against such have been 'on the books,' as they say, for some time, but there are some who question certain officers' enforcement of the law."

Curt raised his eyebrows. "Really?"

Sarah nodded. "Especially Constable David Jenkins. It seems that his methods are largely ineffective. If he even arrests the fallen women, he rarely jails them or charges them fines. If he does fine them, he sets them free to earn the money to pay their fines by the very profession for which they were arrested. It's atrocious!" She gazed at the three of them, expecting their accord. "And he virtually ignores the gambling going on in all the saloons — and not just in Chinatown, either. Every day our menfolk are throwing away their hard-earned money on games of chance." She smiled, blinking rapidly, at Bud. "Not all our menfolk, of course, but even one is too many. Just think of how prosperous each family could be if the money was not wasted on these evil sports."

Curt nodded and settled himself for a long lecture. Sarah went on and on, but he did not for a second allow himself to look bored. Finally, her bosom heaving and her voice hoarse, she talked herself out. She rose from the chesterfield, offering everyone tea.

While she was gone, Curt grabbed the opportunity to get Mary talking. "How've you been, Miss Andrews?"

"Just fine, Mr. Prescott, thank you," Mary replied. She appeared a little stiff to Curt, as though she were determined to keep her nerves under control. "I've been keeping busy in the garden these past few days."

"It's been beautiful weather for gardening, hasn't it?"

"Yes."

"Do you like gardens, Mr. Prescott?"

"Very much."

Bud gripped his knees and leaned forward. "Then you should see what Mary has done in the backyard. She has a way with growing things." He nodded his head at his daughter. "Why don't you take Mr. Prescott out back and show him, Mary?"

Curt heard her quick intake of breath. She looked at her father, as if to be doubly sure he meant it.

"Yes, go on." He waved her off.

"All right," she said and rose from the chesterfield just as her mother was returning with a tea tray.

Sarah eyed them curiously as Curt stood up and followed Mary past her. Bud said, "Mary's going to show him the garden, Sarah. I'm sure the tea will keep for a few minutes."

"Of — of course." She set the tray down on the coffee table. Her smile was a little forced, and the look she cast her husband questioned the wisdom of allowing the garden tour.

Mary led Curt out the back door. The back yard was a little rougher than the front. The grass had been trimmed but the yard was broken with rocky outcroppings. A dense stand of trees fringed the fence, offering privacy and shade. One dogwood billowed with snowy blossoms over the south fence while most of the others were cedar and fir. One oak stood just inside the southwest corner, its pale green leaflets still rolled — the oaks always seemed to be the last to unfurl their leaves in summery splendor.

A small vegetable garden was broken along the south fence, and near it a young apple tree blossomed. A crescent-shaped rock garden rose near the center of the lawn, but Mary led Curt along the fence first, showing him the sweet violets, bluebells, and lilies of the valley blooming in the partial shade along the fence.

"Very nice," Curt told her. "Very nice."

She dipped her head, her eyes flitting away even as a tiny smile curved her pink lips. "Thank you. I can't take all the credit, though. Much of this was already here when we came, just neglected. I've just tidied things up and done a little rearranging."

"I hope you like blackberries," Curt remarked, noting the thick tangled brambles growing between the Andrews' property and the neighbor's.

"We've never had them," Mary replied. "I don't think they grow back east."

"Well, just wait for August, and I guarantee you'll enjoy them."

They strolled along the back fence, and Curt scrutinized the other side. Some low brush, but no brambles. A few yards beyond the fence, the ground dropped off into the very ravine he often walked. How many times, he wondered, had he passed beneath her and not even been aware of her presence? He leaned over the fence for a better look. From what he could see from here, it was steep, but passable.

At the north fence, a huge bush of purple lilacs perfumed the air with their delicate sweetness. Mary stopped to nuzzle a bunch.

"These are my favorites," she said. "We had them back home, too."

He looked closely at her. "You don't consider Victoria home yet?"

She hesitated then shook her head. "It isn't that. It's beautiful here. It's just that this is the first time we've lived anywhere but where I was born. I miss some people and some things. But wherever my family is, is home to me."

He nodded with understanding. Mary led him to the rock garden then, and they circled it slowly.

"Your father's right," Curt said to her. "You do have a way with growing things."

She brushed a hand across her cheek and tucked some stray hairs behind her ear. "Thank you."

Curt could feel her parents' eyes on his back. They had been watching through the kitchen window from the moment the door had closed behind him and Mary. They might like him, but they weren't taking any chances.

"Do you like lavender?" he asked, pointing to the long row of spiky grey-green stems fringing the base of the rock garden.

"Oh, yes, I love it. We used to buy it dried back home. But here, the west coast, seems to have so much more ... life in it. There's always something blooming or growing, it seems."

He nodded and squatted before the stems. Scatterings of purple blossoms were beginning to bloom in earnest. Mary crouched next to him and drew a sprig to her nose.

"It doesn't smell much yet."

He chuckled.

"What is it?" she asked, tipping her head to one side and looking at him curiously.

"Did you know that a sprig of innocent lavender, given by one lover to another, signifies distrust?"

"Does it really?"

Nodding, he cast his eyes over the rest of the rock garden. "And if I were to give you those daisies over there ..." He pointed. "It'd mean we share the same sentiments. If they were mine to give, I would, because I think we do."

Mary's eyes were bright with fascination.

"Or ..." He looked a little further. "That red rose over there means that a lady is pure and lovely, but if a man sends her a yellow one, it means he's a jealous lover."

Her eyes were now fastened on his. "Truly? How charming!" Then she giggled. "It seems odd that a man should know so much about flowers — it's usually a feminine obsession. How did you learn all that?"

"My mother. She was the daughter of a professional gardener — a horticulturist, she called him."

"Oh? Tell me more, please. You hardly ever talk about yourself."

He stood up and held out his hand to her. She looked at it a moment before placing hers in it and allowing him to aid her ascent. He held her hand firmly, feeling the heat prickling between their palms. She must have felt it too, for she withdrew her hand suddenly. Almost glancing at the kitchen window, she tucked the hand into the pocket hidden in the folds of her skirt.

He nearly smiled. She, too, knew they were being watched. He wondered if she might have left her hand in his longer if they were not. They strolled around the garden once again.

"Well," he began, in answer to her query, "my mother was born and raised in Seattle. Her parents were English. And, as I said, they were gardeners, and they had a flower shop as well. My mother used to help her mother in the shop. Their specialty was helping customers send messages of love to sweethearts — through the language of flowers."

"How romantic!" Mary's hands came out of her pockets and clapped together with delight. "And she taught you everything she knew?"

"As much as she could before she died."

Mary's enthusiasm faded. "Oh, yes, Dad told me she was ... I'm sorry."

"It's all right. It was a long time ago."

"But you still have your father and other relatives ..."

"No."

She tipped her head in that curious way again, and his mind searched for a way to put her off questions. They had made a full circle back to the lilacs. Knowing full well that her parents were still watching, he reached up and took a branch in his fingers. It was a limber twig, and at first it resisted his attempt to snap it, but after a deft twist, it came free. He presented the cone-shaped bunch of flowers to Mary, who took them with astonishment, and a hint of disapproval, on her face. He held her eyes with his.

"Purple lilacs speak for a heart experiencing the first emotions of love."

All trace of objection vanished from her face, replaced by a rosy glow. "Mr. Prescott, you shouldn't have ..."

"Shouldn't have what? Given you the lilacs as my secret message or plundered your parents' bush?"

She tore her eyes from his without answering.

He took her elbow lightly. "Perhaps we should go back in now."

She cast a careful glance toward the window. "Yes, I suppose we should."

They walked back inside. Curt wasted no time in singing Mary's praises to her parents while Sarah poured the tea. Neither Bud nor Sarah mentioned the liberty he'd taken with their bush, but Curt could see Sarah struggling with the urge to bring it up. One glance at Bud told him that her husband had forbidden her to do so. Perhaps the old dog did have the balls to keep his wife in check. If he hadn't, it would be a safe bet Sarah would spend the next half hour bawling over one broken branch on one bush.

Curt sipped his tea and turned his eyes to Mary. She still held the lilacs, and now and then she raised them to her nose to smell them. She had small, pretty hands, despite a slight toughness in her skin that had come from everyday work. He could still feel the imprint of her hand in his. It seemed charged with heat, searing its way to his midriff where it disturbed him with an uneasy feeling. He found himself staring at her lips, and his own hungered to taste them. Her pert breasts and the innocent movements of her body were an allure he found hard to resist. He imagined her naked body against his, and his loins stirred.

Immediately, he focused his attention on Bud, redirecting his mind and distracting his body. The last thing he needed was a tent pole in his trousers.

When he left about an hour later, a thin layer of cloud veiled the stars, and the moon was on the wane. The residential streets were empty, and most houses had their lamps turned down already. The air was absolutely still.

The sudden bark of a dog startled him less than his sudden desire for Mary. That in itself concerned him only in its unexpectedness. He had planned to seduce her from the beginning but had considered it in a mechanical, practical manner. That he should suddenly actually want her with an urgency that tried his patience was curious, to say the least.

But it was not a problem. Years of practice in complete self-mastery gave him an edge most men did not have. The rigid discipline was self-imposed. From the moment in his youth when he had decided he would become a professional gambler, he had known the importance of self-control. He had seen the gamblers who practiced it win big and live to enjoy it. Those who ignored its importance rarely lived long enough to regret their oversight.

Early in his career, he had learned to screen every word before it left his mouth, every expression before it reached his face, every gesture before he made it. The slightest twitch of a nerve in his face could cost him the pot, the slightest hint that he might be better with the cards than he professed could cost him his life.

He'd studied people to learn their cards — and their intentions — by their faces and mannerisms. He'd studied their styles, their speech patterns, their way of carrying themselves, and learned to imitate until he was at home with even the stuffiest of characters. He could be as suave as the blue bloods or as coarse as the street-scum.

Besides mastering his manners at an early age, he had also mastered his carnal instincts. The concentration necessary in a serious game was impossible when distracted by the rutting urge.

As for any young man, overriding a stiffened prick and trying to ignore the painted ladies so freely offering themselves to him was more than difficult. Even harder, though, was the jeering he had to withstand once he'd begun to master his baser needs. When no longer able to entice him at their whim, those whores who saw him as merely easy young prey fell to insulting his masculinity to try to shame him into bedding them. He couldn't blame them — they needed the business to survive — but it was no easy task to grit his teeth and put up with it.

Now, however, he was years older and long since passed caring what they or anybody else thought or said about him. As with everything else in his life, he bedded a woman when and where he wanted. Nothing and no one interfered with his work. It was the most important thing in his life.

Without poker, he was certain he would have remained a grimy street rat and grown into one of the derelicts that drank their lives away on Chatham Street. Even thinking of it now, he came close to shuddering. He thanked Lady Luck that he'd been born with a knack for the pasteboards and thanked Charlie Buttons for helping him hone that knack.

The streets of the sporting district were sparsely populated tonight, and the Carlton was little more than half-full when he walked through the doors. Del was singing and strutting onstage. Curt walked up to the bar and ordered a shot of rum.

Willie poured. Curt passed him a coin. "How's business, Willie?"

The bartender shrugged. "Fair to middlin'. It's Del what draws 'em in on slow nights."

"Here's to Del." He raised his glass and downed the shot in one swallow.

Then he pushed the glass at Willie. "Hit me again, mister bartender."

He drank the second shot down and then leaned his left elbow on the bar, scouting the room for potential suckers. Everyone seemed occupied right now, so Curt picked himself a table and sat down alone. Taking his pack of cards from his inside coat pocket, he began to practice. He would never allow himself to get rusty.

By and by, men began to trickle his way until he was doing a fair to middling business himself. Some of them he'd skinned before, and some more than once, but they kept coming back. He'd wager that if he showed them four aces, they'd still bet they could beat him. They wanted to have a good time and didn't care how much money they threw away doing it. They seemed eager to let him take their cash, and he had no qualms about obliging them. Come closing time, he'd made one hundred twenty-three dollars — a good take considering the lack of affluent customers that night.

Del met him at the bar as the last of the saloon's customers dribbled out the door. He bought her a whiskey, and she tossed it back and accepted another. Then she hooked her arm in his, and they walked toward the stairs.

"Mr.— Mr. Prescott?"

Curt and Del turned around together to face the owner of the thin, feeble voice. The man appeared a vagrant: pale, emaciated, and unkempt. His bony fingers trembled as he fidgeted with the tattered woolen cap he held close to his breast.

"I — I gots me a wife 'n' four wee buttons ... They ain't et decent in munts. I ain't had no work in eight. The law's gonna put me in jail 'cause I cain't pay me debts. Phil, at the livery, he told me you helped him out once. I wouldn't never ask 'cept fer the wee ones ..." A tear slipped from one of his lusterless eyes and trickled down to his stubbly jaw.

Without a word, Curt reached into his wallet, removed the entire contents, and placed it in the man's hands. The man's eyes bulged as he stared at the handful of cash. He choked, and a flood of tears burst from his eyes.

"God bless ye, Mr. Prescott! God bless ye!" He grasped Curt's hand and shook it with all the vigor his weakened state would allow.

Curt nodded to him, suddenly feeling a mite embarrassed. Finally, the man let go and turned away. He shuffled toward the door and disappeared into the night.

Del stretched up and kissed the corner of Curt's mouth, and then they linked their arms once again and walked up the stairs.

CHAPTER EIGHT

After brunch on Wednesday, Curt and Del took a stroll downtown beneath bright blue skies. The ne'er-do-wells that hung around the James Bay Bridge and so frightened Sarah Andrews that she would not set foot on the structure did no more than watch Curt and Del as they strolled across the wooden planks. The tide was low, and the mud flats below the bridge stank with ocean debris and all the garbage human beings had tossed into the shallow bay. Seagulls fought over space and feeding rights and never seemed to let up their cacophony. Once across the bridge, Curt and Del wandered past the ornate wooden parliament buildings referred to by many as "The Birdcages," as that was exactly what they resembled.

Curt and Del walked the few blocks to Beacon Hill Park. The city park was far too large to explore completely in the time they had, but they enjoyed seeing how the creation of the gardens was coming along. They walked to the cliffs and gazed southward over Juan de Fuca Strait to the snow-covered Olympic mountains in the Washington Territory. The sea breeze was constant here, salty, clean, and refreshing.

Making a loop through the fine residential homes of the James Bay district, Curt and Del made their way back home. He kissed her good-bye on the boardwalk in front of the Carlton. He was on his way to the Andrews' now, and Del had a rehearsal to make.

When they released each other, Del batted her eyelashes at him flirtatiously, her eyes shimmering like liquid gold. "Think that'll hold you till you get back?"

He gave her a lopsided grin. "How do you expect me to charm Mary Andrews after you've kissed me like that?"

Del smiled, a wickedly self-satisfied glint in her eyes. "Gotta go, darlin'." She pivoted on her high heels and walked through the door, swaying her hips for him as she went.

He watched her for a moment then started up Government Street. Mary was pretty, for a fact, but she had nothing near the raw sexuality that Del had. A woman like Del could keep a man's pole stiff round the clock.

He scanned the street continually, watching for Sarah Andrews. He wanted to be sure he saw her on her way to her committee meeting without her seeing him. Just as he reached the corner at Douglas and Pandora Avenue, he saw her. She was hustling along the north side of the avenue, on the dirt path that followed the black wrought iron fence on that side. The fence surrounded the grounds of an abandoned mansion that had belonged to the long extinct Sherman family, who had once held a number of mining interests from Victoria to Nanaimo. After the founder's death, his grandchildren had squandered the family fortune. They were all gone now, either disappeared or dead. A couple of the grandsons, it was rumored, were murdered in Vancouver for unpaid gambling debts. No one really knew what had become of them. A grand estate their home had once been, but now the house was peeling and overgrown with vines, and the gardens choked with weeds.

Curt smiled as he remembered his boyhood forays into that realm. He used to scale the fence along the rear of the property, where he was screened by trees and shrubs, and then slip amongst the gardens to try to find the flowers his mother spoke of. If he thought he'd discovered a likely prospect, he'd pinch just one from its stem and tuck it in his shirt to take home to her. The rich folks couldn't possibly resent the loss of one blossom from amongst the hundreds gracing their grounds, if they even noticed it. After his mother's death, he would bring the flowers to her grave, to show her he hadn't forgotten.

When the family held garden parties, Curt would steal as close as he could, often tucked into dense shrubbery or perched high in a huge bigleaf maple tree. He'd watch and listen and silently mimic the attendees' speech and mannerisms.

Ducking into the nearest doorway, Curt slipped out of sight from Sarah. But even as his eyes followed her, he felt his attention tugged back toward the mansion's decaying gardens.

His eyes focused on the vining Japanese wisteria overrunning the arbors and trellises on the southwest wing of the mansion. The lavender-colored flowers had faded, but he still recalled their heady fragrance, even though it had been years since he'd lingered beneath them.

What was it his mother had said they meant? Something about friendship and trust ... There was more to it than that, he was certain, but he couldn't quite gather it all back to him just then.

What a pity the place had fallen to such a state of neglect. That no one had yet purchased it was a curiosity to Curt. Real estate was a prime investment these days. Someone should restore it before it crumbled to pieces. It was easy living above the Carlton, but sometimes he grew weary of the limited space of the suite.

He snapped himself from his musings and refocused on Sarah. She held her head high beneath her bonnet, and her small bustle bounced a bit with each stride. Her eyes fastened on the ground as if there was but a narrow path ahead of her, she never saw him. He hung in the doorway of the florist's shop, watching her until she was safely beyond the chance of looking back.

The door opened behind him. "Master Prescott! It's been a spell."

Curt turned and smiled at the old man, not minding that Mr. Drury still referred to him as 'Master' as though he were still a young boy.

"I've a sale on, you know," Drury said. "Got to move out the last of the spring pots."

Even as the proprietor spoke, an idea was forming in Curt's mind. "Still got some hyacinths?"

"A few late bloomers. Few more days, though, and they'll all be wilted. Half price."

"Any white ones?"

The old man nodded. Curt smiled and followed him into the shop. The shopkeeper offered him the choicest plant — it was thick with milky blossoms and smelled like lilacs. Curt bought it and carried out the small pot in his left hand. This was perfect.

He made certain Timberline was clear before walking up the path and knocking on the door. When Mary opened it, her mouth fell open in shock.

"Good afternoon, Miss Andrews. Hope I'm not intruding." He doffed his hat.

She stammered, as if trying to catch her breath before she could speak. "Mr. Prescott —! G-good afternoon. What a surprise!"

"It's such a beautiful day I couldn't stay indoors. And I thought of you — probably cooped up inside, too. I decided I'd come and rescue you."

Her mouth was still open.

"I brought this for you." He held out the hyacinth.

"It — it's lovely, thank you, but ..." She stole a look past him into the street. "I'm afraid that neither of my parents is home. I couldn't possibly let you in."

He slipped a wounded look onto his face. "You're not happy to see me?"

"Oh — of course I am!" An embarrassed smile came and went from her lips. "But —"

"Then take the flowers and let me in before your neighbors have something to gossip about."

As if on cue, a gentleman stepped out onto a stoop a few houses down. Gasping, Mary stepped back and waved Curt in, shutting the door quickly behind him.

"Thank you. Here." He put the pot into her hands.

She was still flustered, but she finally focused on the plant. "It is lovely." She smelled it. "Thank you."

"You're welcome. It's a hyacinth. I chose it because you enchant me with your unobtrusive loveliness."

She stared at him blankly for a second, and then crimson flooded her cheeks. But Curt could tell she was pleased. He hung up his hat. She hadn't yet noticed his gun, which he'd deliberately worn beneath his coat, and he did not intend to hide it from her. The more of the real him he could get her to accept, the more complete would be his mastery of her.

"I don't know what to say ..."

"Don't say anything. Just enjoy it."

She set it down on the hall table and invited him into the parlor. "Can I offer you coffee or tea?"

"No, thank you." He deliberately sat down in her spot on the couch.

She took her mother's place, pressing her back into the corner made by the arm. He let his eyes drift over her. She was wearing a pale green short-sleeved blouse over a dark green skirt. The colors really brought out her eyes.

"Were you busy?"

"No, not really. My mother just left — you just missed her. It's her meeting today."

He snapped his fingers. "That's right. I'm sorry — I really didn't intend anything improper."

"Of course you didn't. I'm glad you came. Really." She smiled, but then it fell away as her eyes rested on his gun belt. "You're wearing a gun. I never noticed it before."

"That's because your father asked me to take it off so I wouldn't offend your mother. Does it bother you?"

"Oh, no. It just took me by surprise. A lot of men wear guns. Even my brother does — did. Dad told you Miles was a lieutenant in the navy."

Curt nodded. "Yes."

"I think you'd have liked Miles. He was very courageous. He was very much his own man. I believe you are, too."

"Thank you."

Mary played with her fingers in her lap, dropping her head forward. "He could always tell my mother to let him be. I can't."

"I imagine it's different for a girl."

She raised her eyes to his. "Yes. It is. We always have to do what everybody else tells us to do. I have very little control over my own life." She stared, frowning, at the cold, dark fireplace. "I'm beginning to hate it."

A slight smile lifted the corners of Curt's mouth. At last, a glimpse inside Mary Andrews. He let her talk.

"That's one of the reasons I help at the school. Fridays, I help Mrs. Blaine with the children, and Saturdays I help her clean the building before church on Sunday."

"It earns you a little money, too."

She shook her head. "No, I'm not paid. She's a kind woman, and I enjoy helping her. And I love children." Her smile returned, and she glowed.

"I see. And you were going to say that it gets you out of the house and away from your mother."

Mary drew a sharp intake of breath, and her cheeks colored as she looked at him. "Please don't think that I hate my mother or anything — I love her, I really do. It's just that she can be so

... demanding. She wants to control every speck of my life. Sometimes I feel like I just can't breathe!"

Stretching his right arm along the back of the chesterfield, he watched her bosom heave with repressed emotions.

"Why don't we take a walk, then? Get some air and stretch our legs."

The light that came to her eyes told him she very much wanted to do that, but she shook her head.

"If I were to be seen alone with you this soon, people would talk. My mother — and my father — would be furious."

Curt lifted his right index finger, indicating the back door. "These houses back onto the ravine, don't they? There's a trail along the creek down there. Nobody'd see us."

Her eyes shifted away from his then back again. She drew her lip in between her teeth.

"Your mother's not even here," Curt pressed her, "and she's holding you back. You're a grown woman. Take some of that control away from her."

Mary started to rise, then faltered, and then finally got to her feet. "Yes, let's go for a walk, Mr. Prescott."

He rose and caught her hand. She peered up into his face. "From now on, I'd like you to call me Curt. And I'd like to be able to call you Mary."

With a giddy giggle, she smiled. "Yes, I'd like that, too."

He smiled. "Thank you, Mary." He released her hand. "Lead the way." He followed her out the back door to the fence at the rear of the property.

There was no gate, so he swung one leg at a time over the fence then held out his arms for her. She hesitated, staring at his hands and the long grass and wild shrubbery on the other side of the fence. Finally, she stepped into his arms.

He hoisted her over easily, making sure her skirt was clear of the pickets before setting her on her feet on his side of the fence.

Deliberately, he slid her down the front of his body. Her face betrayed the natural response within her body, her hands gripping his arms tightly for support. He let her go as though the move had been unplanned and had meant nothing.

"Are you ready?"

She twisted at the waist, checking that her skirt was in order. "Mm-hm."

He turned and walked toward the ravine. She fell behind, her skirt dragging on brush. He halted, and she caught up. She hooked her right hand in his arm and hoisted her skirt with the other.

The ridge fell away down a steep but passable slope, giving Curt plenty of excuses to hold Mary's hands as she negotiated trees and ferns and stinging nettles. She stepped on, instead of over, a moss-covered deadfall, and it crumbled beneath her shoe. She would have taken quite a tumble if Curt hadn't caught her around the waist.

"I'm sorry," she said as she caught her breath. "I'm not used to this."

"It's all right." As he smiled into her face the breeze lifted the leaves of the tree above them, and the sunlight caught her eyes. They sparkled an almost incandescent green. She was breathing through her parted lips, and the temptation to kiss them nudged Curt. He shifted his grip to one of her hands. "Shall we go on?"

She nodded, and they made their way to the bottom and found the path.

"Here we are — safe and sound."

She smiled over the accomplishment as she brushed bits of twigs and foliage from her clothes. Then she looked around. A narrow, shallow creek purled over a rocky bed. In places where the sun made it through the trees, the banks were lined with ferns and other plants. Small boulders were scattered here and there. Some spots were bare brown soil; others were sprinkled with a reddish brown layer of shed cedar needles. Above them along both sides of the ravine, cedars and Douglas firs blocked out most of the sunlight and made the creek and the path seem like the floor of a tunnel. Little breeze reached the bottom, and all was still and silent save for the creek.

"It's beautiful," Mary whispered. "It's like being in church."

Curt chuckled. He could see how she'd think of it that way. He used to come down here a lot as a boy, whenever he needed to be alone to think some problem through. It had always felt a little magical to him. He'd felt renewed after spending a few hours here.

"Let's walk," he said and led the way north, following the path away from town.

They rounded a corner several minutes later. Curt saw the young mule deer first and pointed it out to Mary. She gasped as she saw it. It had come down to water on the other side of the creek. Now it stood watching them, water dribbling from its muzzle.

"Oh — she's beautiful," Mary sighed.

The doe swung around on its haunches and bounded up the slope, disappearing into the woods.

Mary grasped Curt's arm. "This is wonderful. I'm having such a good time."

"I'm glad." He took the hand that grasped his sleeve and knitted their fingers together. Mary smiled and squeezed his hand. He felt that tingling sensation again.

They walked another half-mile to a place where the banks were less steep, and the trees fell away for a small grassy meadow. The sun was high in the western sky and warmed them the instant they stepped into the open. The meadow, surrounded by dense forest, was still very private.

"Shall we sit a while?" Curt asked her.

She nodded, and they sank down onto the thick, soft grass, facing the creek. Mary drew a deep breath of the sweet spring air and hugged her updrawn knees.

"Feeling better?" he asked, leaning on his left hand and propping his right elbow on his right knee.

"Yes, much." She smiled at him. "I feel as free as a bird."

"I'm glad." He beckoned her eyes with his. "I'm enjoying myself too, Mary. I really enjoy being with you."

She blushed and bit on her lower lip.

He chuckled softly. "I wish you didn't embarrass so easily. It makes it hard for me to tell you how pretty you look sitting there, with the sun shining in your hair."

The intensity of his stare drew her eyes to his and locked them there. He lifted his hand and touched her hair. She stiffened and held herself frozen. He leaned over the inches between them and placed a soft kiss on her temple. He heard her sharp intake of breath.

"Are you afraid of me, Mary?" he asked, his breath fanning her ear.

"N-no. That's silly." She hugged her knees tighter.

He dipped his head and placed another kiss on her cheek. Her eyes ran away from his. "Mary. Mary, look at me."

She bit on her lip again then released it as she met his eyes once again. Holding her captive with only his gaze, Curt pressed a brief, warm kiss to her lips. She stiffened again, holding her breath, and did not exhale even after he'd drawn away. He cupped her cheek with his palm to keep her face toward him.

"That was nice," he said softly.

She shivered, at last breathing out, and he sensed that one more kiss would send her running from him. He sat back but held her hand firmly in his. He could feel her anxiety in her rigid fingers. Gently, he stroked them until at last she relaxed and met his eyes once again. There was uncertainty in her gaze, a little fear, too, but there was also a small spark of awakened desire. He believed she was as close to wanting a man as she'd ever come. In time, she would want him beyond all reason, and she would surrender to him. And the spark he saw made him wonder if there was more passion hidden beneath her shy, quiet exterior than he had so far given her credit for. He was definitely going to find out.

Mary let Curt hold her hand because she wanted to hold his, but should he attempt to kiss her again, she would refuse him.

Her insides were still quaking from the tiny pecks he had given her. Her skin burned in each of the three spots his lips had touched. It was the first time she'd ever been kissed by a man. It had been satin magic, like the words he breathed into her ears.

As though he'd tied a tender string to her mouth with his, her lips wanted to follow his and meet them again. His nearness disturbed her in a way she'd never experienced before. The clean, masculine scent of him filled her nostrils and she breathed deeply of it. Her body swayed toward his. But it was the lure of lust, and she could not allow any more of such contact.

She straightened her spine and stared at the rippling creek. It was dancing along, merry and uninhibited. Inside her, there were churning rapids, and she wasn't certain how to negotiate them. Her mother had told her a man might try to make her feel this way some day. Her mother had told her to avoid the rapids, and the only way she could do that was to stay out of the boat.

But Curt made her feel buoyant and alive and, perhaps most of all, liked. He made her feel like she was at least a little bit interesting. Most men, with the exception of her father or her brother, didn't care to hear what she had to say. If they didn't straight out cut her off, they merely sat quietly while she spoke and then went on as if she hadn't. And then some of them wondered why she hardly ever had anything to say. She'd learned long ago not to bother.

But Curt was different. He listened. The sheer excitement of it made her want to tell him everything she could think of, finally able to share her thoughts, her hopes, her fantasies with someone. But she bit the urge back, afraid to go too far in her enthusiasm. He was the last person on earth she would ever want to bore.

"What are you thinking?"

His voice was baritone velvet. She turned her face to smile at him, to gaze into his dark, hypnotic eyes.

"Oh, about everything. And nothing."

He chuckled. "That makes a lot of sense."

She laughed too. "I don't want to make sense of anything right now. I don't want to think. I just want to ... to be."

He smiled at her, his even, white teeth flashing in the sunlight. Then his face dipped closer, and his lips brushed hers. Reflex jerked her face away.

"No. You mustn't."

"Why not? You liked it last time, didn't you?"

She knew she had. But a lady didn't admit to such. A lady shouldn't even enjoy the types of feelings his kisses had engendered. A lady shouldn't even be near a man like him. Suddenly, a dagger of fear stabbed her inside.

"I'm sorry. It's my fault. I didn't mean to lead you to believe ..."

His finger hooked her chin and turned her face back to him. "You think a little kiss like that is wrong?"

"Of - of course it is. We're not married. Not even betrothed."

His hand fell away. "I wonder what you'd think if I really kissed you."

She darted a quick look at him but couldn't decipher his exact meaning. His face was utterly unreadable. "I'm sorry."

"Don't be." He sighed. "You're a preacher's kid — I guess it's only natural for you to think that way."

She frowned. "What do you mean?"

"Nothing. Nothing." He stood up and held out his hand for her. "Come on. Maybe we should get you home."

Her hand in his, she rose, relieved, saying, "Yes, Mother and Dad will be home soon."

He released her hand, and they walked back up the trail without speaking. She had a more difficult time climbing back up the ravine than she'd had getting down, but he saw her safely to her back door.

She stood in the half-open doorway, torn between quickly gaining the safety of the house and lingering with him on the stoop. "Thank you for a wonderful afternoon," she said.

"My pleasure," he returned with a smile. "Perhaps you'll allow me to drop by again."

She bit her lip. "It would be wrong of me to invite you."

He leaned his shoulder against the house in a lazy fashion she found curiously attractive. Her heart began to hammer again. His eyes were dark magnets.

"I meant nothing inappropriate when I kissed you. I did it to show you how I feel about you. If there's something wrong with a man letting a woman know he cares for her, then I guess I ought to be hanged."

Mary's drew a deep breath, but her heart would not settle down.

"Before I go, I have to ask you one more favor. I left my hat inside."

"Oh! I'll get it." She dashed inside and returned swiftly with it.

"Thanks." He pressed it firmly onto his head then pinched the brim as he inclined his head to her. "Until I see you again, then."

She stared into his eyes, trying to discover if he meant privately or properly. He turned and left the yard by way of the back fence. Was he preserving her reputation, or was he demonstrating that he could come and go without being seen?

When he'd vanished below the ridge, she went inside and closed the door behind her. It was time she began preparing the small roasting chicken for the oven, but she paused to bend over the fragrant, milky-white blossoms of the hyacinth. She inhaled deeply of its essence. Her insides quaked with the rashness of what she'd done — taking off with him on the spur of the moment, being alone with him when no one knew their whereabouts. Allowing him to kiss her. It was dreadfully sinful, but her heart sang with the joy of it.

Never had she felt as free as she had this afternoon. For the first time, she had willfully done something she knew her parents would disapprove of. Her stomach knotted at the prospect of keeping it a secret from them. But she couldn't tell them — not ever. They would never forgive her for such conduct. She could hear her mother now, screaming about how she had flirted with danger, of how she was probably already ruined and was too much a fool to know it.

Mary turned her attention to the chicken, placed it, prepared, in its pot in the oven and straightened up. As she lifted the heavy iron door, its springs jerked it from her hand and slammed it shut. She glared at it.

She was not a fool, and she was tired of the safe and dull little box she was forced to live in. She wanted more, some form of excitement, something to get her blood going and make her feel alive instead of merely existing.

Curt made her feel alive. He touched something deep inside her, making her want to cry out with joy. She should have refused even his first kiss, but she hadn't wanted to. And what was wrong, she thought, pressing her hands hard against the edge of the counter, with the little kisses Curt had given her? Dear little kisses that made her all warm inside. She had wanted no man's kisses before, but now she wanted Curt's. And she was curious to know exactly what he'd meant about really kissing her. Could anything be more pleasant than the tender caresses he'd already given her?

Sighing, she slowly spun round, clasping her hands in front of her, and rested her spine against the ridge of the counter. When he'd left, she hadn't outright refused him permission to visit her again. Smiling to herself, she hoped he would interpret the absence of a no as a yes.

CHAPTER NINE

Curt climbed the bank where the ravine joined the one running along Johnson, still wondering why he'd gone and tried to kiss Mary again when he'd told himself to go slow. But she'd been sitting there, her hair glittering in the sunlight, her lips parted in a bewildered but contented smile — looking so utterly kissable that he couldn't help himself. He'd gotten exactly the reaction he'd figured he would, but at least she hadn't run away.

At Government, he caught a break in the horse and wagon traffic and jogged across the intersection. It was early evening now, and the streets were crowded with people going home from their jobs. As he reached the boardwalk on the Carlton's side, he saw Dave Jenkins walking his way. Jenkins must have been off duty, for he was in plain clothes. Curt stopped to wait for him. The constable's eyes were down, and his hands stuffed deep into his pants pockets. Coming down the steps, Jenkins didn't notice Curt until he bumped into him.

"Jesus — sorry, Curt."

"No problem." Curt looked closely at him. "What's the matter, Dave? You look like somebody just gave you a rough time."

Jenkins moved out of the way of two ladies, tipping his hat to them with a polite smile. He swung around to the side of the saloon and backed himself up against the wall. Following him, Curt leaned his shoulder against the wall and faced Jenkins.

"What's up, Dave?"

Jenkins drew a nervous breath and expelled it, glancing around to make sure no one was within earshot. "I just got through a meetin' with the superintendent, the mayor, and the Moral Action Committee." He dug into his vest pocket and pulled out the makings. Creasing the paper first, he began to sprinkle tobacco into it. Most of the tobacco ended up on his boots. "Shit." He started all over and finally got the paper licked and rolled. The match snapped in half when he struck it against the wall. "God damn it!"

"Take it easy, Dave." Curt took the broken match from him and struck it against the wall. He held it to the tip of Jenkins' cigarette while Jenkins dragged on his smoke and got it going.

"Thanks."

Curt nodded. "Now, want to tell me what's got you so spooked?" Jenkins dragged fiercely on his smoke then jerked it from his mouth.

"I'm bein' reviewed, that's what. That goddamn committee's been tellin' the council I ain't doin' my job proper! What the hell do they know?"

"Sounds like more than we'd like them to."

Jenkins eyed him then dragged on his smoke again.

"So what did the powers that be have to say?" Curt prompted.

"For starters, they want me to take personal responsibility for cleaning up Chatham Street. Then burn it to the goddamn ground if I have to. And they're thinkin' of confiscatin' every piece of gamblin' equipment in every saloon an' burnin' it, too. They figger that'll send the sharks off to distant parts."

Curt raised his eyebrows. Then a thought occurred to him. "Did he mention any names?"

"Yeah. Wingbone Wilson and Jim Haggerty. And Fat Johnnie, o' course." He suddenly caught Curt's drift. "No, he never said nothin' about you. Nobody did. But you got a way o' mindin' yer own business an' keepin' yer nose clean. Them other fellas are always in some kinda trouble." He took the last drag on his smoke and crushed it out under his heel. "But I don't reckon it'll be long before yer name does come up, you havin' killed a lawman an' all. Them old biddies won't give two hoots you had no choice."

Curt knew that was true. "Who was doing the most squawking? It wouldn't be the preacher's wife, Sarah Andrews, would it?"

Jenkins blinked in surprise. "Yeah. How'd you know?"

"I have my sources." He wasn't letting Jenkins in on his little game with the Andrews'. He didn't completely trust the constable's mouth when he was this agitated. "Was everybody else taking their cards from her? Or were they all cutting for dealer?"

"She's in charge, all right. No doubt about that. They hang on her every goddamn word like it was the bloody gospel."

A small smile creased Curt's mouth. Good. That was very good.

"What're you smilin' about? If I wanna keep my job, I gotta do what they say. Eventually, that'll mean runnin' you outa town, too. Either I'm fucked or you are. Ain't nothin' to be smilin' about."

"The mayor and your super might just be telling her what she wants to hear for now. They know that this city needs its sporting districts. That's why they let places like the Carlton or fellas like me alone. Despite what Sarah Andrews and her cranky old biddies think, the police do a good job of keeping real problems under control in this town."

Jenkins nodded, so Curt was sure he was listening.

Curt's gaze then became cold and level. "But whatever happens, Dave, I'm warning you right now not to fuck with me. You better decide right now who you're more afraid of: the mayor and a bunch of old women — or me."

Jenkins stiffened, trying to hide the shiver that ran up his spine. He swallowed. "No contest, partner. I'm with you."

Curt clapped him on the shoulder and tossed a casual gaze down the street. "But don't worry, Dave. There's always a way around a poor hand, whether it's bluff, sleight-of-hand, or a Colt .45."

With that, he walked off, leaving Jenkins only mildly comforted.

Del was not in the bar room or backstage, so Curt took the stairs two at a time and found her in the suite. She was reclined on her chaise longue, sipping a glass of whiskey and flipping through a catalogue of women's underclothes.

"You're back at last," she said with a big smile. "Look, darlin' — how d'you think I'd look in this?" She held out the catalogue, her long red fingernail pointing out the item.

He glanced at it. "Real nice."

"White, red or black?"

"Black."

"That's what I think, too." She watched him shed his jacket and vest, yank his tie loose, and unbutton his collar. "Somethin' wrong, hon?"

He dropped into his chair. "I just had a conversation with Jenkins." He told her all about it.

She laid the catalogue down. "Can they do that?"

"It's an election year, so with enough law and enough votes behind them, yes."

Del's face fell blank with awe. "Whatcha gonna do?"

"I haven't decided yet. But it'll come to me." He looked at her glass for a second then said, "Pour me a glass of that, would you?"

He spent a restless night, even after having worn himself out with Del during the first half of it. He rose early and washed and shaved while Del slept. Turning to his bureau for a fresh shirt, he glanced out the window in time to see the Moral Action Committee on another march.

Quickly, he strode out onto the roof for a closer look at the committee members. Many of them were the wives of prominent society men. Others were not, but that didn't mean squat. Chances were, some of their men had to be dirty, had to have their hands in somebody else's cookie jar, their pricks in some other woman's nest. If he could find out who was doing what — or who — he might be able to chip away at the foundation from all sides. Sarah Andrews was the cornerstone, but the entire structure would fall if he could erode enough weak spots.

He went back inside, finished dressing, and left the suite. He needed to have another talk with the constable.

Jenkins was obviously surprised to see him. He got up from his chair, tugging nervously at his mustache. He hadn't forgotten the gambler's warning from the day before.

"Dave, I want you to do exactly what Drake and Todd told you to do."

"Huh?"

"Crack down. Arrest anybody and everybody you find gambling or whoring or causing any sort of trouble on Chatham Street or elsewhere."

Jenkins' brows furrowed, and he scratched his chin. "I don't get you."

Curt poked his badge. "It's not just scum that roll around in the dirt. You've gotta know a few so-called respectable gents who indulge themselves."

Jenkins responded slowly, "For sure, yeah ..."

"So what've you been doing? Charging the whores and the bawds, but you let the high class society men walk away."

"That's the way it's always been done around here."

"Well, it's time that changed." Curt walked away from him and looked out between the bars on the window. He waved his hand, as if to present all the townsfolk to the constable. "These self-righteous prigs are screamin' about us spoiling their prim and proper little town. At the same time, a lot of them are sneakin' out their back doors and into somebody else's. Stick it to 'em, Dave. Charge them as guilty as the working girls. Get their names in the paper if you have to. After all, you couldn't be arresting whores if they didn't have customers keeping 'em whores, could you?" He turned back for the constable's reaction.

"I could get in a lotta trouble for that. I already know a couple public figgers pokin' a whore or two quite regular."

"Who?"

Jenkins hesitated to tell, but the intensity of Curt's gaze dragged it from him. "Zachary Halstead, of Halstead and Werther Investments. There's some I wouldn't touch, at least for now. But, hey, there is Barney Neff, the court stenographer. He's brother to Charles Neff on the town council. And a couple others — just reg'lar stiffs." He chuckled. "And me, o' course."

"Just as long as they're from the 'proper' crowd. We want to rub their noses in their own shit until they're so busy burying it they don't care about ours."

A slow grin spread across the constable's face. "Hey — that's a corker of a plan, partner. It oughta work."

"So keep your eyes open and your spine stiff, Dave. And let me know when you catch your first big fish."

"Sure thing. I'll get right on it."

Curt turned his back on Jenkins' goofy grin and walked out the door.

The next Tuesday evening he was back in the constable's office at the jail after Jenkins approached him in the Carlton. They'd hooked their first fish.

"Curt, meet Barney Neff," Jenkins said as he swaggered towards the first cell. "Court stenographer and family man. Got a wife and two kids and a nice little house. And a hard-on for Tequila Sheila there." He pointed into the other cell.

"Hi, Sheila," Curt said as he approached the forty-year-old prostitute. "Long time no see."

"Likewise," she answered. She met him at the bars and cocked a hip to one side.

Curt jerked his head at the short, balding man in the other cell. "You know this guy?"

"Hell, sure. He's one o' my regulars. Every Tuesday, five-thirty."

Curt turned amused eyes on the stenographer. "Work late on Tuesdays, do you, Barney?"

Jenkins chuckled as his prisoner flinched and flushed. "Maybe ya oughta loosen that tie and take off yer coat, Barney. It'll help ya relax."

His fingers shaking, Barney removed his bow tie. He unbuttoned his brown sack coat but kept it on, as if it afforded him some small measure of protection.

Curt spoke to Sheila again. "So how long has Barney been coming to see you?"

"Oh, nigh about four years now."

Curt raised both eyebrows. "Four years? Gee, Constable, what do you figure that ought to get Barney with these new laws we have now?"

Jenkins crossed his arms thoughtfully and studied the ceiling a moment. "Oh, I'd say if we added 'em all up ... Just a rough guess, now ... Say a minimum fine of ten dollars per charge, times fifty-two weeks a year, times four years ... You're lookin' at over two thousand dollars in fines with or without a year an' a half in jail — give or take."

Neff bristled and squared his shoulders. "That's preposterous! You can't do that! You can't charge me with anything but today —."

Jenkins swaggered before him. "With the right witnesses, I can charge you with anything I damn well want. And you know how good ol' Judge Begbie loves to use the testimony of gals like Sheila. They put away a lotta bad guys. We could keep you in here until the next time he's in town. 'Course, who knows when that'll be?"

The truth of it made Neff blanch. "Please, Officer — if my wife finds out about this — if anybody finds out about this — I'm ruined. Please, can't we make a deal?"

Curt strolled along the bars toward Neff, wagging his finger at him. "Barney, Barney. And you a court official — a very minor one, but still, you should know we can't do that."

"It's done all the time!" Neff cried desperately, rushing towards them. "Why do you think there's still crime on the streets?"

"Oh, I know why, Barney. But you see, the town council's got a bee up its ass on account of the Moral Action Committee. You've heard about that, haven't you?"

Neff nodded. "My wife and sister-in-law are on it."

"You don't say?" Curt cast a satisfied glance at Jenkins. "What do you think they'd do if they found out about this, Barney? They're fighting so hard for the virtues of this town, and all the while you're sneaking around behind their backs, consorting with whores." He pinned Neff with a dagger-like stare. "You're the enemy, Barney."

"No! I love my family!"

"Of course you do. That's why you fuck whores. Had the clap yet, Barney? How about crotch crickets?"

Jenkins sprayed out a laugh while Neff nodded in shame.

"And you love your wife so much you want to share them with her, right?"

Neff reddened. "My wife won't ever get them. She stopped —." He cut himself short and turned his face away in embarrassment.

Curt turned eyes full of false sympathy on him. "Oh, I see. We see, don't we, Dave?"

"We sure do," Jenkins replied with another laugh.

"Well, then that excuses you, doesn't it, Barney? It just ain't enough, pounding your pud in the outhouse. And it does get to aching real hard, doesn't it? So you just can't help going to Sheila to get it greased real good once a week, huh?"

Neff's face grew so red he looked like an overripe tomato about to burst.

Jenkins jumped in at just the right moment. "Aw, gee, Curt. We've done gone and hurt his feelin's. We oughta make it up to him somehow, don't you reckon?"

Curt shook his head. "I dunno, Constable. He is a criminal."

"But he's a nice criminal. It ain't like he killed anybody."

"That's right!" Neff exclaimed. "I never killed anybody!"

Curt crossed his arms over his chest and pretended to think it over. After an effectively lengthy moment, he said: "All right,

Barney. Here's what we'll do. We'll drop the charges and let you go if you persuade your brother to nudge the town council off the committee's wagon. Kill that movement deader than a squashed bug. Think you can do that, Barney?"

Barney sucked in a breath and held it. Finally, he exhaled, nodding.

"Good. And remember to forget this little chat. 'Cause if word gets out that we pressured you, word'll get out about you and Sheila here."

Barney nodded rapidly and bellied up to the cell door. He rushed through it as Jenkins opened it, squeezed past Curt and dashed out the door. Jenkins let out a horselaugh while Curt grinned, shaking his head.

Sobering, Curt inclined his head at Tequila Sheila. "You can let her out now, too, Dave."

With effort, Jenkins swallowed his laughter. "There's still her fine to pay. I did arrest her for prostitution." Anticipating Curt's next question, he added, "She only had what she got from Neff on her."

"How much more?" Curt asked, taking out his wallet.

"Well, she is a repeat offender. Should be another twenty dollars and she should get ninety days —."

Curt shot him a dour look. "No jail time." He thrust twenty dollars at the constable.

"If her madam came to bail her out, I'd get extra just for bein' a nice guy —."

"Shut up, Dave. Let her out."

Coughing into his hand, Jenkins moved to Sheila's cell and unlocked it.

Sheila sauntered out, winking at Curt. "Thanks a mil', honey. I owe ya."

"Forget it."

She scowled at Jenkins, smiled sweetly at Curt, and sashayed out the door.

Jenkins said, "What do we do now, jest sit an' wait?"

Curt nodded. "And keep bringin' 'em in." He pointed a stiff finger at Jenkins. "Don't you let one of those sons of bitches off, Dave. Not one."

"You can count on me."

"Good." Curt turned away from him and reached for the doorknob. As he pulled the door shut behind him, he hoped to hell this was going to work.

Friday afternoon, Curt dropped by during working hours to visit Bud at the saddlery and got himself invited over to the house for Sunday dinner. He knocked on their front door a few minutes after five, and Bud let him in and hid his gun.

As they stepped into the parlor, Mary came to meet them and gave Curt the warmest, most adoring smile he'd ever been given by a woman. A gleam in his eye, Bud laid a hand on each of their shoulders. Sarah bustled into the parlor from the kitchen, and they had to wade through her formal greeting and chitchat like every other time Curt had come over. He'd hoped she would be used to him by now and ready to give up her tedious etiquette. Obviously, she was not.

As they chatted before dinner, Curt took advantage of a lull to try to ease the confines of Sarah's formality. Looking at them all in turn and coming back to Bud, he said:

"We've known each other about a month now, and I don't know about you, but I'm very comfortable with each of you, and I'd like you all to call me Curt from now on."

Bud smiled. "Yes, I've been feeling the same way myself. Feel free to call me Bud if you like. Titles get awfully heavy sometimes."

Curt nodded. He looked at Mary, who was smiling but trying not to show her teeth lest she seem too eager in front of her parents.

Sarah said nothing. Curt studied her closely. She obviously was not too keen on loosening the bounds of propriety. He would make a point of always calling her Mrs. Andrews.

Dinner on Sundays was always roast beef, potatoes, Yorkshire pudding, peas, and carrots, but Sarah truly was a gifted cook. Curt doubted he would ever tire of a lifetime of Sunday dinners at the Andrews'. He had no doubt that Mary was equally skilled, for Sarah and Bud were always touting dishes she'd prepared on her own.

After eating, they returned to the parlor with their tea. Subtly, Curt prompted Sarah to update him on the Committee's progress. He wanted to know if Jenkins' new method of law enforcement was getting back to them.

She set down her cup after a tiny sip. "We're quite pleased with the results of our meeting with the council," she told him. "They've obviously spoken to the offending constables, for we've been told there have been more arrests than previously. Everything is proceeding wonderfully."

He gave her a fake but convincing smile. "Good. I'm glad to hear it. Without strict enforcement, the laws themselves mean nothing."

"Exactly," she agreed.

Softly clearing his throat, Bud said, "But if people would just govern themselves, there wouldn't be any need for laws or officers — or any of the things that go with them. Most people consider laws prohibitive. But if they'd look at the reasons behind the laws, they would see that they are for the common good of all."

"I agree," Curt said with a nod, expecting another lecture.

"I thought you would," Bud replied. "You strike me as the kind of man who has a great deal of self-discipline."

There was a slight delay as Curt inspected the preacher's expression and tone of voice. "Thank you," he answered, finding nothing that told him the preacher might know more than he let on.

Sarah had lost her position as the focal point for long enough. "As long as the police force continues to do its job, we will be happy," she said. "But just in case, I've written a letter to our son's former commander, to see if the Navy can do anything."

Bud frowned at her. "Sarah, we discussed that. I really don't think that will be necessary. I doubt they would even find the situation here worthy of their attention."

"Nevertheless, I would rather err on the side of caution."

Curt's stomach had tightened sharply at the mention of the Royal Navy. While he was certain Bud was right, the last thing Curt wanted hovering around Victoria was a Navy presence on official military patrol. The thought of it brought back bad memories of how they'd used and discarded his mother. It had been a sailor who'd smacked her tooth out. It might even have been one who had killed her.

"Curt, are you all right?" It was Mary's voice.

His eyes had lost focus during his thoughts. He forced them to focus on Mary. "Fine. Fine. Sorry, I was just thinking."

Sarah distracted them both by starting on another tirade over Chatham and Humboldt Streets. Curt only half-listened this time, for she was merely repeating things she had said before, and he was caught up in a whirlpool of memories that he'd thought were left far, far behind him.

He left the Andrews' at around eight o'clock, saying that he'd promised to meet a friend. Del was glad to have him home early. They took a stroll until sunset and then returned to the Carlton. With a bottle of whiskey on the table between them, they settled into their seats in the sitting room and played cards beneath the lamplight. Afterward they fell into bed, made love, and, their bodies entangled, dropped off into separate realms of sleep.

The next evening, the sheep were thin in the Carlton. Curt drilled himself in the manipulations of the cards while keeping one eye open for woolies to shear. Del sang and danced on stage as though the place were packed. When her first set of the evening was through, she joined him at his table. But she did not sit down.

Stroking his shoulder, she said, "Curt, honey, dance with me?"

Curt completed the pass he was half through and set down the deck. The band was playing Del's favorite waltz. It had been a long time since he'd danced with her. He rose from the table, and a big smile lit up her face.

She was still smiling when they took up the pose and began to dance amongst the few other couples on the floor. When the song ended, she asked them for another waltz, and they complied.

Halfway through their third dance, a huge man in a red plaid shirt caught Curt's eye as he came through the batwing doors. Curt watched Wesley Keegan saunter up to the bar.

Del followed his gaze. "He's got a helluva lotta nerve, showin' up in here again."

Curt grunted, wondering if there was a particular reason for the lumberjack's sudden reappearance. Keegan didn't seem aware of Curt's presence. He ordered a beer and slurped it at the bar.

"You gonna show him the door again, darlin'?"

"No. As long as he stays out of my way, I'll stay out of his."

The music stopped, and it was time for Del to get back on stage. She kissed Curt before she left him. The gambler went back to his table. He shifted the chair over a bit, so he could see Keegan from the corner of his eye. Something about the lumberjack raised the hairs on the back of Curt's neck. But, casually, he picked up the pack of cards he'd left on the table and began to shuffle them.

The lumberjack gulped down the last of his beer and swaggered over to Curt's table. He pulled back a chair and clomped a heavy boot down on it. Leaning on his raised knee, he pulled out his oversized bowie knife and started paring his square fingernails.

Curt noticed that the laced boots were new and without calks. But it was the glitter of the abalone handle on the knife that drew his attention. He wondered how a lumberjack could afford a knife like that, even as he concealed his annoyance over the bits of fingernail that fell on the table.

Keegan grinned at Curt, baring a set of huge, yellow-brown teeth. This close, Curt could smell the cheap tobacco the 'jack was chewing on. Curt regarded him coolly, barely taking his eyes from the cards.

"Like that knife, do ya?" Keegan said, his voice coarse, almost a growl. "I got it off'n a fancy dandy gambler I kilt down in 'Frisco."

Curt's countenance remained unchanged, even though he knew Keegan had said it to impress him. Whether or not it was true was neither here nor there.

"Fat Johnnie wants ya to come see him," Keegan said.

Curt raised his eyes to Keegan's briefly. So, Keegan had hooked up with Johnnie. The fat man usually had young boys run his messages. "So you're one of Johnnie's little boys now, are you?"

Keegan bristled, his lips curling into a snarl. Curt saw his knuckles tighten on the gleaming haft. But then the 'jack relaxed and uttered a slow, low chuckle.

Curt fanned the deck. "What does he want? For me to bail him out of jail or something?"

"I'm just deliv'rin' the message. Go see what he wants, or don't. I don't give a rat's ass." Keegan tucked the knife back into its sheath and looped the keeper over it. He dropped his foot to the floor. "He ain't in jail. He's at his place." Hawking, Keegan cocked his head at a spittoon halfway under the next table and spat a black gob at it. He missed the opening, and the slime dribbled down the side of the bright brass receptacle. Without further comment, Keegan walked out the door.

Curt's lip curled in disgust at the lumberjack's lousy marksmanship. Shuffling the pack absently, he wondered what sort of trouble Fat Johnnie was in this time. Or what sort of trouble he thought he was in. The only time that fat ass wanted anything to do with Curt was when he was in trouble. The gambler was more inclined not to go, but with the state of things right now, it might be in his own best interest to keep abreast of whatever might be going on. There certainly wasn't anything to keep him in the Carlton tonight.

Rising, he boxed the cards and tucked the pack away before going out the door. The streets were relatively quiet and a faint breeze cooled his face as he walked.

The riffraff were crawling all over Chatham Street. For the most part he ignored them, and they moved out of his way. Fat Johnnie's place was dark and dank as always and, as he always did, Curt let his eyes adjust to the dimness before stepping fully into the doorway.

Keegan was guzzling more beer at a makeshift table with three shiftless types. He looked up when Curt walked in and jerked his head at Fat Johnnie's office door. Curt knocked on the door and waited a second before entering.

Fat Johnnie was alone this time, his immenseness sprawled over most of the loveseat. He yanked the fat cigar from his mouth with his right hand and took a swallow from the glass of dark liquor in his left. The liquor dribbled down his chin and dripped onto his gold brocaded vest.

"You heard the rumors?" he asked Curt. "The town's plannin' on burnin' us out down here."

"I've heard 'em." Curt crossed his arms over his chest and settled on the only uncluttered corner of Fat Johnnie's desk. "There's a lot of exaggeration going on."

"What're you gonna do about it?"

Curt raised both eyebrows. "What am I gonna do about it? Seems to me this is your end of town, Johnnie. Why don't you deal with it?"

"'Cause I ain't got no policeman in my pocket. You can steer him around us."

"Him, yes. The town council ..." Curt shook his head.

"Then what the fuck good are you? What about this plan you're supposed to have to make 'em back off?"

Curt shot a hard look at Johnnie. "Look, you overflowing bucket of lard, I'm gettin' sick an' tired of playing nursemaid to you and your cronies. You've got some control around here — use it."

"How?"

Curt tossed a glance at the ceiling draped in cobwebs. "That's up to you, Johnnie. But since you're looking for my advice, I'd say you can either clean up this dump you call home or clear you and your people out."

Fat Johnnie's jowls jiggled as he shook his head. "We got no place to go. The same thing'd prob'ly happen again anyhow. And why should I waste my money fixin' up the place for the low-lifes that come in? They don't appreciate the finer things like you and me." He raised his glass to Curt and tossed back the last swallow then wiped his mouth on his sleeve. "My money's my money, and it's stayin' that way. And I'm stayin'. As is."

Curt tossed up one hand. "That's your call. Just don't come cryin' to me if you lose the whole house."

Johnnie's eyes twitched from side to side. He cleared his throat. "You still gonna work on this plan o' yours? You ain't gonna just cut us loose?"

Curt sighed. "If the plan works, it'll work for everybody. If it doesn't, then I lose, too."

That seemed to satisfy Fat Johnnie.

"Is that all?"

The fat man nodded.

Curt rose off the desk and stepped toward the door. Without looking back, he said: "Next time you think you need my advice, Johnnie, don't be sending Keegan to darken my door. You want to talk to me, you hoof it down to the Carlton yourself. The exercise might just clear your head." He opened the door and jerked it shut behind him.

CHAPTER TEN

Wednesday dawned cool and overcast with a blanket of flat grey cloud. By mid-afternoon, the sun had burned the cloud off, but the sudden heat had turned the air unusually muggy and heavy in Curt's lungs as he walked toward the Andrews' home.

There were three people out on Timberline Street, so he walked on and made his approach from the creek. He knocked on the back door. A smile lit Mary's face the moment she saw him.

Sweeping off his hat, he smiled broadly. "Are you going to let me in?"

She did not hesitate this time. As he closed the door, he caught from the corner of his eye her hand rising to touch his arm. But she withdrew it as he turned to face her, without having touched him. Her eyes dropped away from his face.

Still shy, but she wanted him, he was certain. The gestures people almost made were just as important as the ones they actually did. He was gaining ground with her more quickly than he had anticipated.

Placing his hand tenderly on her shoulder, he said, "Mary, I've missed you," and found it odd that, in a way, he actually had.

Her eyes flicked to his face and she sucked in her breath. "I — I've missed you, too."

Bending slightly, he kissed her cheek, near her mouth. Her lips quivered.

Taking her hand, he said, "Would you like to take a walk along the creek?"

She nodded. Without another word, he led her out the back door, lifted her over the fence and guided her descent to the floor of the ravine. They went northward again, wrapped in the silence and solitude of the forest. She queried him about the wild evergreen plants growing along the trail, and he identified sword ferns, salal, and Oregon grape for her.

"Later in the summer, you can eat the salal berries — they taste kind of like blueberries, just some are a little ... 'gamey,' for lack of a better word," he told her. "And the Oregon grape berries ripen later in the fall and winter. They're even sweeter after they get a little frost. But you've got to get them before the birds do."

"How did you learn all this?" she asked him, wide-eyed.

"Just paying attention to the natives as I was growing up. A kid on his own had to eat something."

"Is that why you have such strong concerns about the less fortunate?" she asked, laying a hand on his arm. "Because you had a harsh childhood?"

He shrugged, realizing he'd walked into that opening which would allow her to ask about his life. His mind spun over what he should or should not tell her. "My mother was a prostitute, a whore, Mary," he imagined himself blurting out. "One of those unfortunates you say you would bring into your home. I don't know my father — I am the product of fornication. Are you still interested in knowing me?"

When he did not respond after a few moments, she took her eyes from his face, let her hand slip into his, and walked quietly beside him.

Though they merely strolled, it seemed they made the little meadow more quickly this time. They stood just at the edge of it, gazing out across it. During the week since they'd last seen it, the field had decorated itself with wildflowers of every kind and color. Some were gaily poised at the tips of long stems; others huddled together in small, dense clumps. Both Curt and Mary breathed deeply of the sweet and heady scent of summer.

"Isn't it wonderful?" Mary sighed.

"Uh-huh."

She twirled ahead of him, spinning in circles with her arms stretched out like wings, her hair trailing out behind her like the tail of a spirited horse. Laughing, she turned again and again through the flowers. Watching her, Curt couldn't help a small laugh himself.

"I feel like that doe we saw last week," she cried. "Wild and free, without a care in the world!" She turned once more and bounded through the tall grass, her skirt held high in one hand.

Grinning, Curt followed her at a walk. Near the far end of the meadow, she turned around and ran back to him. Stopping in the middle of the field, Curt waited for her. Her high spirits had already begun to infect him, and the sight of her hair and her breasts bouncing as she played made him feel like a stag in rut. She reached him, letting her skirt down one step too soon and tripping over it, falling against his chest. He caught her, and they laughed together.

Her leaf-green eyes entranced him, and he stared into them as if seeking out her soul. She stared back, and their laughter fell away. His grip tightened on her arms, and she stepped closer, bringing her feet more surely beneath her. Her pink lips were like a magnet to his, and he lowered his head to capture them.

She gasped when their lips first touched and stood rigidly as he slowly explored her mouth with his. Softly pressing, gently tugging, he urged her to respond. Her eyes closed, and her lips parted slightly. Then she sighed, and all her tension seemed to pass out of her with it. Her lips began a tentative taste of his, and the response sent fire racing through Curt's veins. But he held himself tightly in check. To abandon all restraint now would be to overwhelm her too soon.

He wrapped his arms around her, enveloping her, and matched her slow kisses. Gradually she grew bolder, and her arms wound around his neck as a little moan escaped from her throat. Her breasts pressed against his chest, and he pulled her more tightly against him. Sliding his hands up and down her curves, he cupped her breasts, causing her to utter a little animal-like whine. Leaving them, he splayed his fingers over her soft buttocks and ground her hips against him, forcing her to feel his need for her.

She flinched at the first feel of his hardness thrusting against her, but her own body's awakened desire drew her back to it. He could feel the heat of her ardor now. Cupping her head with his hands, he tipped it back and thrust his tongue inside her open mouth. She stiffened at the sudden, intensely intimate contact, but again she gave herself to the experience. His movements enticed her to respond, and her tongue sought his with an instinct beyond her understanding.

Curt drove himself against her, wanting to be in and around her at the same time, to lose himself in her. Her passion was fresh, unblemished by any acquired skills, and headier than anything he'd encountered for a long time. His brain began to fall back as his body demanded dominion over the moment.

Sucking in a deep breath, he pushed her to arms' length. If he didn't stop now, he wasn't certain he could stop. Mary blinked at him through eyes drugged with passion, and her hands gripped his lapels tightly.

"Curt ..."

He couldn't bring more than a grunt from his throat. His breath ragged and his heart pounding like a galloping stallion, he stared at her. Her breath was coming just as hard. Her hair was in disarray, and her lips were moist and swollen.

"Mary ..." He softened his hold on her. "We shouldn't ... go too far."

He saw the question pass through her eyes — what was too far? He doubted she had been given any explicit rules to follow. Probably instructed to allow a man no privileges at all, orders as cut and dried as that.

Her eyes began to focus, and a smile lifted the corners of her mouth. "You would never go too far with me."

"Don't be too sure. You don't know what you can do to a man."

She came close to laughing, but clearly she was still too entangled in her swirling emotions. "With you, I'm sure of everything." She snuggled herself against his chest, her hand slipping beneath his jacket and clasping at the silk backing of his vest.

Her blind trust tugged at his heart. He cuddled her close, feeling a sudden urge to protect her — from himself.

For several minutes, they stood, embracing, and then Mary sighed and lifted her head to smile at him. He smiled back, trying to fight the emotion he knew she could see in his eyes. He couldn't do it.

She began to trace the trim lines of his notched lapels with her fingertips. She toyed with his tie then went back to tracing the lines and seams of his vest, following his watch chain to its pocket.

"What's this?" she asked, trying to determine the outline of the lump in his lower left pocket. He couldn't stop her. She pulled out his derringer. "Another gun?" She tipped her head back to see his face.

He shrugged. "In my line of work, I sometimes carry a lot of money, and it's necessary to have protection."

She accepted that and tucked the weapon back into its pocket. Exploring further, she came across his pack of cards.

"Something to pass the time with on long trips," he explained.

She waggled the cardboard pack between them, feigning censure. "Do you know what my mother would say? She would scold you black and blue for dallying with the devil's Bible."

"Thank God you're not your mother."

They both chuckled as she tucked the pack away again. For some reason, her movements had aroused him again. Her face reddened but she didn't move away. He caught himself, wishing she would reach down and take it, too, from his clothes, but that was too much to hope for yet.

Her eyes turned misty. "I love you, Curt. I know it's awfully soon, but I know I do. You're so wonderful to me — I've never met a man like you. You make me feel so ... so ..." She gazed into his eyes, unable to come up with the right word. Her eyes dropped to his mouth, and she raised herself up on her toes and kissed him.

The bolt of fire that shot into Curt rocked him back on his heels and left him feeling dazed by her kiss. He could do nothing but let her kiss him, surrendering himself to her affection. When she stopped and lowered herself down, he could only gape at her with wonder. She smiled, as if knowing that she had affected him the way he had her.

"Let's sit down," he said, feeling like he'd better sit down before he fell down.

He'd been going to drop right there, but Mary took his hand and led him nearer the creek bank. They sat in the deep grass there and watched the sun sparkle on the water.

Curt noticed a tangle of sweet peas growing just out of reach. He stretched over and pinched off a few stems with multicolored blooms on them.

"For you," he said, presenting them to Mary. "Because I enjoy sharing these simple, delicate pleasures with you."

She blushed, smiling, as she accepted them. Leaning against him, Mary plucked a single stem of clover from the grass and twirled the tiny white flower in her fingers. Then she held it up to him. "Does this mean anything?"

"'Think of me'," he answered.

Putting it in his hand, she said, "Then I give it to you, because I want you to think of me always."

Looking at it, he knew it would be difficult not to think of her. "I will." He tucked the tiny blossom into the buttonhole of his left lapel.

She sighed and laid her head on his shoulder. "I pray we'll be together always."

Always. Of course, that would be what she had in mind. In her mind, why else would a man keep calling on her? And of course, that was what he needed her to think.

"Do you like children, Curt?"

Her question caught him off guard. "Uh — I dunno. I haven't been around them much."

"A kind, gentle man like you would make a wonderful father."

He nearly choked. "You think so?"

"I'm certain of it." She turned her head and smiled up at him. Seeing his disturbed expression, she squeezed his hand and laughed softly. "Don't worry — I don't want too many children. Two or three would be enough."

Two or three children? "You've been thinking a lot about a future together, haven't you?"

She smiled. "You and me in a little house — perhaps just a little outside town. We'd have a garden and lots of flowers. It would be so wonderful! Don't you think so?"

He looked away, up the creek.

"Oh, don't be bashful. It's okay for a man to want those things, too."

Want them? He had no concept of life in that fashion — how could he possibly want those things? But the way she said it, the way she squeezed his hand, made them seem somehow pleasant enough to be wanted. He turned his face back to hers and suddenly felt like a goddamned heel. Her eyes were sparkling with love and dreams that he would shortly destroy for her.

"You don't really believe in God, do you, Curt?"

Mentally, he shook himself and half-turned back to her. Where had that come from all of a sudden? Her hand was warm on his shoulder blade.

He'd never been pious, and he knew he couldn't fake it. "No, I guess I've never much gone for religion. It just gets in the way."

She chuckled softly. "Whatever do you mean?"

He leaned back on his arms so he could see her face and feel the sun on his. "All this faith stuff you church folks talk about. Like no matter what's happening, no matter how bad it is, you trust God to make it all right."

"He will."

"Seems more like an excuse to not take care of things yourself. If something needs fixing, I'd rather fix it myself right then, instead of waitin' on somebody I've never even met who might not even show up."

She laughed, and though it was a good-natured laugh, he suddenly felt a little foolish.

"Don't you get it? God is there to help us through the things we can't take care of ourselves. You only need to ask Him and believe."

He shrugged.

Mary slipped her arms around him and hugged him as one would a confused child. "My dear Curt, you have a lot to learn. But don't worry — there's hope for you!"

"Humph!" was all he could summon in response.

After walking her home and kissing her lingeringly at the back door, Curt made his way slowly along the creek path toward town. His brain felt foggy, sodden — muggy like the air around him. He felt like he'd lost his bearings, tossed around like an autumn leaf in the wind. Rubbing his hands over his face, he strode more briskly, trying to wake himself up, forcing his lungs to pull in this unusually humid air. He hated this kind of weather. He'd mentioned that to Mary, who said this was more the norm for entire summers back east. He recalled few humid stretches in years past here, and they were always short-lived. Thank God.

What would it be like, with a house, a garden, kids, and a wife? Waking up with Mary every morning, going out to a job five or six days a week?

Great crucified Christ! What the hell was he thinking? Chaining himself to one woman and the responsibility of feeding three noisy brats and the droll, day-in, day-out rut of a working stiff? He must be going mad!

He already had a woman to wake up with. He already had all the home he'd ever needed. He already had the work he wanted to do. And he had the freedom to come and go as he pleased and fork a different woman now and then.

He'd lose all of that if he went and got himself married.

He climbed up the bank at the bridge and headed for downtown. Del should be ready for supper about now. She'd look at him like he'd lost his marbles if he told her what he'd been thinking. There was no way he was telling her any of it.

She was sipping a whiskey at the bar when he walked in.

"What's this?" she asked, plucking the clover puff from the buttonhole of his lapel.

He leaned on the bar. "Mary gave it to me. A token of her affection."

There was a sudden discomfort in his stomach as Del crushed the flower on the bar top and tossed it over the far side. "She's fuckin' in love with you already. When's this all gonna be over?"

"Hard to say."

"Well, it better not take too goddamn long. I don't want her gettin' too wound up in you, so's she won't let go."

Curt ran his fingers up her bare forearm. "I'm in control of the whole game, Del. As far as I'm concerned, everything's going like it should." He looked into her amber eyes, hoping she believed him because he wasn't entirely sure he believed himself.

He brought her hand to his lips and kissed her fingers near the big emerald ring he'd given her years ago. "Hungry?"

"Starved."

"Good. So am I. Let's head over to Earl's and get a couple of big steaks or something."

"Sounds good," she said, sounding mollified.

He hooked her hand into his elbow and led her out the door.

It wasn't quite five-thirty, and Earl's had only a few couples seated. Curt and Del settled themselves in their usual spot and waited for service. A few minutes passed before Aimes approached their table. His cheeks were red, and he looked embarrassed. Just before reaching them, he dropped the pad and pencil. He retrieved them, and when he stood before Curt and Del, his knuckles were white, he was gripping the pad and pencil so tightly.

Curt and Del eyed him curiously.

"What's the matter, Aimes?" Curt asked him. "Del hasn't said a word to you yet."

"It — it isn't that, sir."

Del laid her hand on his rigid arm. "Are you sick, honey?"

"N-no, miss." He tossed a worried glance over his left shoulder.

Curt followed the glance and saw Earl Stanbury flutter his hand at Aimes. "What's up, Aimes?"

"I — I'm really sorry, Mr. Prescott, but ... Mr. Stanbury won't allow you to be served anymore."

Curt's eyes fluttered in shock, and his mouth fell open. "What?"

"He — he says you're bad for business."

Del hissed. "That fuckin' sonovabitch." She raised her hand in an obscene gesture at Stanbury. "Whatsa matter, Earl — your wife think you're porkin' me? Well, tell her for me I'd rather hump a dead hog!"

The other customers all stopped eating to stare at her and Stanbury. Curt laid his hand on Del's arm, easing it down. "Take it easy, Del."

Her eyes flashed at him. "We been regulars in here for years — since he opened the goddamn place! Who does he think he is, turnin' us out?"

"Just the owner," Curt reminded her gently. Biting back the bile that threatened to rise in his own throat, he took her hand and urged her to rise. Glancing at the young waiter, he said, "Thanks for everything, Aimes. You're an ace."

"Thank you, sir. I'm really sorry."

"Forget it."

Del was on her feet, but she reached back to snatch up her spangled reticule. Her furious face softened long enough to give the boy an amicable smile, but then it reverted to fury. Curt steered her away from the table with his fingers at her elbow. He moved through the tables toward Stanbury, ignoring the stares of the other customers.

Stanbury began to shift back and forth as Curt approached him. Finding no way to make a dignified exit, he backed himself up against the cash counter. He cleared his throat and straightened his ascot tie.

Curt stepped up close to him, facing the smaller man squarely. He noted the beads of sweat on Stanbury's receding hairline.

"What's the problem, Stanbury? Something suddenly wrong with my money?"

Stanbury lifted his chin and closed his trembling hands on the open front of his black frock coat. "We don't want your kind around here anymore," he said. "And I'm not afraid to do my part."

"Is that why you sent the boy to do your dirty work for you?" Curt's voice was smooth and level, but full of contempt.

Stanbury looked down at his hands, shaking despite their tenacious grip on his coat. "I'm not afraid of you."

"No particular reason you should be." Curt felt Del about to jump in but he held her arm firmly. "So be a man, Stanbury. Tell me your reason for kicking us out."

Stanbury babbled something Curt didn't believe the man himself understood. Stanbury stroked the twist in his mustache as if it were able to give him courage. Then he replied: "Someone's been trying to undermine the efforts of the good people of this town. Influencing decent men to turn on their brothers and aid the cause of the undesirable element. You are well-respected within that community. I, personally, feel the culprit might be you."

Curt fixed him with a penetrating stare. "Don't tell me you're on the Moral Action Committee with all those old biddies?"

"My wife just recently convinced me to join. I've yet to attend my first meeting, but come next Wednesday, I assure you I'll tell them all about my suspicions concerning you." He narrowed his tiny black eyes and sneered up at Curt. "You and your kind are not long for this town, gambler."

Curt half-smiled. "We'll see. We'll see."

He turned away, steering Del, but she jerked her elbow out of his hand and faced Stanbury. She was taller than he was, and she stared down into his bead-like black eyes. He sniffed at her in disgust. Del's eyes dropped to his precious mustache. Sucking a huge wad of saliva onto her tongue, she spat it directly beneath Stanbury's nose.

The restaurateur gasped in horror, staring transfixed at her grin as the spittle ran down his lips. Suddenly coming to life, he wiped it away with his handkerchief. He saw all his customers staring at him. He raised the hand holding the handkerchief and shook it in the air.

"Get out! You just get out!" he screeched, his face flushed red from his starched collar to his hairline.

Del pivoted gracefully and sashayed after Curt, hooking her arm in his as she reached him. He led her out the door.

With a cock-eyed grin he said, "Nice touch."

"Thanks. That two-faced sonovabitch deserved it. Why didn't you punch him or somethin'? Don't it bother you what he just did to us?"

"'Course it bothers me. But I wasn't going to prove his point."

She frowned a moment before his meaning impressed itself on her mind.

Curt suggested they try the new café that had gone up just last week. They headed west down View Street, walked in, and seated themselves. It was half the size of Earl's, sparely furnished and modestly decorated. A waitress approached them instantly with a smile, a pot of coffee and menus. She said good day as she filled the off-white earthenware mugs.

Del stirred cream and sugar into her coffee before picking up the flimsy pasteboard menu. "Ain't got much, do they?"

"No," Curt replied. "But what they have might be good, so try anything you want."

When the waitress returned they both chose a chicken sandwich and vegetable soup. When the girl was gone, Del slurped her coffee and looked over the rim at Curt.

"You ain't said yet what you're gonna do about Earl."

Curt leaned back in his chair and fingered the red- and white-checkered tablecloth. "He is gonna be a problem."

"What are you gonna do? I'd like to see you beat him to a pulp for what he did to us."

"That wouldn't help. It'd probably make things worse."

"If he gets to that meetin' he'll blow the whole thing. You gotta stop him somehow." She swallowed more coffee.

Yes, if Stanbury got to the meeting, he'd pull their legs out from under them. But unless the little rat was bluffing, chances were he was already talking, and people were already listening.

Like a forest fire run up against a peat bog, it might have appeared the committee was gradually being squelched, but underneath the moss it was still burning, burrowing its way through to new fuel. Curt realized he'd been so busy keeping an eye on the trees that a few sparks had gotten past him and kept right on burning. And unless he did something fast, it was going to reach the other side, and then all hell would really break loose.

It was time to burn a firebreak. When the blaze reached the forest, it would have to find it already scorched. It was time to burn Mary Andrews.

CHAPTER ELEVEN

Half in a dream, Mary had prepared dinner mechanically and helped her mother clean up the dishes afterward. Now she sank into her corner of the chesterfield with a shirt of her father's to mend. She began to hum a cheery tune, but her mother looked up in surprise at her, and Mary suddenly felt very loud. The silence fell heavily when she stopped humming.

"Go on, Mary," her father said from his chair. "Hum if you want to. It sounds very nice."

Her mother made no objections, but Mary couldn't bring herself to begin again. It was already spoiled. After threading a needle, she turned the shirt inside out to gain access to the tear in the shoulder seam.

Her mind drifted back again to her afternoon with Curt. How wonderful it had felt to be in his arms! And his kiss — that must have been the real kiss he had meant before. Even the memory of the delicious ecstasy of it made her quiver inside. It had been frightening at first, but then it had felt, oh, so good.

Stiffening, she remembered her vow not to allow him to kiss her again. She'd had it firmly in mind until they reached the meadow and forgotten it somewhere in the breeze as she ran. From the instant she'd come up against his chest and felt the strength in him as he pulled her close ... gazed into his eyes that were so dark yet seemed to smolder when they looked at her ... From the instant his mouth claimed hers, she had given herself over to the feelings he evoked in her.

She felt her cheeks flush hot, remembering her body's response to his. She'd had a vague understanding of lust. Now she knew it firsthand. She knew she had only a vague notion of the secret things men and women did in private, but her body seemed to know all about it and wanted it.

Carefully, she glanced at her father and mother. Was it like that between them? Her mother had never spoken of it directly. She'd made only obscure references to men's lustful natures and to women's duties to their husbands.

Mary stole a look at Bud. Her father, lustful? She could not imagine him being anything but a most tender and gentle husband. She could not imagine him losing his head to lust.

Her thoughts turned back to Curt. Had Curt lost his head with her? She certainly had with him, and she a woman, supposedly not prone to such desires. But for all her searching, she could not find herself truly damaged in any way. At least, not physically. Physically, she felt awakened, alive like she never had before. But censuring thoughts nagged at her. She worried her parents would be displeased. She was certain the Lord was displeased with her. She knew her first responsibility lay in pleasing Him, not herself or Curt. Until she met Curt, it had been easy, and she had wondered what all the fuss was about — self-control was easy. But now she caught herself shutting out the voice of conscience, shutting out the voice of the Lord. She didn't want to be told she was doing something wrong. How could something that felt so good, so right, be so wrong?

"Did something special happen today?"

She looked up quickly at her father, who still had one coarse, stubby finger in the pages of the book in his lap. "You're smiling," he said.

It faded from her lips then returned and faded again. She couldn't tell her father about her outing. Nor could she look him in the face and lie to him. She fixed her eyes on the fireplace.

"I — I just took a walk in the afternoon, that's all. It was a beautiful day and —."

Bud chuckled, holding up his free hand. "Don't apologize, my dear. It's good for you to get out and take some air."

"Where did you go?" asked Sarah, peering at her over the spectacles she used for embroidery and other close, detailed work.

Mary looked at the crisp new handkerchiefs in her mother's lap. Her brother had been gone nearly a year now, but Sarah still insisted on stitching her father's initials on his new hankies so as not to confuse them.

"N-no place in particular. I ... just sort of wandered ..."

"Well, just you watch where you wander — don't go anywhere near the bad areas of town."

"I would never go to those places, Mother."

"Good. You stay in our neighborhood. Where there are respectable people around."

"Yes, Mother."

"A girl can't be any too careful."

"Yes, Mother." Mary drew in a breath to sigh but caught herself and let it out very slowly and silently.

Even after her mother had returned to her embroidery and her father to his book, it was several minutes before Mary began to relax. She tried to concentrate on the shirt but her eyes kept lifting themselves to her father. Twice she nearly blurted out the truth to him.

Not since she was a child had she been so afraid to admit the truth of her wrongdoing. Conscience demanded she reveal her lapse of propriety, but she just couldn't. Not without losing everything — her parents' trust, her moments with Curt.

She should be ashamed of herself. Curt was a gambler, which made it likely that he consorted with bad men and equally bad women. And she was consorting with him. She knew who and what he was but it didn't stop her from wanting to be with him. She knew her father was wary of Curt's motives for befriending them, and she should be, too. But she couldn't help but feel that he wasn't all lies.

She believed he honestly liked her. She believed his concern for rehabilitating fallen women who wished to change was genuine. With all the kindness and tenderness he had shown her, she just could not believe he was evil. There had to be some part of him that she could touch — that she indeed had touched. If only he was taken with her enough that he would change his ways. Then they could stop hiding their relationship, and she wouldn't have to feel so guilty about it.

Yes, she thought, drawing her lip between her teeth. If Curt would forthrightly ask permission to court her, then her parents might see him in a different light. They might see the Curt that she saw. Her heart began to flutter at the thought of it. Yes, if only he would do that!

A smile spread over her face, and she beamed at her father, whose face was still tipped to his book. Yes — then everything would be all right. Then her deception would not really matter. She had to see Curt again and soon.

But how would she find him? With a jolt, she realized she didn't even know where he lived. Her father probably would, but she couldn't ask him without revealing too much. There was no one she could ask without raising too many questions. She was going to have to wait until Curt came to her.

Friday afternoon, Curt waited for Mary. He'd stopped at the livery to pay his horse's monthly board then walked out of town past the little farms on the way to the Garry Oak Church. He stood, concealed in the forest fringing the church-school building, waiting for her to pass by on her way home. He watched the old teacher see her and the children off and then go back inside. Mary walked amongst the pack of frolicking children, smiling and chatting to some as they all went their separate ways. By the time they reached Curt's location, they were all ahead of her. Curt let them all pass then lifted a cedar bough and stepped out onto the road.

"Mary."

Her step faltered, and she turned around, a bewildered look on her face. But it vanished the second she saw him, replaced by an elated smile. She let the children go along home without noticing she'd fallen behind.

"Darling!" she cried, as hushed as she could, and rushed into his arms.

He drew her into the trees and crushed her to his chest. "I had to see you," he murmured. "I couldn't wait."

"Oh, I'm so glad you came. I couldn't wait, either." She lifted her face from his chest.

He dropped his eyes to her parted lips, which were an invitation if he'd ever seen one. Without hesitation, he covered them in a masterful kiss, demanding a response from her. She welcomed him, returning his kiss with equal ardor and holding his head down to hers.

"Come for a walk with me," he said when they broke their kiss.

"I can't. I have to go home and fix supper. Why don't you come?"

He rested his eyes on hers and stroked her hair, which was pinned up in a swirl on her crown. "Wouldn't you rather run off with me?"

A smile spread slowly across her face, and she looked away from him. "You make me feel so wicked ..." Her eyes came back to his. "Yes, I'd rather run off with you."

"Then do it. Let your mother fix supper by herself."

He watched the light dance in her eyes, and then her eyelids dropped, extinguishing it. "I can't. I have to go home." She tugged at his hands. "Come with me. We can stop at the shop and check with Dad first to make sure it's all right — if you'd rather?"

Damn. He wasn't going to win this hand. "All right."

"Good!" She flung her arms around his neck. "I love you. Oh, I love you."

He buried his nose in her hair and breathed its scent deeply. Her body fit into his so perfectly it was intoxicating. The forest floor beneath their feet was covered with reddish-brown cedar needles that were fragrant, free of brush, and soft to lie on.

"Curt?"

"Hmm?"

"Would you ... would you ...?"

"Would I what?" He spread his fingers over her lower back then moved them even lower to squeeze her soft, perfectly shaped buttocks. He ground his hips into hers, and she moaned softly. Damn, but he wanted to fork her right now.

"I shouldn't be asking you ... but there's not time."

He nuzzled her ear and kissed his way down her neck then nipped his way back up. Her body molded against his. Her breath was uneven. Her arms locked around his neck.

"Would you ask my father for permission to court me?"

He lifted his head and searched her eyes.

"I know — a woman shouldn't ask, but ... I just don't feel right deceiving them like this. It has to be out in the open, or I can't see you anymore. And I don't want to stop seeing you. I'd rather die."

He hadn't expected her to come right out and ask him. A ready response eluded him.

Her face drew taut in concern. "Don't you want to? You do want to marry me some day, don't you?"

Marriage again. There was only one answer that would satisfy her. But that demanded an outright lie he couldn't quite bring himself to. "I — I'm just not sure I'm ready right now."

Her eyes dropped. "I see ..." She looked back up at him. "But even if you think you might someday ... you could still ask."

"Perhaps. We've only known each other a month or so — you don't think this is too soon?"

"But courting would allow us to get to know each other even better!" Her smile returned. "So there's no reason you shouldn't ask. And right away."

His gut tightened. There didn't seem to be any getting around it now.

"They'll say yes. I know they will." She pressed a kiss to his lips. "Don't worry. It'll be as easy as pie."

He had no doubt it would be. He checked to make sure the road was clear then lifted the bough and followed her out of the forest. As they strolled down the hill toward town, he marveled at how easy the whole thing had been. These people had admitted his entry into their lives as easily as the ocean admits a river.

If he weren't so good at wearing whatever hat suited the occasion, he would have called it too easy. But the Andrews were trusting, expecting other people to be as sincere and guileless as they were. Easy prey.

Bud welcomed him to take dinner with them. He told them that Sarah was home, so the two of them could go straight on there.

Mary tucked her arm in Curt's elbow as they left the saddlery. He leaned close to her ear.

"And you were nervous about what to say," he commented. "He didn't even ask how we ended up together."

She smiled, a nervous gush of air passing through her teeth. She hadn't had to lie. "Thank goodness. But what if he asks later? Or Mother?"

"You worry too much."

"But I hate lying."

"I'll cover it. Trust me."

She squeezed his arm with gratitude.

He followed her into the house. She waited while he took off his gun and hid it in the drawer before calling to her mother.

"Mother, I'm home! And Mr. Prescott — Curt — is with me."

Sarah hurried from the kitchen, wiping her hands on a dishtowel. "Why, Mr. Prescott — what a surprise."

"We've seen Dad at the shop," Mary blurted out. "He said it was all right for him to come for dinner."

"Fine, fine." The creases around Sarah's eyes and mouth deepened as she studied them a moment. "I thought you were late. Where did you two meet?"

Mary's mouth opened but Curt cut her off. "I had been taking a walk in the country, and suddenly I looked up, and there was Mary." He flashed them both a big smile. "Brightened my day, she surely did."

Sarah's stern countenance cracked, and she smiled at last. "Well, you may stay for dinner, Mr. Prescott." She turned her eyes on her daughter. "I will look after dinner, Mary. You entertain Mr. Prescott until your father gets home."

Curt saw Mary bite back a smile. "Yes, Mother."

Sarah left them, and Curt and Mary sat down on the chesterfield. Curt let her have her spot but sat close to her.

She braced her hands against his shoulders. "You shouldn't sit too close with Mother around," she whispered.

"If she comes back, I'll hear her." He deliberately kissed her lips then chuckled at her as she pulled away, her eyes round and staring, full of dread, toward the kitchen. He kissed her again.

"Curt, stop."

"Shh — she'll hear you."

Her eyes were bright green flashes as she glared at him. "You are so bad sometimes."

He grinned wickedly. "I know. I like to be bad." He captured her lips yet again, but this time kissed her long and lazily until she yielded. When he raised his head, she opened her eyes, and they had a drugged, dreamy look in them. "And you like to be bad, too. You know you do."

She pursed her lips, as if about to deny it, then she said, "Only because you make me want to be ..."

"Just wait until we're married. Being bad gets better than this."

Her eyes brightened immediately, and she clasped her hands behind his neck. "It will be wonderful, darling. I know it will be." She drew a long, deep breath and sighed. "I can't wait for it all to be in the open. It's too hard, trying to lie."

He said nothing, and she looked at him curiously.

"You seem to do it so easily. Do you lie very often?"

He chuckled. "No. Only when I have to."

Concern darkened her eyes.

"If it makes you feel any better," he said, stroking her hair. "I didn't really lie — I just left out a little bit. Life has taught me the hard way that blatant honesty is not always the best policy. People take advantage of you and twist the truth to suit their needs. I've just learned not to give them the ammunition."

She looked into his eyes then turned her face away and stared at the dark, empty fireplace. He'd bet that it used to be so easy for her to tell right from wrong. Her parents had drawn her bold, precise lines all her life, and until now, she was so used to living within them that she never even thought to question them. Now the lines were blurring, and no doubt she couldn't tell so easily anymore. Curt was opening her eyes to so much, yet at the same time, he was closing them too.

He read her thoughts on her face. "Darling? Are you upset with me?" He took her chin with his finger, to make her look at him. "I only did it to protect you. Haven't you ever told a little white lie so you wouldn't, say, hurt someone's feelings or let a mountain be made out of a molehill?"

Hesitantly, she nodded. He pressed a kiss to her forehead and passed his hand through her hair. Then he shifted a couple of feet back from her. Sarah was coming to check on them.

After dinner, the women cleaned up the dishes while Bud and Curt talked in the parlor. Bud talked mostly of his day in the shop. Curt guessed there wasn't much else the old fellow had to talk about.

"I unloaded two dozen hides today," said Bud. "They weigh only fifteen to twenty pounds apiece, but near the end there, they were feeling more like fifty." He shook his head. "I suppose I'll have to start accepting my age. I'm just not twenty anymore."

Bud's serene grey eyes lighted on Curt's, and Curt held them, feeling there was more coming.

"I wish my son had chosen to stay with saddlery. He would still be with us. And I could really use his help now."

"You didn't approve of him being in the Navy?"

"It isn't the ideal life for a Christian. But he was sixteen when he told us he wanted to go. He was a young man. I had to allow him to make his own decisions."

"I guess you did."

Bud sighed, and a thoughtful gleam came into his eyes. "How well do you like what you're doing? Have you ever wanted to do anything else?"

"Honestly, no. It's all I've ever done and all I've ever wanted to do."

"I see. Well, if you ever feel the need for a change, I'd be glad to take you into the business."

Despite Curt's shock, Bud's offer warmed a spot in his middle, and his heart suddenly felt like it was swelling into his throat. He'd never considered another line of work before, but the sincere offer from Bud was touching. "Thank you. I'll keep that in mind." So Bud wouldn't doubt his sincerity, he added, "I will."

The older man nodded and left it at that.

The women joined them a half hour later, and Sarah started squawking almost immediately over how prices had gone up at the mercantile. Mary kept looking at Curt, as if hoping he would interrupt and broach their subject. He was not unaware of her nearly invisible prodding. He nodded to her that he would as soon as he could.

At last, Sarah stopped for breath, and Curt cleared his throat. He made eye contact with both Bud and Sarah then directed his words to Bud.

"Sir, there's something I'd like to bring up."

Bud waved an open palm at him. "Go right ahead, son."

Curt straightened in his chair and chose his words with care. "I've given it a lot of thought, and I've decided it's the right thing to do. I hope you'll agree." He paused deliberately and looked at Mary, who was perched on the edge of her seat, her hands clamped together in her lap and her top lip between her teeth. He looked back at Bud. "I'd like permission to court your daughter, sir."

Surprise rounded Bud's eyes and opened his mouth. He looked at Mary, who now had smiles coming and going from her anxious face. Curt followed his gaze to Sarah, who was staring at Bud with something like terror on her face.

Bud gripped his knees with his hands. "Curt, I — I don't know what to say. I confess I wasn't entirely sure you were interested."

"I am. Very much so."

"Well ..." Bud looked at his wife then over at Mary. "How does this sit with you, my dear?"

Mary seemed afraid to speak or move for fear of falling apart. She nodded rapidly. "I'd love it, Dad. I really would."

A warm smile touched Bud's lips. He lifted his hands and spread them in the air. "Then permission is granted."

"Oh, Dad!" Mary sprang from her seat, bumping her shin on the coffee table as she rushed to fling her arms around her father. She ignored the pain. "Oh, thank you! Thank you!"

Bud hugged her in return, grinning from one ear to the other, the laugh lines deep around his dancing grey eyes.

Mary turned her face to look at Sarah as she said, "Thank you, Mother," to which Sarah merely replied with a nod.

When Mary had let go of him and sat down, Bud reached over to shake Curt's hand. Curt felt the warmth in the firm grip.

"You'll make a fine son-in-law."

"Thank you, sir. I'll do my best." Then he saw the moisture in Bud's eyes and had to look away. There was only one wall he could look at without meeting their eyes, and that was the one with the empty, soot-blackened fireplace. He raised his eyes to the pastoral paintings and wished he could feel as peaceful as they looked.

As soon as Curt had made it past the front gate, Sarah, who had been watching him from the window, dropped the sheer and whirled on her husband.

"Have you gone insane? Allowing him to court our daughter?"

Bud had been standing before the cold fireplace, staring into it, wondering the same thing himself. He turned slowly to face Sarah. "I don't have to allow the marriage. But he might become suspicious if I said no."

He noticed Mary attempting to gain the stairs and the safety of her room upstairs the moment her mother had snapped. Without speaking, he pointed a stubby finger at the chesterfield, and she sank into it obediently.

Sarah waved her hands frantically in the air and shrieked with frustration. "He is filth! I will not allow my daughter to marry filth!"

Frowning, Bud stepped closer to her. "Sarah —."

"Don't touch me!" She slapped at his outstretched hand and backed away from him. "I only went along with this because it was so important to you! I never wanted that — that — gambler in my house! I still don't want him! But I allowed it, and I smiled and pretended to like his company because you asked me to! But this is too far, Richard! This is going too far!"

Bud stayed where he was, letting her rage until she finally stopped flailing the air and stood, her arms crossed and her bosom heaving, near the tiny foyer.

"I understand your worries, Sarah, but I still believe it's safe to continue. Do you think I'd risk Mary if I thought there was any chance of her being hurt?"

The look Sarah struck him with made no bones about her doubt. "Are you very certain? Are you not so obsessed with saving Curt Prescott that you're willing to sacrifice Mary?"

Bud's jaw dropped. He glanced at Mary, whose eyes had shot to his at the same moment. Bud chewed on his lip and drew a breath. He returned his gaze to his wife's.

"Is that how you see it?"

The outrage on her face mixed with self-satisfaction. "As a matter of fact, I do."

Silence fell over the room like sudden death. Minutes ticked loudly by on the mantle clock while none of them moved. The first sound beyond the clock that Bud became aware of was Sarah's breathing, hissing in and out between her clenched teeth and parted lips. He suddenly felt as though he hadn't taken a breath in days and sucked in a deep one.

"Dear God ..." He wiped his hands over his face, but it did nothing to erase the deeply etched lines. "I haven't, have I?"

His wife stared at him in triumph, but Mary stood and came to him, taking his arm.

"No, Dad. You haven't put me in any danger."

He stared at her, his grey eyes lost and searching hers for help. "Haven't I? I invited him into this house. I saw the attraction between the two of you, and I let it develop."

"That's right!" Sarah spat. "You've thrown your innocent daughter to a wolf, all for the sake of your own pride!"

Mary gaped at her mother. "No!" she cried. "No! Dad didn't ask me to like Curt — I did that all by myself. I'm not ignorant, Mother. I know who Curt is just as well as you do — even better. It doesn't make a difference to me."

Sarah sniffed impatiently. "He's taken you in, you little child. Can't you see that, both of you? Am I the only one around here with any sense left? He's up to something! I don't know what it is, but he's after something. Why else would a man like that have anything to do with us?"

"I think he likes us," Mary said.

Sarah sniffed again. "That's what he wants you to think."

Bud patted the hand that Mary had resting on his arm. "Perhaps your mother's right, dear. Perhaps I was a fool to think we could deceive a deceiver."

"But we're not trying to deceive him," Mary told him. "We're trying to help him. He knows what we are."

Bud shook his head. "But your mother may be right. What is he hoping to gain from us?"

Neither Mary nor Sarah answered him. He suspected that they, like him, had no answers, only a lot more questions.

CHAPTER TWELVE

Del was crooning a love song as Curt passed through the Carlton's doors. He wasn't in the mood for a love song. He was in the mood for jaunty, bawdy songs and enough high-risk wagering to get his mind off Mary Andrews.

He even felt like a few too many drinks.

But he drew the line there. His head was muddled enough already. The suckers came to him in droves, and he sheared them without mercy, but it was all too easy and did little to ease his tension.

Shortly after ten-thirty, Dave Jenkins appeared at his shoulder.

"Evenin', Dave," Curt said, without looking up from his cards.

"Evenin', Curt." The constable looked at the three men sitting around Curt's table. All of them were married, workingmen. "Excuse me, gentlemen, but you're all under arrest."

The three of them stared up at him simultaneously. Curt cocked an eyebrow.

"Come with me, please."

Too stunned, too used to obeying higher authority to protest, the three men all put down their cards and got up from their chairs.

"You, too, Curt."

Curt cocked his head and eyed Jenkins. "What?"

"You're under arrest for encouragin' vice."

Curt's voice dropped to a place deep in his throat. "You're out of your mind."

One of the men spoke up. "He never 'couraged us, Officer. We came askin' him to play."

"That don't matter none. He's a professional gambler. This town don't cotton to his type no more."

Curt eyed the flush in his hand. "That go for you too now, Dave?"

Jenkins hesitated a long time. "I gotta take ya in, Curt. It's the law. I cain't very well arrest these fellers and leave you alone, now can I?"

Curt waved his arm around the games room. "What about the rest of them, Dave? Gonna arrest the whole goddamn place?"

"Ain't got that much room in the hoosegow."

A sardonic smile curving his lips, Curt said, "Oh, I get it. This is all for my benefit. You want to arrest Curt Prescott so everybody can see you're doin' a good and proper job. All right, fuck you. Arrest me." He tossed his cards on the table and stood up.

Jenkins gathered up the cards and money as evidence and stuffed them into his hat. Curt saw his eyes drop to the spot within Curt's vest that concealed his derringer. Jenkins' eyes flicked back up to Curt's for a second, and then he turned to the other men.

"Okay, boys, let's go." He ushered them out ahead of him.

Curt followed Jenkins out the batwing doors then strode impatiently past him and the other three to lead the way to the jail. Once there, Jenkins locked the three in the far cell and opened the near one for Curt.

Curt crossed his arms over his chest. "Far enough, Dave. You already made your point back in the Carlton."

Jenkins shrugged sheepishly. "Gotta go by the book. And I need your boot knife and the derringer."

Curt narrowed his eyes at him. Jenkins looked away and swallowed hard. Curt glanced at the cell, aware of the other three men in the next one keenly watching. The last thing he wanted to do was allow himself to be caged. However, for the sake of their plan, perhaps he should play along. For now.

Blowing air out his nose and shaking his head with a snarl, he passed his weapons to the constable. "You son of a bitch."

"Anythin' else I don't know about?"

"No."

Jenkins raised his hand toward the cell. Curt stepped inside and turned to face Jenkins as he locked it. Jenkins fumbled with the key, afraid to take his eyes off Curt but unable to look him in the face. Once he got the door locked, he moved away from the cell.

"You gentlemen'll be here for the night. In the mornin' you can pay yer fines and go."

The three townsmen huddled close together like nervous sheep. Curt eyed them irritably and turned away. He might as well try to get some sleep. It'd make the night go faster.

Sleep did not come except for brief, scattered moments. Curt was up before dawn, pacing the uneven stone floor. Jenkins and the other three still slept when Curt's watch read seven. Grabbing the bars of the door, he shook them vigorously and kept them clanging until the constable showed signs of life.

Mumbling hoarsely, his eyes half-stuck with sleep, Jenkins searched for the floor with his feet.

"Get up, you son of a bitch!" Curt yelled. "It's morning! Open this goddamn door!"

All three in the other cell were awake now, too. One of them called to Curt, "Hey, knock it off, would ya?" Curt turned to him with eyes brimming with such malice that they all shrank back into their blankets. Curt then swung his attention back to

Jenkins. "Come on, damn it — get the fuck on your feet, Jenkins!"

Groaning, Jenkins rose off the bunk, teetering like a notched tree. Rubbing his eyes, he pulled out his watch and read the time. "Jesus, it's only seven."

"It's morning. Open this door, you lazy bastard."

Jenkins stumbled over and unlocked first Curt's cell and then the other. Curt strode out, collected his weapons and threw his fine down on the desk. Before he left, he pointed a finger at Jenkins like a dagger.

"I warned you before not to fuck with me, Jenkins. I know what you're tryin' to do, but you went too far. Don't ever try to lock me up again, or I'll fuckin' kill you."

Jenkins, already looking like a chastened schoolboy, suddenly went very pale. The three men stood behind him dumbly, their mouths hanging open. Jenkins' lips moved a little, but nothing came out. Curt spun on his heel and stalked out the door.

Striding down the street, his hands balled into fists, he mumbled to himself what a goddamned son of a bitch Jenkins was. What a goddamn idiot. So much for any comradeship on this deal. He was going to have to do it all himself. That was how he should've kept it from the start.

He'd never considered himself and Jenkins actually friends, but they'd had an association of sorts. Jenkins wasn't a bad guy — a little addle-headed and lazy — but he was okay. Usually. Damned poor time to go off on his own with a harebrained scheme like this.

He swung around to the alley behind the Carlton, took the stairs two at a time and let himself in. He hadn't meant to slam the suite's door, but he did.

"Who's there?"

He strode into the bedroom and found Del perched on the bed, the night table drawer open, and the small revolver from within it in her hands and pointed straight at him.

"It's just me. Relax."

Exhaling with relief, she laid the gun back in the drawer and slid it shut. Sliding off the bed, she rushed into his arms, clad only in a diaphanous negligee. "Where have you been? I hardly got any sleep last night. You never leave without tellin' me."

He snorted. "You mean it wasn't goin' all around the saloon? Curt Prescott got arrested last night."

She lifted her head off his shoulder and gaped at him with an open mouth. "It was for real? I heard some fellas talkin', but I didn't believe 'em."

"It was for real, all right."

Del's brows drew together. "Did Jenkins do it?"

"Yep."

"That smart-assed sonovabitch."

Curt moved away from her, got out of his jacket and tie, and undid his vest. "We can't count on him anymore."

"If you ask me, we never could," Del said. "He's always only been hangin' around 'cause you're Curt Prescott. He figgered he'd get to be a big shot too if he hung around with you. I never liked him."

Curt grunted and looked out the window. Drawing a deep breath, he let out as much tension as would go with it. Del stepped up behind him and molded her body to his. She stroked his knotted shoulders.

"Want me to make you feel better?"

Sex had been the furthest thing from his mind, but she had a way of always steering his thoughts in that direction. Turning around, he yanked her up against him.

Tuesday evening in the Carlton was dead. It had been a hot July day, the saloon was stuffy, and the handful of patrons had little enthusiasm for any of their games. A thin layer of cigarette smoke hung like a wraith just below the ceiling.

Curt sat at a table working the cards and nursing a beer. Del was onstage. She was wearing black tonight, offset by diamonds at her throat and in her ears and in her pert little hat. She was singing something, but he wasn't hearing the words.

Tomorrow was Wednesday and the Moral Action Committee meeting.

Tomorrow, Earl Stanbury would open his big, fat mouth.

Curt had had Sunday dinner at the Andrews' again, but of course he couldn't get Mary suitably alone. The very second Sarah left the house for that meeting, he was going to have be there to take Mary down to the meadow. And take her.

He grabbed his mug, dripping with condensation, and gulped down a good swallow of the golden liquid. Setting it down, he reached for his thin cigar and took a long drag. He watched Del curtsy and come off stage before the batwing doors parted and distracted him. The gap briefly admitted pale light before the space filled with a large dark form.

Fat Johnnie waddled stiffly up the aisle to Curt's table. Curt could hear him breathing, sucking and blowing air like a congested ox. Fat Johnnie pulled a chair way out from the table just as Del reached Curt's shoulder. Pinching the brim of his maroon bowler hat, Johnnie smiled his wet, flabby smile.

"Good evenin', Miss Delores."

As she looked at the sweat pouring down his bloated face, Del's lip curled, and she didn't bother forcing it into a smile. She sat down at Curt's left shoulder. Fat Johnnie let himself down into the chair he'd pulled back. It screeched in protest under his immense weight.

Trying not to clench his teeth, Curt asked, "Is there something I can do for you, Johnnie?"

"You sure can." He reached inside his coat and pulled out a long piece of paper folded in three. He spread it open on the table before Curt. "Read that."

Curt picked it up with his left hand. It was an official eviction notice from the city.

"He just served that to me this afternoon, the bastard. I spent all this time tryin' to figure out what to do. I gots a month to get out or they'll run me out on a rail."

"Johnnie, I don't think that's possible," Curt replied with a straight face.

Del snickered.

Johnnie eyed her briefly but soon returned his attention to Curt. "Whadda you think I should do?"

Curt dropped the paper on the tabletop. Leaning back in his chair, he said, "To tell you the truth, I don't much give a damn right now. I got more immediate problems."

Johnnie bristled but held his temper. "Like what?"

"Like trying to save all our asses at once. You got a month. I got until tomorrow."

"For what?"

"None of your goddamn business."

Fat Johnnie straightened a little. "Well, me and the boys figger it is our business. You ain't told us squat about this so-called plan of yours. Hell, for all we know there ain't no such plan. For all we know, maybe you and Jenkins is in cahoots tryin' to run us out and take over our operations for yerselfs."

Curt threw him a sneering smile. "Use your goddamn brain — if you have one. I've already got everything I want right here. What the hell would I want with your stinking hovels?"

Now Fat Johnnie grimaced, clearly affronted. His ice-blue eyes flashed, and his pale skin took on a rosy hue. "Sure, you say that, but how do we know?" His Cockney accent surged forth as his anger swelled like breakers smashing against a rocky shore. "Look, Mister King of the Carlton, if we go down, you go down. I'll see to that!" He slammed his fist down on the table so hard Del jumped, and Curt's beer, only half-full, spilled over the rim and dribbled onto the table.

Curt hadn't even blinked.

"Did you hear me, King Shit? I said you're goin' down, too!" Johnnie jabbed a pudgy finger at him for emphasis.

Curt had stared past Johnnie during his tirade. Now, with the swiftness of a striking rattler, he snaked out his hand and grabbed the finger without even appearing to have seen it. In the same motion he stood, bending the finger back until it snapped.

Johnnie howled, his eyes sparking with pain and surprise.

Curt leaned over him. "If you'd had a mother, you maggot, she'd have taught you it isn't polite to point."

Bent over his injured hand, still in Curt's grip, Fat Johnnie stared up at him, his eyes wild with fear. He did not appear in the least bit reassured by the lack of emotion on the gambler's face. Curt knew there was no hint of tension or anxiety betrayed by his features, but even he could feel his fearsome anger like a sour smell in the air. No doubt Johnnie felt it too.

"Never threaten me, Johnnie." He twisted the broken finger, and Fat Johnnie screamed. Then Curt released the pressure but kept a firm grip. His hand, lean, sinewy, and dark against Fat Johnnie's fleshy, soft, white one, looked small, but it vibrated with a focused power the larger one did not possess.

Curt's voice dropped to that low spot in his throat and came out cold and menacing. "I'm sick and tired of all your whining and bellyaching. I want it to stop now. You boys elected me nursemaid all on your own. If you expect me to solve your problems for you, you'd better sit back and let me do it. Get in my way, and I'll run you out of town myself. And believe me, if I do it, you won't be leaving on your feet, let alone on a rail."

The fat man quivered and swallowed.

"Do we understand each other, Johnnie?"

Fat Johnnie nodded, his jowls jiggling.

Curt released his finger. "Now get the hell outta here."

Fat Johnnie scrambled from his chair, knocking it over with a clatter. His broken finger cradled in his other hand, he hoofed it out the door.

Del grasped Curt's arm, her eyes flashing with excitement. "You sure showed him! Imagine him tryin' to tell you what to do!" She hugged him and pressed a kiss to his cheek. "That's the Curt I know!"

Something inside him flinched, and he eyed her. Did she mean he hadn't seemed himself lately? He certainly hadn't felt it. But he hadn't realized it showed.

"I need a drink," she said, standing. "Want another one?"

He nodded. She picked up the mug he had and took it with her to the bar. When she came back, she wiped the table with a rag borrowed from a waitress. Then she sat down with him, and they both sipped through the froth.

"So," Del began. "What are you gonna do by tomorrow?"

He sighed. "What do you think?"

"Fuck that Andrews girl."

He nodded.

"'Bout time. This whole thing's draggin' on too long for me."

He regarded her closely. That's what everyone around him seemed to think. He'd figured them to be too impatient, unable to understand the need for delicacy. But perhaps the problem did lie with him. Maybe he was being far too patient.

He watched Del pivot her mug back and forth in the ring of moisture around its base. Her eyes traveled back and forth between it and his face.

"Is she really pretty? I ain't never seen her."

"Pretty enough."

"Are ... are you gonna like doin' it to her?"

"I suppose. Some."

She pressed her lips together and moved them nervously from side to side.

He put his hand on top of hers. "But I can tell you right now, it won't be the same as with you. There's nobody like you."

A tentative smile brightened her face. She met his eyes. "There's nobody like you, either. You're my Curt. There ain't been nobody I even wanted to be with since you. Promise or no promise."

He smiled and pressed a kiss to her cheek. "I know."

"And we'll always be together, right?"

His eyes widened a little. "Of course we will, Del. Always."

When Del had finished her beer and gone back onstage for her next set, Curt left the cards alone and watched her sing for the few as though they were a full house. Whether the song inspired pain or pleasure, anguish or rapture, she made each and every one of them feel it. Damn, but she was good. He could think of more than one time he'd seen tears in tough men's eyes. She'd even brought him close once or twice, but he hadn't cried since his mother died.

He downed the last swallow of yet another beer. It was after midnight, and his bladder was nagging him too hard to ignore any longer. He got up from the table to go up to the water closet. The bar room shifted before his eyes like a mirage. Damn. Now he recalled why he hated drinking too much. During his first youthful forays into alcohol, he'd been a lot worse off than a little dizzy. He failed to find the attraction in doing that to himself again and hadn't been really drunk since. He didn't like feeling like he'd lost control; he hated the possibility of losing just a fraction of his edge.

Taking a deep breath, he headed for the stairs, but they looked like too much trouble. He thought of the alley. Everybody else did it there — why the hell shouldn't he? Moving on, he made his way down the hall and out the backdoor.

It was pitch black outside, and what starlight made it into the alley was of little aid. He stopped, holding the door open, listening. Somebody was laying a stream up the wall opposite the delivery dock. Whoever it was passed a long, noisy fart and grunted with self-satisfaction.

Curt stepped down to the dirt and walked the few yards to the other side. He unbuttoned his fly and pissed for what seemed like forever. The other fellow staggered back inside without a word. Curt did his pants back up and turned around.

He got a glimpse of a huge figure before pain exploded on the side of his head and sent sparks flying behind his eyes. A second clout made his knees give out, and he sank to the dirt. He felt the cool earth on his cheek and then nothing more.

He smelled urine. Foul, rotting garbage and urine. Instinctively, he wanted to move away from it, but he had to drag himself out of a deep, dark void before he could even open his eyes.

It was just as black on this side of consciousness. His head was ringing with pain. Forcing his muscles to obey him, he pushed himself up until he was sitting. The alley was empty, silent save for the dim rhythm of the music from inside the saloon. He shifted to be more comfortable, and his hand brushed something smooth and cool. He picked it up. It was his wallet. Empty, of course.

Damn. He'd had over a hundred fifty bucks in it. He hadn't been robbed since he was a kid in the streets, and it had been another kid from the streets who'd robbed him.

He found his hat and climbed unsteadily to his feet, wondering how long he'd been out. Staggering through the door, he started down the hall. The lights in the bar room seemed at the end of a long tunnel, but they were very bright, searing his eyeballs until he had to stop and look away.

Come on, Prescott, get hold of yourself. You can't walk in there like this. He propped himself against the wall and waited for his head to clear some. Maybe he should just head on upstairs and fall into bed. That would be the easiest thing to do. There was no action in the Carlton tonight anyway. Outside maybe, but not inside.

Collecting himself, he made a beeline for the back stairs, slipped around the banister, and took one step at a time. He hoped no one noticed him like this. Del would find him. He let himself into the suite and went straight for the bed. He dropped down on it, rolled onto his back, and was instantly asleep.

When he awoke in the morning there was a dull ache in his head, but otherwise he felt better. Del was curled up along his side. His boots were off, and his suit jacket, but he was in exactly the same position as he had been when he fell asleep. He stretched, and Del lifted her head from his chest.

"You're alive," she remarked.

He managed a groan in return, nothing more.

"I almost thought you were dead when I found you. I couldn't wake you up. You never sleep like that. Hell, if I dropped a pin out on the hall carpet you'd hear it and wake up just like that." She snapped her fingers.

He raised his head a little and squinted at her. A cold compress slipped to the pillow.

"What happened to you?" she asked, gently replacing the cloth over the ugly lumps on his skull.

He dropped his head back into the pillow and laid his forearm over his eyes. "I got hit over the head in the alley — twice. Whoever it was stole the money from my wallet."

"You didn't see them?"

"Just a glimpse. Not enough to tell."

"Jesus. Never woulda thought somebody'd try a thing like that with you."

"Me neither. But things are changing in this town." He withdrew his arm and stared pensively at the ceiling.

Del felt his mood shift. "We ain't gonna let it get us. It won't change us."

He hoped she was right, but he was beginning to feel like there wasn't a damn thing he could do about anything.

CHAPTER THIRTEEN

They lazed in bed a couple of hours then shared a bath and dressed. It was while he was pulling his boots on that Curt noticed his knife was gone.

On the way out for brunch at the new café, they checked the alley but the knife wasn't there.

"I'm sorry, lover," Del said as they gave up.

He shrugged. "It wasn't anything special. I can replace it." Offering her his arm, he said, "Let's go," and led her from the alley.

After eating, they left the restaurant, and Curt let Del walk back to the Carlton on her own while he walked in the opposite direction toward the Andrews'. This was it — today it had to happen.

Under the heat of the summer sun, he browsed in the window of the florist's, waiting for Sarah to go by. Old Man Drury waved at him through the window, beckoning him to come in. Curt hadn't planned on it, but he didn't want to hurt the old fellow's feelings.

"Beautiful afternoon," the florist said as Curt stepped through the door, which was propped open.

"Yep." If you liked it this hot, Curt thought. He couldn't wait for this odd hot spell to pass.

"Anything in particular that you're lookin' for, Master Prescott?"

"Actually ..." Even as he was about to say no, Curt's eyes swept the store for possibilities. Flowers might help, actually. Set the mood. Soften her up.

"Got a lovely selection of roses, I do." The old man moved over to the display to show them to him. "Every color and kind."

Not wanting to arouse curiosity by checking for Sarah, Curt resisted the urge. He walked over and looked at the flowers. "You sure do."

"A rose is always a lady's favorite."

"True."

Off to one side were potted tuberoses. Impulsively, he pointed at them. "I'll take a bunch of those."

The old man smiled and moved toward them. "The pot or just a few blossoms?"

"Just the blossoms. Until I know whether she likes them or not."

"Very good." The florist took the cuttings and wrapped the tall spikes of fragrant white flowers in paper. "Remember to keep them in water all the time — and make a fresh cut when you get them home. If she likes them, you can come back and get some to plant in the garden next spring."

Curt nodded, taking the bundle and paying him.

"Thank you, Master Prescott. Always a pleasure."

Curt thanked him in return and said good-bye. As he left the store, he scanned the street for Sarah. At first, he thought he'd missed her, but then there she was, bustling up the hill toward the church. A flock of children was coming down the hill, running, yelling, and rejoicing in their summer freedom.

Curt started down the road and quickly made for the creek to approach the house from the back. If there was ever a time he couldn't risk being seen, it was now. As he swung his leg over the fence, he noticed the lilac bushes. All the flowers were withered a rusty brown. Too bad, he thought. He liked lilacs.

The lavender was blooming as he walked by the rock garden on the way to the door. Its unique scent filled the air he was passing through. A slight smile tugged at the corners of his mouth. There was always something blooming in these parts.

Mary opened the door for him before he could knock.

"I knew you'd come," she said, hovering close to him like a hummingbird around a flower heavy with nectar. She was wearing a burgundy skirt and a pink blouse and had her hair long like the first time he'd seen her.

Even as Curt stepped into the middle of the kitchen, he sensed something was off. "What's wrong?" he asked her.

Her eyes flitted away.

"Mary, did something happen?"

She leaned close, her body brushing his for an instant before she took a step back. She wrung her hands. "Oh, it's just my mother. I was hoping to spend Friday with you again. But Mother has already decided that I should come to her silly knitting circle." Her eyes flashed. "I don't want to spend all afternoon listening to those — women — gossip. They've nothing good to say about anybody. I want to be with you."

"What does your father say?"

"He doesn't know yet."

"He helped you get out of the Committee, didn't he?"

"Yes."

"Maybe he'll do the same with this."

She met his eyes, and the fervor slowly evaporated from hers. She nodded. "Yes, he might."

"So cheer up. Everything'll work out fine. Smile for me."

She did, and it was then that she appeared to notice the bruised lump on his temple. "What happened?"

He dodged her touch. "I got robbed last night."

"Oh, my goodness! Are you all right?"

"Yes. Just a little embarrassed."

"Embarrassed?"

"I should have been paying more attention. But hey — these are for you." He held out the little bouquet.

She took it and held the blossoms beneath her nose. "Mmm, what are these? They smell so good."

"Tuberoses."

"I've never seen them before. They're lovely, Curt. Thank you." She squeezed his hand. "Do they mean anything?"

He allowed a coy smile to curve his mouth.

"What?" she asked, eyeing his expression curiously. "What is it? Tell me."

He dropped the smile and stared into her eyes. "They mean we'll share dangerous pleasures."

Her mouth opened in shock, and then a rush of rose filled her cheeks. Clasping her hands in front of her, she swayed her torso back and forth, blinking demurely. "I thought we already had ..."

He took her shoulders in his hands. "But there is so much more ..." He dipped his head to kiss her. She allowed him briefly then twisted out of his grip.

"I'd better put these in water. Then we can go down to the creek."

He smiled as he watched her stretch, reaching for a slim vase from a cupboard above the counter. She had a nice figure. Nicer than he'd sometimes given her credit for. She dipped the vase into the basin of clean water and then unwrapped the flowers and stuck them in it. Coming back to him, she practically pulled him out the door.

"Hurry up. I want to get away from here. I want it to be just me and you and the meadow."

Raising both eyebrows, Curt lengthened his stride. At the fence, she turned into his arms without hesitation, and he lifted her over with ease. At the bottom of the ravine, the shade and the cool air welcomed them, enveloping them in solitude and silence.

"I wish we could stay down here forever," Mary said as they paused to make certain they were alone. "I don't ever want to go home again."

He knew she'd change her mind once he'd had his way with her. Then, she wouldn't want to be with him at all. Then she would despise him for seducing her. She'd forget all about marrying him and that little house and the two or three kids. She'd never want to see him again. His gut knotted and pushed his heart into his throat. He set his jaw and forced it back down.

When they reached the meadow, they sat in the tall grass beneath a spreading bigleaf maple. A dragonfly hovered near them briefly, staring at them with its huge compound eyes before darting away. Mary leaned her shoulder against Curt's.

"I cannot wait until we're married. Then I can get out from under Mother's thumb." She turned her face upwards and gazed at the canopy of broad green leaves and the specks of light that broke through.

"Did you two have a fight over something?"

"Yes. I suggested at lunch that instead of casting the unfortunates out of our community, perhaps the committee could raise funds to build a shelter of some sort to help people find their way again."

"And she objected."

Mary nodded. "She refused to even present the idea to the others."

"Maybe you should be on the committee, after all. Maybe you could make them listen."

Her face betrayed both her desire to do just that and her fear of her mother's reaction to such a move. She tugged at the grass without tearing it then ran her hand through it.

"Dad never said anything about how long we had to be engaged," she said, changing the subject. "Maybe he'd let it be short."

"You know your father better than I do," he said with a shrug.

Something in the tone of his voice must have alerted her, for she looked him in the face. "Are you upset about something?"

"No," he said quickly. "I'm just impatient, like you are."

She hugged him, and her hair tickled his nose. It smelled clean, fresh, and so delicately feminine that he had to breathe it deeply into him. His heart swelled up inside his chest as though he had brought her inside of him, and he was loath to exhale, lest he lose her.

He felt her fingers toying with his string tie. She pulled it loose, giggling like a child with a new game.

"Aren't you hot in all these dark clothes?" she asked.

"Uh-huh." Hotter than she knew. Just having her this near was arousing him. He tried not to think of her that way, but she began unbuttoning his vest.

"We ought to loosen you up," she proposed and undid the top three buttons of his shirt.

Jesus, what was she doing? This was not the Mary he'd known two months ago.

"You can take off your jacket — I won't mind. This is an informal get-together, you know." She smiled, a teasing glint in her eyes.

He debated within himself for a second. The heat and his reason for being here won him out of it. He tossed his vest aside, too. He saw her watching him, her eyes coming to settle on the crispy dark hairs at his open collar. She wanted to see him. He decided to oblige her and took off his shirt.

Her cheeks colored at the sight of the dark hairs sprinkling his naked chest. He watched her green eyes run over his sinewy arms. After a momentary struggle, her eyes inched lower, following the ventral strip of hair from his breastbone to where it widened and disappeared beneath his belt. His arousal was obvious. He saw desire spark in her eyes even as her face flushed with embarrassment. Reaching for her hand, he took it and spread her fingers, pressing her palm into the hairs just left of center on his chest.

"Feel my heart beating, Mary. You make it race like that. You do."

The rigidity in her fingers softened as she felt the leaping pulse beneath his taut skin. "Mine is beating like that, too."

He met her eyes. Before she could react, he covered her left breast with his hand and pressed it gently. Her hands came to push it away, but they faltered as the sensations he caused began to invade her. He watched as pleasure washed over her face.

A soft moan escaped her but she wouldn't look at him. He shifted his seat to be closer to her. Tipping his head, he took her lips with his and reached for her right breast with his hand. For the briefest instant she melted against him, but then suddenly she pulled away.

"No — you mustn't."

He searched for her eyes. She kept them down, away from him, and plucked at the grass with her hands.

"Don't you like it? Did I hurt you?"

"You ... didn't hurt me."

"You didn't like it."

She twisted her face away, staring at the creek that was only a trickle now in the middle of summer. Curt knew she'd liked it. She was just afraid to admit it. He stroked a strand of her honey-brown hair, entwining it in his fingers.

"Will you refuse me when we're married?"

She slowly turned her face back but still could not look at him.

"Will you?" He cupped her cheek in his palm, lifting her face so he could see her eyes. They were a dusky green in the shadow of the leaves above their heads. With a feathery touch, he caressed her ear with his fingertips then slowly traced a trail down her throat. She trembled.

"Will you refuse me, Mary?"

Her eyes flitted to his at last, and he saw fear in them, and confusion. Then she lifted her arms and set them around his neck. The fear and confusion vanished, and she sparkled once again.

"No. Of course not." She brought her face closer to his and kissed him right on the mouth.

It was a soft kiss, giving without being demanding, and the sensation shot into his very fiber, transfixing him. She withdrew and met his eyes then came to him again. He followed her lead with slow and loving kisses until he began to feel almost delirious. The feeling surprised him, for it was unlike any he'd ever felt before. Not that he'd never kissed a woman easy before, but it had never felt like this. It was a feeling he hoped would never end.

Groaning, he gathered her into his arms and pressed her back into the deep bed of summer grass. Her arms tightened around him, and she welcomed his tongue as he deepened the kiss. With minds of their own, his hands explored her, and his body surged with desire as hers stirred with awakening passion. He undid her blouse buttons at her throat, but there were only three. Without hesitation, he tugged at the blouse where it was trapped beneath the waistband of her skirt. Her chemise came out with it, and at last he felt her bare skin.

She gasped at his naked touch and looked down to see what he was doing, but he recaptured her mouth and drew her back into the whirlpool of sensation.

When she relaxed, he slowly slid his hand upward to fondle her breast. She started again, but gave in with a little animalistic cry of delight. Slowly, slowly, he lifted her blouse and chemise above her breasts to finally see them.

"Mary ... you are so beautiful."

Her fingers slid into his hair, and she looked as though she were about to cry. Lowering his head near the fabric, he began to kiss his way down between her breasts. His hands had done their work, and her nipples were erect and ready when he took one in his mouth.

Mary's body writhed with new ecstasy, and she cried his name and held him more tightly. As he teased and pleasured her, he felt her hands begin, tentatively, to travel and explore his shoulders, arms and back, to touch and stroke his taut, hot skin. He told her how good it felt, and she became bolder, sliding her hands down his lean flanks as far as she could reach.

His blood raced, and he molded himself tightly to the curve of her thigh, pressing her legs apart with his knee. He began to stroke her legs, inching her skirt up. Her summer drawers were in his way but there was only the one pair, and his hand found its way through the opening with ease. He slid it down inside to stroke her sensitive inner thigh. Beneath her velvety skin he felt her muscles tense, and she closed her legs, but he did not relent; gradually she softened, her muscles rippling now with delight.

Sliding upward, he traded her breasts for her mouth as he moved his hand to her private place. Her body jerked. He drove his mouth against hers, drew her tongue into a dance with his, and eased his hand into her folds. She was hot and very wet, and a few strokes were all it took to open her legs wider. He caressed her very slowly until she writhed against him, her body begging for his. God knew he was more than ready to oblige.

As he worked himself free of his pants he still could not get over what, for a woman of her class, was a shameless response. It thrilled him as much as it surprised him, fueling his desire for her like kerosene thrown on a campfire. His earlier notions of a diffident preacher's kid weren't entirely accurate. Though confident in his ability to sway her, he had thought it would be a battle much harder won.

"Curt. Curt, darling, I love you." Mary hooked her hands around his neck and drew his face toward her. He could not resist and gave her the kisses she wanted.

She loved him. With a jolt, the weight of it suddenly hit him. She was not like any of the other women he had ever bedded. She was no whore. She was no bored little rich girl, looking for sex as entertainment. She was not playing the game with him, feigning chastity yet leading him on to a conclusion they both wanted from the start. Mary's desire for him grew naturally out of her love for him.

Some of the drive drained from him, and his kisses became less demanding. He noticed her hair strewn through the green grass and a small twig sticking to her shoulder. He brushed it away.

If he took her, there would be no indignant ruffle of tousled feathers merely to keep up appearances. There would be heartbroken, soul-wrenching anguish. She had let him go this far only because he had deliberately confused her values, because she was upset with her present circumstances and looking for a way out. If he ruined her, it would kill her.

He stopped kissing her, took his hand from her moistness, and rested it on her hip. The breeze cooled his sweat-slicked flesh, but Mary's fingers warmed him with their gentle caressing.

If he took her, he'd never see her again. But if he didn't, his whole life was sure to fall apart. He needed her; she was his edge, his ace in the hole. If he didn't play it, he'd lose the game. He'd let down Del. The others could all go to hell, but Del was counting on him. He closed his eyes tight and tried to block it all out. He didn't want to think about those problems, that world, right now. He just wanted to be with Mary.

"Curt, my darling." She caressed his cheek and ran her fingers through his hair again. "My love. You make me feel so wonderful."

He focused on her face and saw the love streaming from her eyes. She was flushed from her arousal but glowing with love. Maybe, since she loved him, she could forgive him. He had to do it. If he didn't, all these past weeks would have been a waste of time and effort. He had to play out the hand.

Mary snuggled closer to him, uttering a purring sound. He found her private place again and lowered his head to her naked belly and breasts, kissing and nipping her until she writhed beneath his hands and cried out his name. He rolled on top of her, and her legs admitted him as her arms wrapped around him. Reaching down with one hand, he guided himself through her clothing as he watched her face — he wanted to see her expression when he entered her.

The moment his manhood touched her silken flesh she stiffened, and his second attempt to penetrate her made her eyes widen with terror. Some deep, inner woman-instinct had alerted her to her danger. Her arms let go of him, and she pushed against his chest.

"Curt — what are we doing? Stop — please stop!"

He arched his lower back once more before it was too late, but she began to fight him in earnest, struggling, pushing, and trying to close her legs.

"Oh, don't — please!" Tears filled her eyes, and she choked and began to cry, pushing at him one instant, covering her face with her hands the next.

Staring down at her, Curt clenched his teeth, angry that she had to suddenly come to her senses. Damn it, now it was either rape her or concede defeat. Cursing aloud, he heaved himself off her.

Mary buried her face in her hands, sobbing almost hysterically, her whole body wracked with shaking spasms. He tried not to look at her, but his eyes kept going back to her of their own accord. Finally, he could no longer bear watching her cry and shifted over to take her in his arms.

She screamed and kicked, bashing at him blindly with her fists until he gave up and moved away. Struck with guilt and a sense of helplessness, he turned away and got dressed.

Fully clothed but having left his collar open, Curt dropped to his rump in the grass a few feet from her. She was still crying. She'd drawn her knees up to her chest, wrapped her arms around them, and had her face buried in her skirt. She'd rolled herself into a tight little ball like she was trying to disappear.

Curt studied the deep azure sky then every leaf and stem of every nearby tree. Then his eyes fell on the creek, trickling merrily past them on its way to wherever it was going. He heard its cheery song — it had no care for what had transpired here.

He realized that Mary had stopped crying and turned his head to look at her. She was still all curled up. He contemplated his next move. There was only one he could make.

He got up to cross the few feet separating them then squatted down beside her. Laying his hand softly on her shoulder, he said, "Mary ..."

She turned rather suddenly into his arms and fell against his chest, knocking him onto his buttocks. He wrapped his arms about her and stroked her hair. He was about to apologize when she spoke.

"Oh, Curt — I'm so ashamed! I've never —. What you must think of me now?"

Stunned, he could summon no words. Mary lifted her head and looked for his eyes.

"Can you ever forgive me?"

He looked into her puffy red eyes and brushed away a strand of hair stuck to her tear-stained cheek. She looked like she'd been ravished, with her hair all a-muss and her clothes awry. She looked sullied, brought low as a whore. And he'd done that to her. An ache began to eat away at his heart.

"There's nothing to forgive. You've done nothing wrong." He pressed a kiss to her forehead.

"But I have," she insisted, her hands gripping his arms as though to let go meant certain destruction. "I allowed this to happen. I — dear goodness, I wanted it ..." She shook her head. "I'm no better than a —"

"Don't say it," he said. "You're not a whore. I did this to you, Mary; you didn't ask for it."

"Oh, Curt, you mustn't try to put this on yourself. I led you on. I wanted you to kiss me, to touch me. I need you so badly, I forgot everything. I'm no good for you now. I'll never make a good wife for you now."

He took her by her upper arms and shook her firmly enough to make her look him in the eye. "Yes, you will. We didn't go all the way, Mary. You stopped it in time. You're still a virgin."

Her eyes looked doubtful.

"You are. Trust me. I wouldn't ... lie to you about something like that." All the half-truths he had told her came rushing into his mind like a backwash full of debris. He shut his eyes tight and pushed them away. When they were gone, he opened his eyes again and found her staring at him in confusion.

"I want you too, Mary. You weren't in this alone. I'd have gone too far if you hadn't stopped me. It'd have been my fault. I should be asking you to forgive me."

Gratitude brought a tentative smile to her lips and a fresh tear to her eye. She lifted her hand and touched his cheek. "I love you so much. Please say you still love me. I need to hear you say it."

His heart was so close to bursting, he couldn't stop the words from leaping out. "I love you. I'll always love you."

All doubt vanished from her face, and she flung her arms around his neck. "Oh, thank you! Thank you!"

He held her tightly to him and buried his nose in her hair. It smelled like fresh grass. She felt so good against him in a way that wasn't even erotic. He wanted to hold her like that forever. Then suddenly panic rushed up, swamping him with a need to get away. Fighting to keep it at bay, he put Mary to arm's length.

"We'd better get you home. You need time to cleanup."

"I don't want to go. Let's just stay here like this forever."

"We can't. You have to get home."

Frowning, she nodded that he was right. Rising to their feet together, they righted her clothing and hair, made her as presentable as possible. Curt tucked her hand in his arm and led her home.

CHAPTER FOURTEEN

Curt climbed down the ravine alone after leaving Mary safely at her door. Once at the bottom, he halted, stuffing his hands in his pockets and studying the brown clay soil along the path. Not since he was a kid had he felt this scared and unsure of himself. What was it about Mary that had thrown him for a loop and made him abort his own plan?

He raised his eyes to the canopy of foliage blocking out the light of day. Long, dry, grey-green strands of old man's beard moss draped from the lower tree branches, reaching for him. He suddenly felt very old and very tired.

What the hell was he going to do now? He'd been holding a royal flush, and he'd gone and folded. What a goddamn jackass. What was he going to tell Del? That he'd discovered he actually loved Mary Andrews? That he had gambled on their future and threw in his hand? She wouldn't understand.

The whole thing was such a goddamned mess he didn't know which end was up any more. He couldn't face Del right now. His feet turned and started walking north as if of their own will. A pair of ravens played tag through the trees above him, cawing and croaking, perching as if to watch him and then flying ahead again. He walked right on through the meadow, trying not to see it, and into the seclusion of the woods on the other side. After another half mile, he scaled the bank and came up directly east of the cemetery. Stooping to pluck a few wildflowers, he waded through the tall grass and rounded the little enclosure. He unlatched the gate, and it swung open easily and soundlessly.

He squatted before his mother's grave and laid the flowers gently on the center of the mound. A sparrow flitted over his head and landed on the fence beyond the headstone. It twittered, and another joined it. Then the pair took flight again together.

"Why do I come here?" he asked the headstone quietly. "You can't tell me anything."

He sighed and pushed his hands against his knees to rise. Walking from the graveyard, he tugged the gate closed behind him and headed for the road.

As he wandered the streets of the city, he found himself near the livery. Just down the street, Phil the liveryman and Bud Andrews were standing outside the saddlery together. Curt was about to skirt around the back of the corrals but Bud saw him and waved at him. Phil turned his head and waved his hand as well. There was no avoiding them now. He walked straight to them, wondering if Bud knew yet.

Bud lifted his hand to the hostler's shoulder. "Curt, you know Phil, my neighbor from the livery?"

Curt nodded. Phil smiled brightly, extending a hand to shake with Curt. Curt gripped the man's hand almost absently.

"We shor do know ourselves," Phil said. "Mr. Prescott keeps his horse with me. And he's the one staked me to this place nigh two years back. Don't want to think where I might be if not fer him."

Curt saw the startled look on Bud's face. He looked away. "Wish you wouldn't go spreading that around, Phil."

Phil clapped him on the shoulder. "Naw, go on with ya! I ain't ashamed to admit I needed help. And I got it, too, thanks to you. I'll always be beholden to you."

Curt met his genuinely grateful eyes. "You paid me back a long time ago. No need to be beholden."

Phil turned his eyes to Bud's. "And no int'rest, neither. Takes a gambler not to charge a feller int'rest."

Curt shot a look at Bud to see if he'd picked up on the implication. The preacher tipped his head curiously, but Curt saw no conclusion drawn in his eyes. Something inside Curt tugged at him to tip his own hand, and he couldn't resist it. "You were a safe bet, Phil."

Shaking his head, Phil went on, "By golly, I ain't the only one, neither. He's helped lotsa folks when they needed it. I guess you make it easy, it ain't so hard to give away."

Curt cast his eyes up the road again, itching to get a move on.

Bud watched him closely. "I always suspected my future son-in-law was a generous man."

The black man's eyes popped. "Son-in-law, you say?" He smiled at them both with lights dancing in his brown eyes. "Well, by golly, I didn't know he was a-courtin' your little girl!"

"You're the first to know." He squeezed Phil's arm. "Keep it to yourself for now, would you, Phil? Nothing's been announced yet."

Curt met the preacher's eyes again. Bud couldn't know yet. Surely, he wouldn't admit his daughter was betrothed to a gambler if he knew.

"I will, parson," Phil said then grabbed Curt's hand and pumped it up and down. "Congratulations — I hope I'll be gettin' an invite to the weddin'!"

"You and all your family," Bud assured him.

Phil let go of Curt's hand and suddenly sobered. He looked at Bud. "You know, parson, I just gotta say I think it's a right nice thing you're doin', lettin' this weddin' happen."

Curt flinched. He had thought for a minute there that he might yet escape this one. Oh, well, what did it matter — if Bud didn't learn it now, he'd learn it in a couple of hours anyway.

"What with your wife headin' up that committee 'n' all — which, pardon me, I can't wholly swallow. There's good gamblers, and there's bad gamblers — they's folks just like the rest of us. I'm just right pleased to see you a-seein' that."

Bud's mouth opened, but nothing came out. He looked from Phil to Curt.

Curt had a hard time looking back.

At that moment, Phil's eldest son approached. "Papa, can you come have a look at this horse?"

Phil gripped his shoulder. "Sure, boy." He shook with both Bud and Curt and said good-bye before walking away with his son.

His absence thickened the tension in the air between Curt and Bud. For a moment, neither of them spoke. Then Bud said:

"I think you and I should have a talk."

Curt cast a glance down the road for freedom but turned and followed Bud inside the saddlery. Bud walked down to the counter and laid his hands on top of it. Curt breathed the smell of leather while Bud gathered his thoughts.

"You're a professional gambler."

For the first time in his life, Curt felt guilty about it. He watched Bud's profile as he answered, "Yes."

The creases deepened around Bud's eyes and mouth, and his fingertips turned white on the countertop. "And you deliberately kept it from us."

Curt hesitated only slightly before answering. "Yes."

"Why?"

Drawing a deep breath, Curt searched for words that would make it sound less depraved. "I ... didn't think I'd stand a chance if you knew."

"Stand a chance for what?"

Curt pinned his eyes on the shelves behind the counter. "To ... get to know Mary."

"You didn't know Mary existed before the first time I invited you for supper." He turned his face to Curt's then. "Did you?"

Curt shook his head. "No."

Bud's mouth pressed into a grim line, and his normally serene grey eyes took on a granite-like cast. "Why, then?"

Curt half-turned from him, unable to look him in the eye. His mouth was ready to spit it all out, but his gut knotted at the prospect. Gritting his teeth, he studied the neat rows of saddles and bridles and other equipment. The sudden realization that he was behaving like a coward shook his jaw loose.

"The committee. I wanted to see what I could do about the committee."

A long minute passed before Bud said anything. "So you have no interest in Mary beyond using her as a way to gain information."

Curt shook his head slightly, summoning the courage to face Bud again.

The saddler's eyes regarded him as a stranger. "It's a very cruel thing you have done."

Curt nodded. He saw the hurt in Bud's eyes, the betrayal, and it cut him more deeply than he would ever have thought possible. "I-It was wrong ... I'm sorry."

Bud's eyes penetrated his. "Are you?"

The gambler's jaw clamped shut on him. He forced it open. "Yes."

Bud turned his shoulder to Curt again, and Curt saw his jaw working as he ruminated over everything. "How can I believe you?" the preacher asked him at last. "How do I know which things you've told us are the truth and which are lies? How can I ever truly trust you?"

Curt stiffened all over. He had no answer for him. He looked around the shop again, as if somewhere on the walls, there might be written an answer. "It's over," he began hoarsely. "I gave it up this afternoon. I couldn't go through with it."

Bud met his eyes briefly then straightened up a few articles on his counter that didn't need straightening up. His silence pained Curt.

"I know I must look like a real heel to you now," he said. "And I guess I am. But your wife and her committee threaten everything I know — the only life I've ever known. Can you understand why I'd want to stop her?"

After a brief moment, Bud nodded. "You were just trying to protect yourself."

"Yes."

"But the way of life you're trying to save is wrong," Bud told him, looking him straight in the eye. "Ultimately, it hurts you and everyone around you."

Shaking his head, Curt answered, "I don't see how. I've never deliberately tried to hurt anyone."

"But you take money from men who sweated to earn it. You trick them into losing it — it's like stealing."

Curt shifted his feet, redistributing his weight on the plank floor. "I don't force them to gamble. They come to me of their own free will."

"Like weak souls to the devil's embrace." Bud stepped out from behind the counter and faced him squarely, his hands on his hips. "You're a crook— you cheat men out of their money with tricks."

"I do not cheat," Curt said distinctly. "I don't use cold decks or mirrors or any of the fancy gadgets a fella can buy. I rely on my own skill and my gut instinct. I trained for years to learn the moves — everything I do is right out in the open where a sharp man could see it." A small grin cocked the left side of his mouth. "There just aren't too many men who are that sharp."

"And that excuses you?"

Curt held Bud's gaze and shrugged. "It's how I make my living. If it makes you feel any better, I do lose once in a while."

"Only to your peers, I imagine."

Again, Curt shrugged. "We all have our betters."

"Meanwhile the unskilled get swindled."

Sighing heavily, Curt walked through the saddles and leaned on the white sill of one of the little windows on the south wall. "I won't make any excuses for what I do. I like my work — it's never let me down. As long as I stay sharp, I'll stay flush, and I'll stay alive. I don't have to sell myself body and soul to some jackass boss to use me up in some lame job while he gets rich. I won't do it."

Bud followed him and stood a couple of feet away. "And you had no fear of that — until my wife's committee threatened you, you mean."

Curt shot him a vulnerable look. "Yeah." Then he turned his eyes to look out the window again. A tiny wisp of a breeze teased his face with a hint of coolness.

They stood in silence for several minutes, and then Bud leaned his right shoulder against the wall and faced Curt.

"I've a confession to make myself," he said softly. "I've always known who you are. Right from the first day. Even when you pulled your gun on me in the cemetery."

Curt was sure his face betrayed his astonishment then dawning acceptance of the probability. Of course. In this town, how could they not have heard of Curt Prescott. A self-mocking grin cocked one corner of his mouth. It was he who had been the fool.

"So you had an angle, too, eh, parson?"

Bud nodded. "I was hoping to guide you to Christ. Not that I believe you're particularly evil ... I just think you're ..."

"Misguided?" Curt finished for him, one eyebrow rising into his forelock.

"Yes."

"I guess I can see how you'd see it that way."

A cariole pulled by a black horse rattled past. Curt watched it out of sight. He wanted to say something to Bud directly, to make it very clear. But it had never been easy for him to bare his soul to anyone. He didn't like to feel vulnerable. As a boy, he'd learned quickly that it was the people who knew what was inside of him that could hurt him the most. So he'd stopped showing himself to people. But there was something new inside him now, something that wanted to come out of the dark, hidden place and into the bright light of day. It wanted to be known. And he feared that, if he didn't show it to Bud, then Bud would never believe in him again.

Staring out the window, he began tentatively. "I know I started out wrong ..." His voice was little more than a hoarse whisper. "But ... somewhere along the line everything changed. I want you to know that I could never hurt Mary." Shaking his head, he turned to look Bud in the eyes. "That's the last thing I'd ever want to do."

A point of light flickered in one of Bud's eyes, and he straightened off the wall. He studied Curt's face for a long moment then said, "I believe you." He took one of Curt's hands in both of his. "May God forgive me if I'm wrong, but I believe you."

A grateful smile came to Curt's face, and even though he was uncomfortable with the preacher holding his hand, he endured it. "What are you going to do? Are you going to tell Mary?"

"She already knows," Bud replied.

Curt was so shocked he stepped back involuntarily, breaking the hold Bud had on his hand. Mary knew? But she'd —.

Bud cut off his thoughts. "I think, though, that you should go to her and confess." He placed a hand on Curt's arm.

Curt did not move away. "If she already knows, what difference would it make?"

"It would assure her that her faith in you is not misplaced."

"Faith?" Curt drew himself up and faced Bud squarely. "What kind of faith could Mary have in me?"

"She sees the man you've buried inside you. She sees the one who has compassion for others. She sees the man that loves her."

"I'm not sure that I do," Curt said, suddenly feeling defensive.

"Aren't you?"

Curt tried to hold the preacher's eyes, but he couldn't. He looked out the window. He felt Bud's hand grip his shoulder.

"Stop hiding from love, Curt. It's not as scary as it seems."

The hell it's not, Curt thought. He considered a moment then asked, "What if I do love her — and I'm not saying I do for sure, 'cause I don't know myself — would you let her make her own decision? What if she does want to marry me? Would you let her be seen around town with a gambler?"

"I think there's another question that should be answered first," Bud told him. "Do you have any real intention of marrying her?"

That knocked Curt a little off balance again. He had to answer honestly. "I don't know." He stroked the smooth white paint on the sill with his fingertips then rubbed the trace bit of dust off on his pant leg, frowning at himself even as he did it, for the powder blemished the suit. "If you'd asked me that even yesterday, I'd have said no. But now ... now I really don't know."

A small smile warmed Bud's features. He gripped Curt's arm. "That's all I can ask of you: an honest answer. Thank you for giving me one."

The bell jingled over the front door, and a cowboy strolled in. Bud called hello but paused a moment longer with Curt.

"Come for dinner tonight, and we'll all get reacquainted and sort this out."

Curt grimaced. "Your wife's going to be a walking hornet's nest. I don't know how you've kept her quiet this long."

"Don't worry about Sarah. I can handle my wife. Just come."

"All right."

Bud squeezed his arm once more then went to attend his customer. Curt watched him for a second then let himself out of the shop.

The late afternoon sun was sinking toward the hills in the west, and he could feel the air beginning to cool as he walked toward home. He felt as though he'd been braised over hot coals, yet at the same time, he felt an enormous sense of relief. Things were bad, yes, but maybe not all that bad.

He walked into the Carlton and ordered a beer. Hooking a boot heel over the brass rail, he sipped it slowly, savoring the taste. Motion caught his eye, and he looked up to see Del hurrying from the hallway to meet him. He smiled.

"Lover!" She threw her arms around him. "It's over now, isn't it? You took care of everythin'!"

With only a slight hesitation, he said, "Yeah. It's all over."

She hugged him tightly again and pressed her cherry-red lips to his cheek. Then she stood back, her fingers linked at the back of his neck. "So tell me — did she fight to the bitter end, or did she take to it like a bitch in heat?"

A pang of disgust stabbed at his gut.

"Did you break it to her folks yet?" Her eyes glittered like molten gold. "I'd give my left tit to see the looks on their faces." She tugged on his lapels. "Come on, spill it! I'm dyin' to know what happened!"

He hooded his eyes and wiped all expression from his face. "Let's just say they know who they're dealing with now."

She shrieked with delight and with a little jump hugged him again. "Oh, darlin', now everythin'll be just like it used to be!

You don't gotta spend any more time with them whitewashed goody-goodies. You're all mine again."

He was about to tell her that he needed to go over there again tonight when three men came through the batwings. Their shoes echoed loudly in the near-empty saloon. Curt and Del watched the constables approach them. All were in full uniform and wearing their sidearms. The third one looked young and carried a shotgun.

They stopped before Curt, and their leader drew himself up to his full height. "Curt Prescott, I hereby place you under arrest for the murder of Police Constable David R. Jenkins."

Curt blinked at him in surprise. "What?"

Curt's jaw fell slack. Del gripped his arm tightly. Jenkins was dead? Murdered?

"I haven't killed anybody," he said.

"We shall see," the officer replied. "I hope you will come with us peaceably."

The young man with the shotgun raised the muzzle a little. Curt eyed him. He saw fear in the boy's eyes. The kind of fear that made for a finger too quick on the trigger. Curt wasn't about to get his guts blown all over the bar by some new recruit having a hard time keeping from pissing his pants.

"All right." He raised his hands away from his body and let the officer pat around for his derringer.

As they cuffed Curt, Del eyed the three men with daggers of contempt in her eyes. "You're makin' a big mistake," she spat at them. "Curt Prescott never murdered nobody."

"As I said, madam, we shall see."

They signaled Curt to move, one senior man leading and the other two following behind Curt. The nervous one brought up the long shotgun like a barrier when Del made to come along. Curt told her to stay. He'd get this straightened out in no time.

The constables marched Curt down the streets, through the doors of the police barracks directly into the first cell and immediately locked the door behind him.

"So how was he killed?" Curt asked.

The officer eyed him suspiciously then went over to Jenkins' desk and picked something up. He brought it back to the cell and waved it in front of Curt.

"He was stabbed in the back with your knife. This is your knife, I'm told. It has your initials on it."

With a grim shake of his head, Curt said, "Yeah, that's my knife. It was stolen Tuesday night along with some money."

The constable exchanged glances with his comrades. "Naturally, you'd have a story like that. Do you think we're fools?"

"What kind of a fool would murder somebody and then leave his knife sticking in him — especially a knife with his own initials on it?"

The man considered that. "Someone suffering from supreme overconfidence, I would imagine. It was, rather amazingly, broad daylight. Even alleyways are not that dark in mid-afternoon. Perhaps you were surprised. By a witness. You had no time to retrieve your weapon."

"If I was close enough to stick him with it, I was close enough to yank it out."

The officer returned the knife to the desk and then paced before Curt. The other two merely stood together a few feet away, letting the officer run the show.

"Mr. Prescott. We have a saloon full of witnesses who saw you arrested by Constable Jenkins. We have three men in particular who heard you threaten his life —." He waved his hands about. "— in this very place. What do you say to that?"

"It's true," Curt admitted, sticking an elbow between two bars and leaning on it. "But I was angry. I would never have done it. I didn't do it."

The constable stopped pacing and faced him squarely, folding his arms across his chest. "We also have one man who says he saw you do it."

This was starting to stink more and more like a set-up every minute. "Whoever he is, he's a liar."

"That's possible. We don't know that much about his character. He's only been in town a few months, but he's caused no major disturbances."

"Mind telling me who?"

The man deliberated a moment, looking at the other two as if for input. The one with the shotgun shrugged while the other nodded.

"A lumberjack by the name of Wesley Keegan."

Curt threw back his head and stared at the rafters. It figured. "You question Keegan, and I'll lay you odds you'll find Fat Johnnie involved somehow or other."

The officer's eyebrows rose into his hat. "We're aware they are associated. Mr ... 'Johnnie' is without doubt an unsavory sort. I take it you don't care for each other."

"You take it right."

The man's hands swung down, and he clasped them behind his back. Then he began to pace again. "Very well, Mr. Prescott. In all fairness I shall ask you this: Where were you this afternoon?"

For the first time during the conversation, Curt hesitated.

"Mr. Prescott?" His inquisitor stood still again, his eyebrows reaching higher than before as he waited for Curt's answer.

"About what time?"

"The good Dr. Helmcken estimates the murder occurred sometime between one and three p.m."

He would have been with Mary. Then alone before talking with Bud and Phil. "Around four, I was at the saddlery."

"And before that?"

"I ... was taking a walk."

"Was Miss Delores with you?"

"No."

"Was anyone with you?"

"No."

The officer sighed and shook his head. "This does not bode well for you, Mr. Prescott."

No kidding, Curt thought.

"Pastor Andrews will of course verify your visit."

Curt nodded.

"Very well. I shall go and speak with him." He turned to his two constables. "Gentlemen, please remain here, and see that Mr. Prescott does as well."

Curt watched the man go out the door then turned his back on his two guards. He had no doubt that Bud would support that he was there. But what about beforehand? The preacher didn't know about his walk with Mary. And Curt couldn't tell him, or them, about it. Victoria wasn't exactly a one-horse town, but it wasn't big enough to dissolve a rumor like this one, either. If word got out about him and Mary, it would ruin her life, and her family's life in this town, forever. There was no way he was going to let that happen.

CHAPTER FIFTEEN

Mary and her mother were setting the table when they heard Bud invite a visitor into their home. Mary followed her mother into the parlor but hung back out of the way. She sat next to her mother after her father invited the police officer to sit down. Oddly, it annoyed her that the policeman sat in the chair Curt always took.

"Again, I must apologize for intruding upon your meal," the officer said to Bud. "But it is a very serious matter."

"Don't think anything of it," Bud assured him. "What can I do for you?"

The man linked his fingers in front of him and cleared his throat. "You are acquainted with a young man named Curt Prescott?"

"Yes," Bud answered levelly.

Mary's attention snapped to the man's face. Her mother shifted uncomfortably, smoothed her skirt over her knees, and plucked at a piece of lint on the cushion next to her.

The officer continued. "You probably are not aware that Constable Jenkins was murdered this afternoon."

Sarah gasped, her hands flying to her great bosom. Mary and Bud stared at the policeman with disbelief.

"Mr. Prescott is the prime suspect in that murder."

Bud's eyes fell to the rug.

Mary watched as her mother's hands began to wring and her face to draw tight. Mary shook her head slowly but emphatically. "You must be mistaken, sir. Curt could never kill anyone."

The officer turned sympathetic eyes on her. "I'm afraid that is not true, my dear. Two years ago, he killed a visiting U.S. Marshal on official business in Victoria. But of course, you and your family were not living here then."

Mary sank back into the corner of the couch. Curt had killed a man? A marshal? And now he might have done it again?

"Granted," the man said, "There were — extenuating circumstances. Prescott shot Marshal Stone in self-defense. I merely state it to illustrate that he is capable of killing."

Mary looked for her father's eyes. They were downcast, and he appeared deep in thought. Then he raised his head to look at their guest.

"What is it we can do for you, Officer?"

"Mr. Prescott claims he was with you from approximately four p.m. until four-thirty."

"He was."

"And we can place him at the Neighborly Cafe before the time of the murder. But from approximately one p.m. until four, he cannot prove his whereabouts. The officer was stabbed with Mr. Prescott's boot knife between one and three p.m."

No longer able to contain herself, Sarah leapt to her feet. But she had barely begun to shriek when Bud waved her with two emphatic fingers back to her seat. Her face was red with indignant rage, but she mustered control and sat down.

Even as Mary watched her mother prepare her theatrics, her thoughts were on Curt. He had a knife as well as his two guns? He was a man prepared for danger and prepared to use deadly force against it. For the first time, she began to wonder seriously about who this man was that she had fallen in love with.

"Unless we can find someone to substantiate his whereabouts before he came to you, I'm afraid Mr. Prescott will be formally charged with murder." Shaking his head, the officer added, "A police officer murdered, practically on the heels of Governor

James Douglas' passing yesterday. A heart attack, apparently. You may not know, being new here, but that old man fathered this province. He will be sorely missed. I fear great change is upon us all."

Curt charged with murder? Mary's hand flew to her mouth, and she bit on her bottom lip. Curt was innocent — and she knew where he'd been all afternoon.

The policeman rose from the chair and stepped toward the door, with Bud and Sarah seeing him out. Mary leapt to her feet and started toward the door. She opened her mouth to call the man back, but her mother turned around sharply and frowned at her with such ire that Mary was abruptly petrified. She watched dumbly as the constable put on his hat and went out the door.

Slowly, they returned to the table and finished setting it, but when they sat down Mary had no appetite. She watched as her father pushed the food around his plate with his fork. Sarah cut her meat up into tiny pieces and raised one daintily to her mouth. But abruptly she dropped her fork back to the plate with such a clank both Bud and Mary winced, certain the plate had been cracked.

"Will you heed me now, Bud Andrews?" she demanded. "I've told you that young man is dangerous. Get him out of our lives."

"We don't know that he took the officer's life."

"Of course he did it."

"We don't know that, Sarah."

Sarah flung up her hands. "I don't believe this! You're defending him! You're sitting right there at our table defending him!"

Mary said, "But, he's right, Mother —."

Sarah's eyes flashed at her. "You keep quiet! This is between your father and me!"

Bud shook his head and put down his fork.

Sarah shivered deliberately. "To think that murderer was right here in our home." Again, she shivered.

"Curt would never deliberately hurt anyone," Mary told them, ready for her mother's anger again. But this time Sarah ignored her.

Bud pressed his palms against the table and rose to his feet. "Sarah, it's a wonderful dinner. But I'm afraid I'm not very hungry anymore." He walked slowly into the parlor and sat down in his chair.

"Mary, get your father his tea."

"Yes, Mother." Mary went into the kitchen, poured her father's tea, and stirred just a sprinkle of lemon into it. As she passed the dining room table on her way to the parlor, her mother brushed by her with their untouched plates, nearly causing her to spill the tea.

Bud took the cup from Mary with a grateful smile. "Thank you, dear."

Mary turned away to help her mother clear the table, but Bud caught her arm with his free hand. "Mary, sit down."

He pointed to the spare chair, the one she thought of as Curt's. Mary settled into it and waited for him to speak.

"Mary, I've discovered Curt's motive for befriending us."

The odd tone in his voice made her uneasy. He set his teacup on the tall parlor table next to his chair. Leaning toward her, his elbows on his knees, he seemed to be searching for the right words.

"There's no easy way to say it," he began in a hushed voice. "But he admitted it to me himself this afternoon. His intent was to find some way to destroy your mother's committee."

"But he seemed so interested!"

Bud held up one hand. "Shush, my dear. I don't want to let your mother in on this just yet."

Mary clamped her lip between her teeth. Then she started again, this time more quietly. "I thought he really liked us ..."

"So did I, as cautious as I was. I suppose I should have had more of your mother's suspicion."

Mary's limbs froze. All she could move were her eyes. She stared at her father, then along the wall with the pastoral paintings, and then down into the cold black heart of the empty fireplace. Her hands loosened briefly, only to grasp the clawed arms of the chair and squeeze them until her knuckles turned white. Inside, she felt like a tree deeply notched and ready to fall.

"Are you also trying to tell me ... that he doesn't love me?" She caught her breath and held it.

Bud drew a deep breath and let it out slowly as he answered. "No. I believe he does. He hadn't planned on it in the beginning, but he does love you now."

Mary let out her breath, and her hands loosened a little. "What should I do? How am I going to know what to do?"

Sarah came back into the dining area for more dishes and eyed the two of them curiously.

"She'll be with you in a minute, dear," Bud said then waited until she'd returned to the kitchen. "That's up to you. I can't tell you how much you love him. I can't tell you if you're willing to forgive him for deceiving you and your mother and me."

Mary searched his eyes. "Do you forgive him?"

Bud pressed his lips together. "I'm still working on it. I know, as a pastor, I should be able to forgive as Christ would, but as a man, it's a much harder job sometimes. I want to forgive him. I believe he's a good man underneath. I also believe some of the things he's done are wrong, but I'm not to judge him. I can only try to guide him. But I can't lead him anywhere he's not willing to go."

Mary contemplated his words. Then, hesitantly, she asked, "Is it wrong for me to love him? Is he evil? Would I sin against God if I wanted to love him?"

Bud reached out and covered her hand with his. Mary felt the roughness of his skin as he patted her hand. "Love is never a sin, my dear. Besides, we each have sin inside of us, Mary. It just takes different forms in different people."

Mary looked at her father closely, finding it difficult to believe he had ever sinned.

"Love him according to God's law, and you will not stumble."

A warm sweetness welled up inside of Mary as her father's words rang true in her heart. Then, suddenly, fear seized her. She grasped her father's hand with both of hers.

"Dad — I have to go to him! Now!"

Bud's eyes questioned her. "Why? What can you do?"

Mary drew a shaky breath and straightened her spine against the back of the chair. She lowered her voice. "I can tell the police where he was this afternoon."

Bud stiffened.

Mary went on, afraid to waver and lose her courage. "We went walking together, along the path by the creek." She saw the astonishment on Bud's face and the disillusionment that followed it. She squeezed his hand tighter. "It's all right — nothing bad happened." But she could not tell him only half the truth. "We came close, Dad. I admit it. But we stopped. Please believe me."

He looked into her eyes a long time, still struggling to absorb the unexpected information. At last, he said, "I believe you. You've always been honest with me."

She sighed, smiling with relief. "May I go, Dad? Please, let me go."

"Yes. By all means. You must. I should go with you." He started to rise.

"I'll be fine — thank you!" She jumped up and hugged him. "I love you, Dad. I love you."

"I know. I love you, too. Now hurry."

She released him and rushed out the door.

The half hour walk to the police barracks seemed an eternity to Mary. She couldn't seem to move her feet quickly enough without breaking into a flat-out run. Being the supper hour, there were few people on the streets, but she dared not run and call attention to herself.

A few blocks north of the jail she began to notice the undesirable element, as her mother called the whores and ne'er-do-wells who sometimes strayed from their dens of iniquity onto the city streets. Her mother's training made her look away, ignore them. But she began to sneak closer looks as she realized that these people were the ones her father was trying to bring God's light to. Were these the people Curt came from, the world he lived in? They seemed as different from Curt as they did from herself.

Instead of blocking out the rollicking piano tunes rolling out of the saloons, she opened her ears to them. She heard the laughter. She winced at the profanity. She wondered if Curt ever used language like that.

He didn't seem like a gambler, or at least not like the kind she had heard stories about. He was not flashy like the ones described. He wore no brocaded vest, no enormous gold watch chain or equally huge diamond stickpin in his lapel. He was neither pale nor emaciated. It struck no fear into her heart to gaze into his enchanting eyes.

Had he charmed her so that she could not see the danger lurking behind those eyes? She'd seen them dance with laughter and stare with keen intensity. When he looked at her, she felt like she was the only thing alive near him, like he had focused his entire attention on her. What if he should wish to harm her? She imagined being trapped in the grip of those eyes, unable to fight or flee, completely at his mercy.

Her breath caught in her throat as she made a link between the story-book description of western gamblers and Curt Prescott. The way he moved. The way he felt. Not the way he felt when she touched him, but the way he felt just being near her, the air he had of always being completely at ease yet ready to strike like a coiled snake if threatened. Despite his cool exterior, in him she sensed power — intense, focused, controlled power. And she knew she was drawn to it.

And yet, lately, she'd sensed a restlessness in him. She'd thought he was simply as anxious for them to be married as she was. But perhaps it was something else. Perhaps he'd been in a hurry to get something over with. If he'd come to destroy the Moral Action Committee, he must have been anxious to get it done.

At Fort Street, she turned toward the harbor, almost walking in front of a freight wagon rumbling by. Jumping back, she pressed a hand to her thumping heart and willed herself to breathe. When it was truly safe, she stepped down to the street. It wasn't far now, and she tried desperately to sort out her feelings, which were becoming increasingly jumbled by the minute. As she stepped into the alcove entrance of the police barracks, a lady-of-the-evening brushed by her. The woman was tall, blonde, and dressed in royal purple from head to foot, except for her black ruffles and ruching. Her purple hat was accented with a black ostrich feather and black lace. She had a spangled black reticule looped around one wrist and a silver tussie-mussie with dried flowers spilling out of it bouncing on her bosom. Mary admired the little cornucopia as the woman turned in front of her and reached for the doorknob with a hand adorned in an elbow-length black silk glove.

The woman turned her head and eyed Mary with a strange sort of smile. "You comin' in here, too, honey?"

Swallowing, Mary nodded nervously. "Um — yes."

"Suppose you got some sorta complaint to make — like maybe you don't like the way I dress?" She turned out a long, shapely calf. Her thigh parted the slit at the top of her skirting, revealing even more of her leg. "Does that offend you, Miss Priss?"

Mary gathered her courage and looked her straight in the eye. "What you wear is your business. Now please let me by."

Del raised her eyebrows. "Oh, are we in a hurry?" She kept her hand on the doorknob and blocked the way with her body.

"I have business inside."

"Well, then we got somethin' in common, 'cause so do I. 'Course, you'll be wantin' some old policeman, while I'm comin' to see a real man. Ever heard of Curt Prescott?"

Mary flinched, and the woman's reaction made it clear that she had noticed. "So you have, eh? Well," she said, drawing herself up to her full height and thrusting out her chest. "I'm Del. I'm his woman."

Mary knew she had a horrified look on her face, but she couldn't compose herself. Her eyes dropped away from Del's.

"Whatsa matter, honey? Jealous?"

Mary looked up again as Del traced her own curves with her palms. She was indeed a beautiful woman, lithesome and graceful with curves in all the right places. Her side-swept hair, exactly the same flaxen shade all over, looked thick and luxurious. Her skin was nearly white and without blemish. Her face was flawlessly painted, accenting her perfection without overpowering it. She oozed sexuality. Mary could understand any man being drawn to her.

"Nice, eh?" Del remarked. "Sorry you don't measure up, honey. I guess some of us got it, and some of us don't."

Mary could only look at her. She could find no words to defend what she felt were her own inadequacies.

Del flippantly waved a hand at her. "Aw, don't worry about it. Someday some man'll want you. He won't be a real man like my Curt, but he'll have to do, won't he?"

Anger flared suddenly in Mary, and she balled her fists at her sides. "For your information — !" She cut herself short, realizing what she was about to say. Collecting herself, she said, "Please let me by now," and reached for the knob.

"Lovely evening, isn't it, ladies?"

Mary started and turned her head to see who had spoken. A uniformed officer had approached them from the street.

"Yes, it is," she replied, hoping she didn't look as flustered as she felt.

He eyed Del suspiciously. "Is everything all right?"

Mary cast a glance at Del. For a moment she could not speak, and the amusement on Del's face only served to weight her tongue. At last she stammered. "Yes, everything's fine. We just arrived at the door at the same time, that's all."

"As long as you're certain ..."

"There is no problem," Mary insisted, hoping the officer would give it up and go away.

"All right then. Have a pleasant evening, ladies." He turned to go then looked back. "Oh, and I just want to say that was a fine sermon your father gave last Sunday, Miss Andrews. I'm looking forward to next Sunday's worship."

"Thank you," Mary said. "I'll pass that on to him for you." The man tipped his hat and strolled away, leaving Mary breathing a sigh of relief. She turned back to the door, but Del still blocked it. When Mary looked up, she found golden eyes staring at her intently.

"You're Mary Andrews, ain't ya?"

When Mary didn't reply immediately, Del's eyes narrowed to gilded daggers.

"Ain't you?"

So suddenly and forcefully did Del take her by the arms and shove her that Mary had no chance to resist. She stumbled backwards off the steps into the dirt street. Del ran her right around the corner and up against the brick wall on the far side where the departed officer wouldn't see them if he happened to turn his head. Mary looked around for help, but no one could see them from this angle.

"So you're the little chit my Curt's been spendin' all his time wooin'! Hell, I'da thought you were prettier."

Mary winced as Del's nails, right through the gloves, dug into her upper arms. The rough brick scraped at her back. "Let me go."

As though she hadn't heard, Del asked, "So, what was it like gettin' fucked by a stud like Curt Prescott? Did you scream, it was so good? Or do you like to moan?"

Mary's cheeks flushed red-hot, and she looked away from Del's eyes.

"Or are you so cold he had to fuck you dry?"

Mary shut her eyes tight, hoping neither to see nor hear her.

"Naw," Del said. "He made you real wet, didn't he? I can tell. So tell me, bitch — how'd you like my man?"

Breathing erratically, Mary fought down her fear and embarrassment and looked Del squarely in the eyes. "Leave me alone. I have nothing to say to you."

Del's lip curled, and she shifted her grip on Mary's arms. "Is that why you're comin' down here? To get Curt hung for what he done to you?"

"Curt did nothing to harm me. And I am coming down to save him, not to see him hanged."

Del's skepticism was obvious on her face. "You're lyin'. When Curt says he's gonna do somethin' he does it. He fucked you, and you hate him for it."

Gritting her teeth against the foulest word she believed she'd ever heard, Mary shook her head. "He did not — do anything wrong to me. I asked him to stop, and he did."

"Horse shit! When Curt gets goin', there ain't no stoppin' him. He's all man, and when he wants it, he takes it."

"Maybe so. But he stopped for me. He respects my wishes."

Del thrust Mary into the wall and let go, taking a step back from her. She glared at her with such animosity that Mary found her stare more painful than bashing into the wall.

Del laughed dryly. "Well, maybe you just don't excite him enough. After all, you ain't really his type. I'm his type."

"Well, maybe his type is changing," Mary blurted out without thinking.

She saw Del's eyes widen but was unprepared for the slap that snapped her head around and made her fall back into the wall.

"You bitch! You lyin' bitch! He's mine, and you ain't never gonna take him away from me! You got that?"

Mary felt Del's finger jabbing her shoulder only distantly. Her cheek stung with pain, and her ears were ringing from the slap. She refocused on Del's face, determined not to cower.

Del stood before her, her hands on her hips now, her bosom heaving with anger. The realization hit Mary suddenly, and she had to speak it.

"You love him, don't you?"

Del's face betrayed that Mary's words had unsettled her. Her hands left her hips and moved through the air at her sides as if unsure of where to go now. "Of course I love him," she stammered. "You don't share the same man's bed for years if you don't love him."

"Not even if you're desperate?" Mary asked softly.

Del half-turned from her. "Maybe at the start. But he's a good man. He takes good care of me. He never hits me — and boy, I had a lotta that before I met him. And he never forces me. If I don't feel like it, he doesn't make me ..."

Del's and Mary's eyes met, and they shared an uneasy look into each other's hearts. Del broke the gaze first.

"He loves me. I know he does. So you just better forget him, 'cause he's mine." She crossed her arms below her breasts and stared out toward the street.

Mary's heart went out to her then. It was obvious, even given the woman's rough way of showing it, that her love for Curt was genuine. "What's your real name?"

"What's it to ya?"

"I'd just like to know, that's all."

Del faced her but did not uncross her arms. "Delores. I already know yours."

"That's a very pretty name," Mary said sincerely. "It sounds musical. It must be nice to have been born with such a pretty name. Sometimes I think mine's so plain, just like me."

Del looked her up and down. After a moment she said, "So, you really came to help him?"

"Yes."

"How?"

"I can tell the police where he was this afternoon. He was with me."

Del's crimson lips parted in shock. "You'd tell 'em that? Don't you care what everybody'd say about you?"

"Of course I care," Mary answered gravely. "But I can't let Curt suffer for something he didn't do. The truth shall set him free."

Del looked at her a long time. Then she glanced around herself, as if to make sure no one else was near.

"All right," she finally said, her normally full lips thin and tight. "I'll let you go in first. But only 'cause you can give him a for-real alibi."

Mary had barely taken half a step away from her when Del jabbed her twice below the collarbone with a fingernail. "But you mind me — you betray Curt and me, and I'll make you pay, I swear. Got it?"

Mary winced as Del's finger twisted and bored into her flesh. "You don't need to threaten me. I came here to help Curt, and that's what I'm going to do." She resisted the urge to rub the sore spot Del had left her with.

"You better."

Del pivoted without waiting for Mary and strode back to the street. Hesitant at first, Mary decided to follow her. Del stood impatiently outside the station's door, her arms crossed below her bosom. Stepping into the uncomfortable zone of Del's angry aura, Mary grasped the doorknob, gathered all her courage, and stepped inside.

She'd never been inside the police barracks and jail before — she'd never had a reason to. The jail guard pushed back his chair, the wooden legs scraping the hardwood floor with a screech that made her already jangled nerves wince. She watched him come around from behind the desk toward her. She looked for Curt and noticed the second guard in the corner with a shotgun. Beyond him she could just see Curt, standing close to the stone wall at the back of his cell. He was in his shirtsleeves, and his back was to her. He was staring out the window.

"Miss Andrews — what brings you here?"

She saw Curt turn around sharply. He met her eyes and came toward the bars. She tore her eyes away and faced the policeman.

"I've come to tell you that you can let Curt Prescott go. He couldn't have killed Constable Jenkins —."

"Mary," Curt warned her, curling his hands around the bars. "Don't."

She bit on her lip and met his eyes again. "I have to. I can't let them do this to you. You're innocent." She noticed how the hardwood floor ended at the cell, and the floor that Curt stood upon was stone like the walls.

"Think about yourself — your reputation. Think about your family's."

"We've done nothing to be ashamed of," she told him. "People can think what they like. We know the truth."

"I still can't let you do it. They'll never let you forget it."

Mary approached the cell, and the curious guard made no move to stop her. She covered Curt's hands with hers. "I don't care. I love you. That's all that counts."

Behind her, the two guards exchanged glances. Their slight movement drew Curt's eyes. He couldn't forget their presence like Mary had. "No, you don't," he told her. "You just think you do."

"Please don't tell me what I do or do not feel," she said. "I love you, and I'm telling the police the truth. You have no choice in either case." With that, she tore herself away from him and faced a third officer who had just joined them, the same policeman who had come to their home.

"What truth is that?" the arresting officer asked from behind her, his brows furrowed deeply in curiosity.

"The truth that Curt was with me all afternoon. He couldn't possibly have killed Constable Jenkins."

"Damn it, Mary!" Curt cursed behind her. She ignored him.

"You must understand I find that very difficult to believe, Miss Andrews." The officer stepped around her, making a small circle around the room.

"Do you think I would risk my reputation on a lie to save someone I hardly know?" Mary asked, following him. "Someone everybody in this town seems to be against?"

"Not everyone, Miss Andrews. As far as criminals go, I don't believe Mr. Prescott qualifies, but I must do my duty by the people of this city."

"Yes, I know. But what I told you is the truth."

He eyed her, his cheek twitching as he considered her words. "Would you sign an affidavit to that effect? And are you prepared to testify the same in court, should it come to that?"

"Yes." She lifted her chin to emphasize her conviction.

"Then you are a most brave young woman, Miss Andrews."

The officer went over to the big desk and brought out some paper as Mary found Curt's eyes. He was looking at her with such profound love and sadness that Mary felt tears come to her eyes. She brushed them away with her hand and took the seat the policeman offered her.

When she'd finished writing her statement and had signed it, she passed the paper to the officer. "Can he be set free now?"

"There would be the matter of bail," he replied. He stepped up to the shelf behind the desk and took down a small book. He flipped through its pages a minute then turned back to her, pointing at a figure that made Mary's breath catch in her throat.

She had no means of getting that kind of money.

"In my wallet," Curt said from the cell.

The officer rummaged through Curt's valuables and took out the money.

He moved toward Curt to let him count it. Curt waved him off. "I'm sure you're an honest man. Just mark me paid and let me out of here."

Mary clasped her hands in front of her, barely able to contain her enthusiasm. She watched as Curt gathered his clothes and met the jailer at the cell door. He stepped out the second it was unlocked and came to her. She looked up into his eyes, feeling her own brimming with happy tears. He touched her face softly with his hand.

"Thank you."

She smiled. He gazed at her a moment longer then moved to take his weapons from the officer. He was not allowed his boot knife, but he tucked the derringer and other valuables into his pockets. Then he came back to her.

"I trust you won't leave town," the officer said.

"Not a chance," Curt replied, and Mary thought she detected more conviction than was needed in his voice.

She bid the policemen good day then let Curt take her arm and lead her out the door.

Del was still there. She threw her arms around Curt's neck. His arm left Mary's to encompass Del. Surprised despite all she now knew, Mary hung back, feeling acutely embarrassed. A moment later, he loosened his hold on Del and smiled at them both.

"Let's go," he said, and she followed the two of them up the street.

Mary kept pace with Curt and Del but kept her eyes down, not wanting to catch the gaze of anyone who knew her. It was easier that way, too, not to see Curt's arm around Del.

It had never occurred to her that there might have been another woman in Curt's life. Why hadn't he told her about the tall blonde woman?

They came to a stop outside the Carlton Saloon without one word being spoken. Releasing Del and facing Mary, Curt inclined his head at the batwing doors.

"This is where I live."

"Me, too," Del added, wrapping both her arms around Curt's mid-section.

Mary stared up into Curt's dark eyes, searching for something, some flicker of emotion that told her she would see him again. There was nothing in his eyes. Although not cold, they held no warmth, either. There was absolutely nothing in them.

Had Del not been standing there, she would have asked him the question in her heart. But with the tall, voluptuous blonde hanging on him so possessively, Mary felt like an unwanted intruder. And Curt was doing nothing to make her feel any differently.

Swallowing hard, she found her voice. "I guess I'll be going now ..."

"Just wait," Curt said. "I'll see you home." To Del, he said, "I'll be back soon. Why don't you go inside and have a drink? Relax for a little while?"

A flash of ire in Del's golden eyes told them both she was not happy with that, but she did not argue with Curt. He squeezed her hand and then turned and took Mary's elbow with his hand. "Let's go, Mary."

They walked in silence, far too aware of the scattering of other townsfolk on the streets around them. The silence only intensified Mary's anguish. This hurt was a hurt more terrible than any she'd ever felt. Even when she realized his initial intentions for her — it had been a shock, but it had not hurt like this. Perhaps because then she still had hope that he truly loved her. Now she felt cast aside — used up and cast aside.

The tears broke through as they reached the old mansion on Pandora Avenue. She faltered and halted in front of the hedges near the rusted gate. She felt Curt's hand take hold of her shoulder, but she couldn't look up at him until she'd gotten herself under better control.

"Mary, I owe you a big thank you. That was very brave, what you did back there."

His gratitude was not was she needed to feel. "Why?" she began awkwardly. "Why didn't you tell me about Delores?"

Her blunt question must have thrown him off guard, for he actually stammered a bit before replying.

"I — I couldn't. You wouldn't have —."

"Wouldn't have what?" she asked, fresh tears stinging her eyes.

He gave her the clean handkerchief from his jacket pocket. She accepted it and dabbed at her eyes.

"You wouldn't have understood."

"Wouldn't have understood that you could court two women at once? How could you make me believe I was the only one? How could you let me believe you'd marry me? And all along you had her waiting for you?"

He didn't answer.

"Do you love her?"

He shrugged. "I guess."

And what about me? remained caught in her throat. She looked away and stared at the peeling black paint on the wrought iron fence surrounding the estate, at the hedges and trees and grass and flowerbeds, all overgrown and gone wild from years of neglect.

"Such a lovely place this must have been once," she said, her back to him.

"It was." He paused then continued. "When I was a kid, I used to sneak across the grounds and climb up into that great big maple over there near the terrace." He pointed. "In the summer the leaves were so thick I could just sit up there and hide and watch all the fancy people come and go. They had a lot of garden parties. I learned how educated people talked and behaved, and I learned to imitate their manners and the way they carried themselves. I figured that if I wanted to be successful like them someday, I'd better start learning right then."

Mary clasped her hands in front of her skirt. "You learned well. I believed all that you said about your mother's family. It would never have occurred to me that you'd raised yourself on the streets."

His hands nearly went to his hips in what looked like annoyance, but he seemed to stop himself and gather up whatever emotion threatened his composure.

"Everything I told you about my family is true. All of it. I just left some things out. Like how my mother got pregnant by a military man, and the fellow was conveniently reassigned. She went looking for him, refusing to believe he had really abandoned her. She never found him. The strain was too great for her. She lost that baby. And she was too ashamed to go home to her very proper English father. She tried to fend for herself, but it was only a matter of time before she had no choice but to prostitute herself."

Mary gazed at the side of his face and saw a muscle in his jaw working, like he was still fighting for control. Her heart swelled in her breast, and she felt tears of compassion shimmer in her eyes. "Oh, Curt ..." Suddenly she hugged him, hoping he would feel her true love for him and be soothed by it. "And you don't even know who your father is?"

He shook his head. There was a long silence between them as he stood stiffly in her embrace, and the sun dipped below the pointed tops of the evergreens to the west.

"So you see why I can't abandon Del. It would ruin her. I won't let what happened to my mother happen to her."

Mary could not encourage him to do so. "But what about me, then? What about us?" The instant the words escaped her lips she felt wretchedly selfish.

"I don't know. I know what you want me to say, but I can't ... I can't tell you what you want to hear when I'm not certain it would be the truth."

Her throat seized up, and she nearly choked on the agony bursting her heart. Her fists went to her mouth, and she bit down on her trembling lip. "I — need to go home," she managed to utter before she choked again. She started walking, refusing to break down any further in front of him.

He followed only a half a step behind and saw her to her gate. He raised his hand to touch her hair, and for a tiny second she leaned into his palm. But then she shook her head and fumbled with the latch. She closed the gate between them and walked up the slate path. He stood by the gate, watching her. Her hand on the doorknob, she turned her head and met his distressed brown eyes, searching for one last meeting with hers. She faced the door again, but could not bring herself to enter. Her parents would want to know all about what had happened, and she just couldn't face that right now.

Glancing back, she saw Curt had begun to walk back up the street. With a breath of relief, she hurried around the side of the house. Careful to avoid being seen through a window, she found a spot along the wall where she fit between the shrubs and settled herself in, her back supported by the wall, her arms around her updrawn knees. Silently, she cried.

As Curt and Mary disappeared around the corner beyond the old mansion, Del turned on her heel and swiftly strode back toward the Carlton.

The little bitch. The little bitch was still after him.

The evening shadows were long before Del reached the front doors of the saloon, every person stepping back from her and her palpable seething wrath.

Somehow, she would find a way to get rid of that little Andrews girl for good. Even if it killed her.

CHAPTER SIXTEEN

As Curt shut the suite door behind him and Del, the fact of having just betrayed Mary in the worst possible way rose up and swamped him like a rogue wave. He'd had to make the decision on the boardwalk not to treat Mary in any way that would upset Del. But he felt like such a heel he couldn't stand it any longer. He leaned back against the door.

"You ain't feelin' sorry for her, are you?" Del asked him, dropping her reticule on the table beside her chaise longue. She plucked at the fingertips of her black gloves and inched them off her hands. She dropped them next to the reticule. "You did too good a job on her — she thinks you love her."

He swallowed. "I know." From the door, he watched her kick off her shoes and plunk herself down on the chaise longue. Then she suddenly bounced back up again.

"Hey — I wanna know somethin'." She pointed a sharp purple fingernail at him. "Did you do her or not?" Cocking her hip to one side, she stuck one hand on the high side and waited for his answer.

He couldn't say anything. To distract them both, he hung up his jacket and hat on the rack in the corner.

"She says you didn't. She says she told you to stop, and you did."

Curt looked away from her probing eyes.

Del gazed at him intently. "You didn't, did you?" She took two steps toward him. "Why the hell not?"

"She wasn't ready —."

"Horse shit! Any woman in a hundred feet of you is drippin' like a fuckin' waterfall!"

"She asked me to stop," he admitted.

She frowned in disbelief. "So you didn't? Because she asked you to stop? What kinda reason is that?"

He captured her eyes with his and held them. "It's the same as like you and me, Del. I've never forced you, either."

"Yeah, but you love me." Del stared at him, waiting for a response. He gave none. Then her mouth dropped open, and she stepped closer to him, halting in the center of the emerald green carpet. "You love her?" She tipped her head sideways, her finely plucked eyebrows pressed together and low over her eyes. "You can't love her! Not someone like her?"

She was too close for comfort. He broke from the foyer and strode toward the bedroom. She leapt in front of him, cutting him off. "Tell me! Tell me you don't love her!"

He couldn't look at her. She grabbed his forearm, and he felt her nails through his shirt.

"Maybe. I don't know."

Her nails dug deeper until they hurt him.

"That ain't no answer! Either you do or you don't!"

"Damn it, Del!" he swore, yanking her hand off his arm. One small spot of blood stained his sleeve. He strode on into the bedroom with her right on his heels. He jerked off his tie and vest and threw them on the bedside chair. "It ain't as cut and dried as that!"

"The hell it ain't!" she cried. "You can love me or you can love her — not both of us!"

He spun around and glared at her, and she glared back, her eyes practically spitting sparks. After a long silence, her expression softened, but just a little.

"Just tell me how come?" she asked plaintively. "How come you gave up? You were gonna save us all."

"I can't!" he snapped then felt sorry for yelling at her. "I ain't Jesus Christ, for God's sake. I'm one man against a system that's changin' faster than any of us can keep up with." He shook his head with exasperation. "I thought maybe I could. But it's just too damn big, Del."

She stared at him with something near horror on her face. "Never thought I'd see the day when Curt Prescott'd back out of a fight."

Her words pained him even though he tried not to let them. "There's a difference between backing out and knowing when to throw in your hand. Sometimes you just gotta fold, Del. When you know damn straight you can't win the round."

She sliced her hand through the air. "I seen you lose thousands of dollars at one shot and not even bat an eye! What's there to lose by forkin' that little bitch? You don't lose nothin'— we don't lose nothin'! So she won't be a virgin no more — so what?"

He dropped his eyes and examined the carpet beneath his feet. There were tiny bits of lint here and there and one white thread near the corner. "It's important to her," he said, raising his eyes to Del's. "What you or I think doesn't matter. She's got a right to be how she wants to be."

She scowled at him skeptically.

"Can't you respect that? Can't you at least imagine how important it is to her?"

"No!" She spun away from him as if to stalk off then whirled around to face him again. "You know what I think? I think you been hangin' around her and her preacher father too goddamn long! I think you soaked up some of their religious slop!"

He cast his eyes to the ceiling and crossed his arms over his chest. "Bud Andrews never tried to force me to see things his way. Sure, he talked about God some, but he never tried to convert me."

"You been converted, and you don't even know it!" she accused him.

"That's horse shit, and you know it."

"One day he'll even have you goin' to church if you don't watch it."

"Now you're getting ridiculous."

She raised her eyebrows and stuck her hands on her hips. "Oh, really? I suppose he ain't never asked you to go?"

"He has. But I said no."

"How long can you keep sayin' no?"

"Until hell freezes over."

She locked eyes with him, and they stood there, at opposite corners of the carpet, both at a loss for what to say next. After what seemed like eons of silence to Curt, he stripped off his shirt and took a fresh one from the top drawer of his bureau.

"I suppose you're gonna see her again."

He had barely formed a "no," let alone vocalized it, before she strode past him toward the door.

"Shit! Do what you damn well want! Just remember — I can do what I damn well want, too!" With that, she twisted the doorknob viciously and slammed the door behind her.

Stunned, Curt stared at the closed door. How the hell had things ended up here?

Rubbing his face with his palms, he realized he hadn't shaved in a day and a half. He could really use a bath. But that seemed like too much work right now. He walked out onto the balcony and exhaled his irritation forcefully into the air.

The streets were busy with the usual weekday evening activities. He had to think about it a second to recall that it was Thursday. Reluctantly, he understood Del's anger. But what made him angry was not really Del. It was his failing her by not following through with his own plan. It was his failing her by giving her cause to fret over his commitment to her.

It was his failing Mary by not being the man she'd fallen in love with. It was that he'd been set up for Jenkins' murder.

It was just too coincidental that his knife should be stolen and then used for that particular crime and left so conveniently as evidence. Sure, it could all be mad coincidence, but he doubted it. And the only party he considered fool enough to even attempt it was Fat Johnnie.

That fat pig of a man was becoming too much to put up with. Curt was sure Johnnie had instrumented the whole thing. Despite Johnnie's lack of control over his own impulses, it was unlikely he'd actually stuck Jenkins himself — he'd probably gotten Keegan to do it. And it was probably Keegan who had hit Curt over the head in the alley.

Curt's jaw ground, and a scowl darkened his face. There was no way he was waiting for the police to sort it all out — he would confront Fat Johnnie himself and wring the truth out of him.

Grabbing his jacket and hat off the coat rack he exited the suite. The piano tunes he'd hardly noticed while in his private quarters now jangled up the stairs. He descended quickly and was about to cross the hardwood floor when a crash from the kitchen stopped him in mid-stride.

"Get out of my way, you stupid little bitch!" It was Del's voice.

"Leave offa me!" a female voice screamed back. "I ain't done nothin' to you!"

There was a slap and a wail of rage, and suddenly, it sounded like a brawl had begun. Curt hesitated then altered his course for the kitchen. As he pushed through the swinging door, he saw Del holding a waitress by the hair. The waitress was bent low, trying to ease the strain on her hair, but Del kept twisting it tighter, oblivious to the girl's cries and the slaps and punches she was receiving from her.

"I'll show you to get in my way!" Del shrieked.

"Del —!" Curt began. He was ignored. He stepped closer, careful to avoid the pots and broken dishes all over the floor. "Del, let her go."

She finally heard him and glanced up. She said nothing, but the way she glared at him told him to butt out. She was enjoying her power over the smaller woman, and he wasn't to interfere.

"Del, come on. It's not Natty there you're mad at. So leave her alone."

"Fuck you!" she spat at him, so venomously that he was taken aback.

Still holding the girl by the hair, she faced Curt more squarely. "Who the hell do you think you are, Curt Prescott? What makes you think you can do this to me and everything'll be just peachy? I've given you everything, and you just keep on takin' and takin' ...!" Suddenly her voice cracked, and she released Natty, who scurried for the backdoor.

Del's shoulders caved in over her chest and began to shake. She brought her hands to cover her face as she began to sob. "I love you, you sonovabitch. Don't you know what that means? Am I so stupid I still love you when you can't love me back?"

Curt's throat suddenly went dry, and he swallowed. "No, Del. If anybody's stupid, it's me." He picked his way through the pots and dishes and took her shoulders in his hands. "I'm the one who doesn't know what the hell he wants anymore."

She looked up at him, her face smeared with teary make-up tracks. She locked her arms around his neck and cuddled her face on his shoulder.

"I'm sorry I haven't always been the man you wanted me to be ... but I ... Hell, I don't know why. But it doesn't mean I don't ... love you. I do love you, Del. I always have. And I'll never stop."

"Oh, lover ..." Del crooned, squeezing him tightly.

He held her closer, breathing deeply the musky, perfumed scent of her. They'd be all right, he told himself. They'd be all right.

Curt led Del upstairs with a steaming cup of tea and settled her comfortably on her chaise longue. He explained to her his suspicions about Fat Johnnie and Wesley Keegan and then rose and reached for his hat.

Her teacup rattled in its saucer on her lap. "But you're not goin' down there now? It's gonna be dark soon. It's dangerous down there."

He quirked the left side of his mouth in a half smile. "I can handle those two."

"But, Curt —." Standing, Del stuck her tea down on the side table, oblivious to the way it slopped over the rim of the cup into the saucer. "Please don't go — not now. Not tonight. I couldn't stand worryin' about you."

He placed a hand on her waist and looked into her golden eyes. They shifted back and forth from his, genuinely uneasy. Her hands clung to his arms with a desperation he hadn't felt from her before.

"I'll be fine, Del. You just drink your tea and relax then go on down and do your show for all those boys waiting for you. Before you know it, I'll be back—."

"No, please."

"Del." He held her eyes firmly with his until she acquiesced.

As he reached the corner of Store Street and Chatham, he halted in a dark corner and withdrew the bundle hidden beneath his coat, tucked under his left arm. He buckled the gun belt around his hips and ran his thumb over the rounds in the bullet loops, despite knowing they were all full. Then he pulled the Colt clear and thumbed the cylinder, double-checking. He slid it back into the holster, satisfied.

Del slid behind the bar to fetch herself a glass of water for backstage but couldn't help pausing to stare at the bright glare that seemed to overwhelm the doorway to the street. How did he expect her to just extinguish her worry? At least he wasn't headed up to that little wench's house. The thought of Mary Andrews refueled her vexation. She grabbed the pitcher and a glass and poured. Someone bumped her arm from behind, and water sloshed over the rim of the glass and splattered on the plank floor.

Cursing, Del turned to see Natty reaching for an empty tray and smirking. "Ain't there nothin' that you're good for?" Del asked, wiping her wet fingers on her skirt before taking a drink from the glass.

Natty smiled back with an odd grace to the venomous twist on her lips. "Oh, lots," she replied.

"Like what?" Del asked, though she turned to walk away without waiting for an answer.

"Like I'm good for gettin' information out of men that could be real useful to the right person."

Halting, Del frowned at her. "What's that supposed to mean?"

With an air of innocence, Natty swiveled her torso from left to right a few times. "It means I had a customer last night that was braggin' about somethin' you might wanna know about."

Del narrowed her eyes at the girl. "Then spit it out!"

Natty waggled her finger at Del. "Not so fast. My information ain't free. But it is for sale. Say, ten bucks."

"I'll tell you how much it's worth when I hear it."

"Bein' snotty just puts the price up. Now I want twenty."

"It can't be that important," Del huffed and turned to go.

"You'll wish you thought different after Wes Keegan sticks his big old beautiful knife in your lover boy's back."

"What?" Del spun back to face her.

Natty held out her hand, palm up. Impatiently, Del dug into her cleavage to pull out what cash she had on her. She slapped the whole lot into the girl's hand.

Natty took her time counting it. "There's only thirteen." She shrugged. "But I guess you can owe me, seein' as Curt's such a sweet fella."

"Spill it!" Del spat.

"Well, as I said, I was pleasurin' this lumberjack friend of yours, and he started braggin' about how he was gonna cut Curt Prescott up real slow before he finally let him die. Then he said he'd come and take his pleasure with you before he cut you up, too, just to get even for that trick you played on him. Unless you proved mighty special in bed — then he might wanna take you home with him. I told him you weren't worth the trouble for either one."

Del barely heard the girl's snide comment. "When's Keegan plannin' on comin' for Curt?"

"Oh, he ain't gonna come for him. They know he'll come for them, sooner or later. And they'll be waitin'."

Del's throat went so dry it choked her.

Willie's voice boomed from the kitchen. "Delores! You're on in five minutes!"

Del tried to swallow and took a sip of water to ease her throat. She had to go after Curt — show or no show. Willie could go hang himself.

But Curt had refused to listen to her already. He'd probably just tell her to go home and stay out of the way.

"Natty, you gotta go warn him!"

The girl shook her head. "In case you hadn't noticed, I'm workin'." She made to brush past Del.

"Wait!" Del grabbed her arm. "I got more money upstairs." Just then, a better idea occurred to her. "I'll give you a hundred bucks if you go fetch the new preacher's girl and get her down there to talk Curt out of it — but you gotta go now."

Del's urgency erased any doubts Natty may have held about her sincerity. "Okay — but why the preacher's girl?"

Del waved her off impatiently. "Those preacher folks are good talkers. Just go get her and show her right to the Bull's Pride Bar. She won't know where it is. When you get back here, I'll have your money."

Natty smiled, and her body wiggled with the pleasure of her reward. "Okay, but where do I find this girl?"

Del's heart stopped as she realized she really didn't know the exact house. Then suddenly she remembered something Curt had told her. "It's Timberline Street, and there's a sign on the gate. You can read, right?"

Natty's lip curled at her.

"Never mind — just go!"

She watched Natty go, her heart beating madly in her chest now. She'd have gone herself, but she didn't believe that Mary would trust her. Willie shouted for her again. She guzzled the rest of the water in her glass and shouted back at him. "I'm comin'!"

Curt's gut agreed with his logic, telling him odds were he'd find both Fat Johnnie and Wesley Keegan in the Bull's Pride Bar. If they didn't put up too much of a fight, he'd deliver them to the police in one piece. If they chose the hard way, the condition they arrived in would be entirely up to them.

He paused in the doorway of Fat Johnnie's rat hole, allowing his eyes to adjust to the perpetual dimness. Only then did he step inside, and the vermin scurried out of his way.

They were expecting him.

A roar from behind him served as no warning, for the instant he heard it, he felt hands grab him like steel claws and yank him back outside. Spun around like a child's toy, he barely had time to see Wesley Keegan towering above him before the huge man's fist slugged him square on the cheek. The pain shot through his entire skull as his body took flight. He came down hard on his back on the front steps.

Keegan gave him no time to recover. Through a sparkling haze Curt saw him rear over him like a great bear, his paws reaching for him. Twisting his shoulders, he spun himself prone off the steps. He landed on his stomach in the street and sprang to his feet. Keegan roared again and leapt off the edge after him. Curt pulled his gun and pointed it at the lumberjack's belly.

Keegan came up short, staring at the gun in the flicker of the oil lamp hanging from the corner post. He began circling Curt, as if trying to figure out his next move.

"Give it up, Keegan. I'm taking you to have a chat with the police. You're gonna tell them how you killed Jenkins."

Halting with his back to the alley, Keegan threw back his big, square head and laughed a booming laugh. "Figger yer pretty bright, don'tcha, gambler? Well, ya weren't bright enough to 'spect me to be waitin' fer ya out back o' the Carlton, that night, were ya? But I gotta admit, luck was with me that time. I'd been watchin' you and waitin' fer some time just outside them nice big windows the Carlton's got." He chuckled. "By the way—how's them lumps on yer head? It was two I gave ya, warn't it? Hard-headed, you are." He snickered at his own joke. "But if you want me to go down fer killin' somebody, let's make it you." He reached his right hand across his body and dragged his big abalone-handled knife from its leather sheath.

The size of it amazed Curt just as much as it had the first time he'd seen it.

"I got tired of cuttin' down trees. Cuttin' down men is easier."

Just as Curt wondered how Keegan hoped to take him while he was holding a gun, the big man dove at him with a speed Curt had not thought possible for a man his size. On pure reflex, Curt pulled the trigger, and flesh and abalone shell sprayed into the air. Keegan howled and grabbed at his mutilated hand. His thumb was entirely gone. He tore off his own sleeve and began to wrap the hand, even as his eyes searched the dirt behind him for the knife. The blade was intact, but the abalone shell handle was shattered.

"Leave it," Curt commanded him as Keegan reached for the weapon with his left hand. "It doesn't have to go any further than this. Just come with me, and we'll get the doc to look after your hand."

Securing his grip on the damaged haft of his knife, Keegan straightened up and backed away, deeper into the dark alley, pain and rage twisting his features. "I'll go see the doc myself after I take care o' you. 'Course you got that gun there, and that ain't exactly fair. Let's say you an' me go at it hand to hand. Unless ye're yellow as yer whore's pretty hair." He smiled his ugly, rotten-toothed smile and waved the knife in front of him. "When I'm finished with you, I'm gonna head on up to your place and fuck the livin' daylights outta your whore. Don't mind tellin' you, I'm hung like a horse — she'll be screamin' before I'm half done."

Curt mocked him with a sneer, not allowing the threat to hit home. Keegan wanted him to lose his cool. No way, Curt thought. No way.

"Come on, gambler. Come on."

Hand-to-hand with that monster? Even with one of those hands half blown off, Curt didn't like the odds. He stepped cautiously into the mouth of the alley after Keegan. Glancing away from the lumberjack, he wondered where the hell Fat Johnnie was. There was no sign of him.

Keegan grinned, exposing his yellow-brown teeth again. He was no longer showing any signs of pain. Curt pivoted to keep facing him as the lumberjack circled him. He would not take his eyes off Keegan now.

Suddenly the lumberjack rushed him, roaring like a grizzly. Curt sidestepped him and, grasping the butt of his Colt with both hands, rammed it into the small of Keegan's back. The 'jack's back arched, and he grunted, but then he swung around, his right arm extended like a log boom. A split second too late, Curt saw it for the distraction it was. He jumped back from the oncoming knife in Keegan's left hand, but the blade sliced him deeply enough across his forearm that he dropped his gun.

A scream caused them both to whip their eyes to the street. Curt immediately recognized Mary and Natty and stole the fraction of a second it took Keegan to focus on them to grab the knife in both hands and twist it into the lumberjack's gut.

Keegan's face contorted in shock and agony. He stumbled, and Curt shoved him backward, lest the big man topple forward and crush him. Keegan's legs gave out, and he collapsed in the dirt, his hands grasping the metal haft of the knife that was sticking out of his belly. He sighed with a sound that was part groan and then was still.

Curt picked up his gun and looked toward Mary. Natty was running away toward home. Mary stood transfixed, one hand over her heart, the other over her mouth.

Curt took one last look at Keegan and then walked toward her. "I'm sorry you had to see that," he said trying to holster his gun with his left hand. Finally, it was in, and he stood before her, searching her eyes with his. He lifted his good hand and touched her shoulder. "Mary, you shouldn't be here. Why are you here?"

She tore her eyes away from Keegan's still form and looked up at him. "The girl — Natty —came to tell me you were in trouble. She thought I could help."

Strange, but he didn't pause to think about it. He took her arm and led her toward the front street. "It's dangerous. You shouldn't be here."

"I — . Curt, I —." Her eyes focused on the blood running down his arm, dripping off the tips of his fingers and into the dirt. "Your arm! We've got to do something!" She turned him into the lamplight, and he let her help him out of his jacket and roll back the sleeve of his shirt. The wound was deep enough not to be taken lightly, but he could still move all his fingers.

"I'll be all right."

"We've got to stop the bleeding." She tore the ruined sleeve along the knife cut and completely off at the shoulder. He let her wrap a tight pressure bandage around his forearm.

"Good job. Thank you."

"You're welcome," she said, taking his left hand. "Now let's go."

He stood his ground. "I'm not done here yet. But you go — .I don't want to have to worry about you."

"Curt —."

He passed her his jacket. "My wallet and stuff's in here. Keep it for me until I get back."

Her eyes flashed at him. "I'm not going without you."

"Yes, you are." He gave her a nudge that was not nearly as strong as his growing impatience. "Go home before you get hurt. Go get the police if you have to, but go where it's safe. Now."

She locked eyes with him momentarily, but he did not waiver. Finally, she acquiesced. "All right. But I'm bringing help."

"Fine." It was all he could do not to yell at her, what with his concern for her coupled with the pain in his arm and his worry that Fat Johnnie could come out of nowhere before she had gotten away safe. "Go."

She hesitated again then touched his face with her palm, careful of the huge bruise forming there. Stretching up on her tiptoes, she kissed his cheek. "I love you."

"I love you, too. Now go."

This time she did. He watched her for a moment then turned to finish what he'd come to do.

Del belted out the last word of her song and curtsied to the applause, whistles and hoots. She never got enough of the adoration, but she turned and left the stage sooner than was usual at the end of a set.

Curt still wasn't back, and she hadn't seen Natty return. That little tart had better have done what she'd been told to do, or there'd be hell to pay, Del swore to herself.

She couldn't stand waiting any longer. What if Natty couldn't find the Andrews girl, or the Andrews girl wouldn't come? What if Mary did go down there and screwed something up? It wouldn't keep Del up nights if the foolish little wench got in the way of a stray bullet. But what if she got Curt shot?

Del cast a look around the bar room for Willie, didn't see him, and decided not to waste time finding him and explaining everything. She strode out the door and headed for Chatham Street, her worries mounting.

Curt was too careful, too smart to get hurt. But they could have ambushed him. And what if that Andrews girl did catch a bullet? Curt would figure out how she got wind of where he was — he would know Del had arranged it. If she lost him to that Andrews girl, it would not be by her own doing. She would not drive him away with an action he could not respect. He might never say so, but it would always remain between them. She'd been a fool not to go herself. She had to get down there and make sure things didn't go wrong.

Outside the door of Fat Johnnie's saloon, Curt paused to eject the single spent casing and slipped in a fresh round. He set his Colt firmly in his right hand and supported it with his left. It hurt like hell, but it was going to have to do.

He drew a breath to steady himself. Then, using only memory as a guide, he burst through the front door, hit the floor and rolled back to his feet, coming up near the bar as a shot sliced through the air where he would have been, had he waited for his eyes to dilate. Instantly he located the shooter, sighted him, and pulled the trigger. The bullet punched a neat hole in the bartender's forehead. The man's head jerked and lolled back as the rifle slipped from his fingers and clattered on the floor. He was dead on his feet, slithering to the floor almost as an afterthought.

Curt leveled the gun again as six swill rats scurried for the door. None of them was a threat. He turned his back on them and headed for Fat Johnnie's office. Shoving the door open with a foot, he found the room empty. A thump and shuffling noises above his head turned his attention to the upper floor. The staircase began just behind him, the first three steps leading from Fat Johnnie's office door up to a square landing. From the landing on up was a straight climb with solid walls on both sides. Not a particularly inviting route. Replacing the spent shell first, he steadied himself and took the first step.

Slowly, he took one step at a time, placing his foot carefully, silently cursing every creak in the old wooden stairs. He paused at each one to listen for any sound above him. His eyes swept the top of the staircase ceaselessly. When a shotgun muzzle appeared on the right, he threw himself to that side and flattened himself to the wall. The walls shook with the deafening report, and the far side became a pockmarked mess. Before Fat Johnnie could reload, Curt charged the rest of the way up and brought his gun to bear on him.

"Drop it, Johnnie!"

"I don't think so, Prescott. I already got a fresh shell in before you made the top." He pointed the muzzle at Curt.

Curt doubted the truth of that. He was certain he'd have heard the hinge action snap-click into place. But he wasn't taking any chances. He scanned the dim hallway beyond Johnnie. A few doors, all closed, and faint light from a back exit.

"So then, let's talk," he proposed. "What's your gripe, Johnnie? Why'd you have Jenkins killed?"

"He was sellin' us out! I tried to reason with him but he wouldn't listen."

"You made a mistake, Johnnie. A big one."

"Says you! I don't listen to you no more!"

Curt saw Johnnie's pudgy hands fuss with their grip on the shotgun. His broken finger was on the mend, but no doubt still sore.

"I get rid of Jenkins, and I get ridda you, and I'm the one what runs this town! From Chatham to Humboldt — the whole thing!" Johnnie steadied his shotgun finally, gripping it tightly beneath his arm. The fingers supporting the stock were going white.

"You're wrong, Johnnie. Things are changing in this town, and they're not going your way."

"The hell they ain't! I'll make 'em!"

"Okay, Johnnie, but who's gonna back you up by doin' all your dirty jobs now that Keegan is dead?"

"Wrong again, gambler!"

Both Curt and Fat Johnnie looked down the stairs in surprise. Curt's surprise turned cold and leaden in his gut when he saw Wesley Keegan with Mary in a chokehold and his bloody knife at her throat. Keegan's shirt was soaked with blood, and some was smeared on Mary's blouse and skirt. *It had better be all Keegan's*, Curt thought. *Oh, God, please don't let him hurt her! Please!*

That fleeting moment of panic was unacceptable. He had to get control of the situation. "Mary, are you all right?"

She nodded as best she could, but he could tell she was truly terrified.

"Get your ass down here, runt," ordered Keegan. He wasn't just holding Mary, he was leaning on her — heavily. "But first you give my partner there your pistol."

Fat Johnnie tossed away the empty shotgun. It clattered heavily on the floor. He held out his hand for Curt's weapon, a cocky grin on his flabby wet lips.

"You let the girl go, and I'll give you my gun."

"No dealin', gambler," Keegan said. "I'm callin' the shots here."

At that moment, Curt caught sight of Del slipping silently between the rickety tables. She'd taken off her shoes, and she had her derringer cocked and ready in her hand.

Curt let his eyes lift to Fat Johnnie's. The red-haired man wouldn't see her as long as he stayed where he was. Curt kept his gun pointed at him. "You gonna let this lumberjack call the shots in your own place, Johnnie?"

"He's workin' for me. He does what I say; I give him a loose rein on how he does it."

Del was nearly close enough to be accurate with the derringer.

"You're losing a lot of blood, Keegan," Curt said. "You need help now, or you won't last much longer."

"Long enough to get you outside and cut you up like a hog in front of the whole street. Then they'll see you ain't nothin'! Now git down here!" The effort of shouting must have caused him considerable pain, for he doubled over, bending Mary with him.

Del closed the gap then, pointed the derringer at his face and pulled the trigger. The .41 caliber boomed, and half of Keegan's throat opened up. Choking on the blood filling his throat, he dropped Mary as he spun to face his new threat.

As Curt swung the Colt to finish Keegan off, Fat Johnnie rushed him, toppling Curt into the wall and crushing him beneath his weight. "Damn you, Prescott! I'm gonna fuckin' kill you!"

Curt heard Del scream with rage as she fought Keegan. He got a glimpse of the lumberjack grabbing at her and falling on top of her, and then he heard the derringer's second shot go off.

But he was pinned beneath Johnnie, whose pudgy hands had clamped around his throat. The gambler's lungs screamed for air, and his spine felt ready to snap against the edge of the stair he was lying on.

Gritting his teeth against the pain, he forced the muzzle of the Colt to point at the only part of the big man he could manage. He yanked the trigger, and the bullet tore through Fat Johnnie's lower flank. The big man screamed and partially rose to his knees, off Curt just enough that the gambler could lift the Colt and fire again. The second bullet penetrated just below Johnnie's sternum. Fat Johnnie went suddenly silent and stared down at Curt with wide-open eyes.

"You're dead, Johnnie. The game's over."

He watched the pale blue eyes lose focus and begin to glaze. Then a putrid stench reached his nostrils as the fat man voided both his bowels and his bladder. Tottering like a sawn tree, Fat Johnnie finally overbalanced and toppled down the stairs.

Mary scrambled out of the way. The floorboards shook as the big man hit bottom on the landing and came to rest on his back. Curt stumbled down after him, his gun ready, but Johnnie's eyes stared sightlessly at the ceiling. He was dead.

So was Keegan this time. Curt holstered the Colt and dragged the lumberjack off Del. She was covered in blood and breathing with difficulty. Curt lifted her shoulders to help her sit up, but she cried out in pain.

"What's wrong? Are you hurt? Where?" He scanned her limbs, fearing something had been broken in the struggle with Keegan.

Mary knelt down next to them. "Can I help?"

Del barely glanced at her. "It hurts here," she told Curt, putting her hand between her breasts.

Curt carefully opened her garments, fearing broken ribs. What he found chilled his heart.

Del coughed and wheezed, and blood appeared at her lips. Mary gasped, one hand flying to her heart, the other to her mouth. She looked at Curt then back at the huge knife wound.

"What can we do?"

He stared at the mortal wound then lifted his eyes to Del's face.

"I'll get the doctor!" Mary cried, rising.

Curt grabbed her arm, and she sank back down. He shook his head. Del stared at him, her breathing becoming more and more uneven.

"So, that's ... how it is ..." she said.

"Del, I —."

"It's not ... your fault. I tried — I'm sorry." She began to choke, and he gathered her in his arms.

Mary took one of Del's hands in both of hers. "You didn't just try — you saved us both."

Del's golden eyes filled with liquid as she turned them from Curt's to Mary's. "You better ... look after him ... good. Or else." She grasped one of Mary's hands and struggled to place it on one of Curt's.

Curt and Mary exchanged a quick glance before both of them looked back at Del.

"Del, I love you," Curt declared, fighting back the tears stinging his eyes.

Her eyelids fluttered. "I know." Her breaths came quick then, quick and shallow until abruptly they stopped. She released one final sigh and went limp in Curt's arms.

"Del!" Curt cried, cradling her closer as Mary draped sympathetic arms around him. Del's left hand slipped from theirs while her right released its hold on the silver tussie-mussie pinned over her heart.

Curt carried Del from that place to the office of Dr. Helmcken. He knew she would be safe there. It was well after midnight by the time the doctor finished cleaning Curt's knife wound and stitching it closed. Curt draped his suit jacket over his good shoulder instead of fighting his way into it and walked Mary home. She'd insisted on staying with him. They spoke no words to each other, and he left her at her door with no more than a meeting of their eyes in the soft light of the porch lantern.

He'd told the doctor all about the events at the Bull's Pride Bar. Helmcken was a good man and agreed to inform the police on Curt's word not to disappear. Curt hoped all the killing over this business was finished with. It was high time things got back to normal. Trouble was, without Del, things would never be normal again. He felt ancient as he climbed the carpeted stairs inside the Carlton, the events of the day swirling in his mind's eye, his tired eyes not wanting to see the interior of the empty suite. He stopped in the hallway, staring down at the doorknob, the key heavy as a gun in his hand. Finally, he jammed it in the keyhole, twisted it, and walked through the door.

CHAPTER SEVENTEEN

Curt felt anything but normal as he took his hat in his hands and stepped over the threshold of the little Garry Oak Church. The hot August day brought out the pleasantly pungent smells of wood oil and varnish. Outside he'd had to keep his head down, shading his eyes lest they squint and tear up in the brilliance of the clear day. But inside, the light streaming through the rows of small windows along each side was softer and easier on his eyes. The rows of walnut pews before him were empty, and the aisle led his gaze toward the pulpit and an unobstructed view of Del's casket.

Bud appeared from a doorway off to the right, beyond the casket, and came to him. He took Curt's right hand in a kind, firm grip. "How are you doing, Curt?"

Curt heard himself say, "Fine," and allowed the parson to guide him to a seat in the front row. Bud sat with him and spoke to him, but Curt barely heard his words. His eyes kept going back to the wooden casket, covered with flowers donated by the old man at the flower shop. Curt frowned, trying to recall the man's name, but he kept coming up blank.

Bud's eyes rose from Curt's just before Curt felt a soft touch on his shoulder. Curt looked up to see Mary try to smile as she slid onto the pew next to him. She squeezed his hand. Motion beyond her drew his attention, and he saw Sarah Andrews cast him a brief glance and seat herself on the other side of the aisle.

Slowly, people began to fill the doorway, and Bud excused himself to go and greet them. Mary stayed next to Curt, her hand holding his. He began to look at the people arriving instead of at the casket. Willie had come, having closed the saloon for the entire day. A few of the waitresses Del had known had come, along with several regular patrons Curt recognized. When they stopped coming, the church was far from full, but it was a turnout Curt felt Del would have found agreeable.

He turned to the front as Pastor Andrews began his service. Bud had not known Del, but his words were kind, gathered from those who had known and appreciated her. He spoke briefly then invited any who chose to come up and share their memories of her.

Willie came and spoke of her talent, her passion for entertaining, and her professionalism, and how she could have been a big star but chose to stay in the place she called home. He credited her with helping to make the Carlton the success it was.

A couple of the girls came up together to share a story that had them both chuckling and crying as they related it.

When no one else rose, Bud turned his eyes to Curt's. Curt looked back at him, a hundred thoughts tumbling inside his head and pain overshadowing them all. He had thought that he might speak at the end, to tell them of her and how her life had made a difference in his, but his voice failed him. He shook his head at Bud and lowered his eyes to Del's casket.

Bud said a final prayer, and then the people began to file out the door. Curt took a lead position as the appointed pallbearers approached the casket and helped carry Del to the site prepared in the graveyard next to his mother.

When he stepped back, Mary was once again at his side, silently slipping her arm around his. Insects buzzed lazily in the heat. Somewhere off in the meadow, birds twittered and flew.

Bud's voice drifted in and out of Curt's conscious hearing. Del's voice was in his inner ear, laughing, singing, saying his name. When the pastor was done, Curt laid the bunch of wildflowers he'd picked earlier on top of Del's casket and whispered, "Good-bye, Del. I love you."

The gatherers drifted away after shaking Curt's hand until the only ones remaining were Bud and Mary. Sarah had not spoken to him and stood well outside the fence, waiting for her husband and daughter.

Bud shook Curt's hand one more time, embracing it in both of his. "You're welcome to come home with us. Have a meal. Stay as long as you like."

"No, thank you, parson," Curt answered, his voice gravelly but finally obeying him. "I think I'll just take a walk."

"Would you like some company?" Mary asked, squeezing his arm.

He shook his head. "Not this time." He stepped toward the open gate, and they followed him. Once out on the road, he put on his hat and touched the brim with his fingers.

"Thanks for everything, parson. I'll see you." He gave Mary a nod and then deliberately gave a tip of his brim to Sarah, who pretended she hadn't seen it.

He turned then and began to walk up the road away from town, where it climbed the slow hill and disappeared around the bend into the forest.

A few weeks later, things in Victoria began returning to normal. The death of James Douglas had rather overshadowed the deaths of Del and Jenkins and the two criminals, and the townsfolk seemed to forget even the young constable rather easily. In the Carlton's bar room, Curt still overheard men talk of his own role in the demise of Fat Johnnie and Keegan when they weren't aware he was near.

He hadn't seen a single Committee march since Del's funeral. The town had hired another young constable but appeared to be taking its time getting around to dealing with any issues of vice. Curt figured they were waiting for things to settle down awhile before stirring up the hornet's nest again, if ever.

The town council had absolved Curt unanimously of any connection with Jenkins' murder. They laid no charges regarding his carrying of a weapon within the city limits, nor in the discharge of his weapon, and actually thanked him for ridding Victoria of two of its more troublesome citizens. However, while the conflict might be over for the town, Curt still felt as though he had unfinished business sitting heavily on his shoulders.

He sat nursing a beer in the Carlton around noon on Monday, his playing cards lying idle on the table before him. He'd chosen a table on the south side of the door and close enough to the windows that he'd get plenty of light. The tables immediately around him were empty. He had an unobstructed view of the front door, and his peripheral vision would keep him aware of the hallway to the back door. Sometimes, from the corner of his eye, he'd swear he saw Del rehearsing a dance number on stage with the band, or striding toward him, her eyes dancing and her golden hair bouncing, but they were only fleeting shadows and still too easily replaced by the dark specter of her dead in his arms.

A stocky figure appeared in the doorway, hazy through the smoke filling the bar room. Curt fought to focus on it and recognized Bud Andrews. With a jolt, he sat up and stared as if he couldn't trust his eyes. Bud looked around the room until he found him. He came over to the table and took off his hat.

"Curt. Hello. How are you doing?"

"Parson — hello. Have a seat." Curt pointed at the chair opposite him.

"Thank you." Bud pulled it back from the table and sat down.

Curt stared at him, unable to believe the preacher was actually here in the saloon. He noticed a small handful of cut flowers in Bud's hand but passed over it without concern. "What brings you in here?" he asked carefully.

Bud set the clippings on the table and covered them with his grey hat. He hitched his chair a little closer. "You do."

A smile almost made it to Curt's lips.

"I don't like to make assumptions," Bud said slowly, "but we haven't seen you since the funeral. Are you all right?"

A smile, at once amused and nervous, quirked one corner of Curt's mouth. "Perfectly."

"Have you chosen, then, to return to your former life?"

"I never left it, Parson."

Bud's response came after a second's hesitation. "I see." His fingertips brushed the brim of his hat. "I had hoped ..."

Curt gave him a minute to continue, but Bud did not go on. Curt swept his left hand over the bar room. "You hoped I'd give all this up and change my spots and marry your daughter and become a good, decent, church-going, God-fearing person."

An embarrassed flush colored Bud's cheeks, and he looked away toward the windows.

"I wouldn't hold my breath if I were you."

Bud's soft grey eyes suddenly hardened and turned back to Curt's. "You can be very cold when you want to be."

Curt shrugged and leaned back in his chair. He regarded the preacher without expression.

Bud leaned toward him, his elbows sliding over the smooth polish toward the center of the round table. "You don't know what it is you want, do you? Maybe for the first time in your life. And you're scared."

Scoffing, Curt looked away.

"Whether you intended to or not, you opened up a side of yourself to us I don't think these people ever see." Bud turned his hand toward the scattering of men in the bar. "It's that Curt I'm appealing to." He paused, realizing he'd raised his voice a tad too high. "Mary is heartbroken, Curt."

Curt felt tension tightening the skin around his eyes. He drew hard on the thin cigar he'd left, forgotten, in the glass ashtray and stared toward the stage where Del should have been. "I'm sorry," he said as he breathed out the smoke. Finding himself unable to hold Bud's eyes, he turned his face away and stared out the window.

"At the very least you owe her an explanation. Tell her why you haven't called on her even once in three weeks. Tell her why you've apparently turned your back on her after the ways she has supported you."

Curt answered with deliberate nonchalance. "I don't need anyone's 'support'." Slowly, he turned his eyes back to Bud's.

The older man's eyes plainly showed his hurt. His face seemed taut, the lines and creases deeper than they had been even a few moments ago. "Liar. Fool."

Curt felt a tightening between his heart and his stomach, as if something was pulling the two together and lashing them into one constricted lump. His eyes shifted to the stage, not wanting to see Bud's face grim and without color. The parson linked and unlinked his callused fingers.

"Hard on you, bein' in a place like this," Curt commented. "And this is one of the best places in town."

Staring at his hands, Bud swallowed and cleared his throat. "I know. I've been in every one of the saloons in town, more than once."

Curt stared at him with surprise.

"But they had no use for a man of God. Oh, some of them tolerated me, let me speak. They mocked me with applause. But they never listened. I was physically thrown out of more than one establishment." He looked up from his hands to see if Curt was listening. "This was before you returned and came into our lives. I'm ashamed to say it, but it's been some time now since I last tried to preach in the saloons, in the places where God's presence is needed more than any other in this town." He dropped his eyes to his hands again.

Curt did not need to look at Bud's face to know his pain. He could feel it. "Must've been kind of hard on a man who takes his work as seriously as you do."

Bud did not look up. "But I failed in that part of my duties. I've half a mind to try again, but I know the reception will be the same."

Curt regarded him silently for a minute and then voiced the thought that came to him. "Is that why it's so important to you that I give up my life and marry Mary? Am I just a project for you?"

Bud's eyes lifted to his quite suddenly. "Goodness, no!"

Curt leaned forward and locked eyes with Bud. "Are you absolutely sure about that?"

Bud swallowed and then slowly shook his head. "I suppose you're right ... in a way. But it's more than that, Curt. I care about what happens to you ... personally, as a young man. I don't want to see you suffer."

"You're talking in a Biblical sense again." Curt shook his head. "You'll never get me to believe in that stuff, parson." He held out his hands to show him the room around them. "This is all there is. But even if you're right, even if you could prove otherwise to me beyond any doubt, I still wouldn't follow your God. You've told me that a man is too weak to prove himself worthy of God, that he could never measure up no matter how hard he tries, no matter how 'good' he is, that he'll always fall short. So then, what's the point, preacher? What's the goddamn point? If I can't measure up, I'm damned. And you've told me I can't. And if your God is merciful like you say he is, he'll accept me for what I am. He'll forgive me for being ... misguided, for making mistakes."

Bud suddenly interjected. "But ignorance of the law and deliberate disobedience are two different things. You're an extremely disciplined young man. You could do it if you chose to."

"But I don't choose to," Curt said. "And that's the whole point. I like my life. I like my freedom. I'm not handing it over to some God that might not even exist. What a fool's bet!"

Bud stared silently at his fingers, scratching nervously at the calluses.

"And what I really don't get is that you know who I am — you've always known and from the beginning you've encouraged a relationship between Mary and me." Curt shook his head. "I really don't get it."

"You seemed a decent fellow to me, the night you saved me from further humiliation right outside this very saloon." He indicated the batwing doors with his hand. "I confess it started rather selfishly ... I thought ... I thought if I could open your heart to Christ, then the others might follow. I realize now it was complete foolishness, but ..." He looked down and ran his fingers over the grain marks in the table. "I suppose on some level I hoped a romance with Mary would encourage you to change. Love often does just that ..."

Curt leaned forward and stared piercingly at Bud's eyes until they met his again and revealed his disconcerted expression. "Do you realize the dangerous position you put Mary in? Do you know what I could have done to her?"

Bud's face reddened, and he looked away. He studied the bar room, his fingers interlocked so tightly his gnarly knuckles were whitening.

"What kind of a father deliberately exposes his daughter to that?"

"I — I didn't know you planned to —" Bud stammered, his grey eyes flicking to and from Curt's brown ones.

"It never crossed your mind? Never?"

Bud wrung his hands and looked away. "Maybe I didn't want to see ... maybe I was so intent on saving you that I forgot about Mary. She has a lot of inner strength, and perhaps I trusted in that too much. God forgive me, it may be." He buried his face in his hands again, but not before Curt saw a tear slip from his eye.

The preacher was fighting desperately to maintain control. Curt reached across the table and gripped his arm. "Don't kick yourself too hard, parson. Guess it proves you're only human, too." He smiled good-naturedly.

After a moment, Bud's hands came away from his face, and he grasped Curt's arm in the same fashion. "Thank you, son." He let go as Curt withdrew his grip.

There was a lengthy pause, during which Curt became aware once again of the noisy bar room and of the scrutiny the two of them were under by some of the patrons. He cleared his throat and straightened in his chair. A moment later, he asked Bud, "You still want me to see Mary?"

Bud nodded.

"Why? Still hope to convert me?"

"No." Bud hesitated then continued. "I want it because Mary wants it. She loves you. But she's hurt, she's confused, and she's a little angry. She does understand that you're hurting and need time to come to terms with your friend's passing. She just wants to be there for you. She wants to help you through it. She believes she meant something to you, but she feels used and discarded. And make no mistake — I'm angry with you for that. But I know there's more to you than that. I know it, and Mary knows it. And I know how you feel about Mary."

Curt came close to squirming in his chair. "You do, huh?" He fished out a new cigar, lit it, and dragged on it deeply before dropping the match in the ashtray.

"Don't start trying to bluff me again," Bud told him, pointing a stubby finger at him. "Maybe you can bluff your way through a poker game, but you can't fool me."

Is that so? stuck in Curt's throat. The old bugger was sharper than he'd given him credit for.

Bud breathed a heavy sigh and spread his palms on the table. Pushing himself to his feet, he picked up his hat and regarded Curt a long moment. Then he pointed his hat at the bunch of dried flowers. "Mary knew I was coming here today. She asked me to give those to you. I'm not certain why she'd want to give you flowers when you've hurt her so. Perhaps they'll mean something to you." He stuck his hat on his head and started to leave then stopped and looked back at Curt. "She's bringing me a late lunch at the shop today. Consider coming by. If you don't want to keep up your relationship with her, just tell her that. Tell her something. Don't leave her never knowing."

Curt gave him no response of any kind. He couldn't. His voice had fled him again. At last, Bud turned and walked out of the saloon. Curt stared after him a long time then dropped his eyes to the clippings. Picking them up, he examined them closely.

A single sprig of lavender in full bloom. A tiny bunch of evening primrose. A single white rosebud. And a note tied around them all. He unrolled it. It read: *Thornapple*. Perhaps she could not find one. His breath stopped halfway into his lungs, and he held it. With her flowery message, Mary had made it plain that she now distrusted him, and she accused him of inconstancy as well as having a heart that was ignorant of love. The thornapple she had been unable to obtain declared his charms deceitful.

He almost grinned. She had learned well.

Damn it. Too well. Even Bud had not brought to the surface all the pain and guilt he'd been feeling over her. Now her little message hit him where it hurt the most, a place he'd tried to hide even from himself — his heart.

Damn it, he wanted her, and part of him did want to be what she wanted. He didn't understand how she could make him even consider having a wife and a little house and maybe even kids. He'd never even thought about that before, never considered changing himself to please anyone else. Fleetingly, since he'd asked Bud for her hand, he'd had the feeling he could actually do it. But he'd been too long a rogue, and there was too much that bound him to this life. He didn't want to leave it. But he knew that if he wanted Mary, he'd have to. He didn't know that he could do that, now or ever.

But Bud was right. Regardless of his decision, he owed Mary the truth. Tomorrow. Maybe tomorrow he'd feel like dealing with it. Cursing aloud, he nearly pounded the table with his fist, but men had already turned their heads to stare at him for his outburst. Snatching up his playing cards, he bolted from the table and nearly vaulted up the stairs to the suite. Locking the door behind him, he strode straight to the bedroom and threw himself upon the bed. He was so tired, so tired of it all. He just wanted to let go, to stop having to try to sort it all out, to make it all make sense. He closed his eyes and threw his arm across them, blocking out the daylight that burned through his lids.

He'd had so many restless nights that sleep claimed him quickly and deeply, swallowing him into a black, empty void. Later, images of Del and Mary flitted in and out of his mind. Even in his dreams, he was trying to push them both away, but the images kept coming back, like waves to a shore.

Half-awake now, he became aware he was dreaming but felt unable to move his body or alter his thoughts. The dream had him, carried him along and tossed him about like driftwood in his own sea. Even at his most restless, even when he was preparing to leave on a poker circuit and anticipating the possibility of bedding a new lovely or two, he had never been so distracted by thoughts of another kind of life or another kind of woman, especially while making love with Del. Del had always made every other female cease to exist when she was here.

Except for Mary Andrews.

He fought his way to the surface of his mind, clawed his way landward and lay, exhausted, on the pebbly shore. He shifted in the big bed, still feeling strangely adrift without the need to disentangle his limbs from Del's to stretch out on his back. He did not want to open his eyes. He wanted to lie here and sleep forever.

With a grunt of disgust, he threw the bed covers clear of himself and stood up on the floor. He tucked his white shirt back into his charcoal trousers, ran his fingers through his tousled hair, and left the suite. Treading down the carpeted stairs to the bar room, he found the rollicking piano tune irritating, the half-filled saloon overcrowded. He headed straight for the kitchen, knowing there was likely a girl or two in there preparing the day's fare, but they would leave him alone. He helped himself to a cup of fresh coffee, nodding a greeting to the girl kneading dough on the flour-covered counter. He took his coffee back out to the bar room, pulled up a chair in a far corner, and sat down.

Why the hell couldn't he stop thinking about this thing with Mary? He should be able to just turn it off like he'd always done with anything that disturbed him. This nagging gnawing at his gut was unacceptable.

Impatient for his coffee, he tested the heat in the cup every minute or two. He found the brew was excellent when he was finally able to drink it. He finished the first cup, got another, and was still churning inside when he downed the last mouthful.

This was ridiculous. He wasn't shaking this off just sitting here. He had to get rid of it. He needed to do something. Shoving himself back from the table, he stood and strode out the main door of the saloon.

Half a block from the Carlton, Curt became aware of his appearance — unwashed, unshaven and, for him, half-dressed. His step faltered once, as he considered going back to first make himself more presentable, but then his sure stride resumed as he rejected the idea. It was unnecessary. Both Bud and Mary would accept him as he was.

Just knowing that made him feel freer than he had in a long time. He snorted at himself for being overly concerned with his appearance. It was important at certain times to present the perfect image, but this was not one of those times. For this particular moment, he could just be who he was, without the artificial armor of the image.

Along the street he noticed a few people giving him second looks as he passed them — they were not used to seeing him less than immaculately dressed, and their faces betrayed their surprise and momentary confusion over just who it was they were looking at.

Despite the rushing in his veins, it seemed to take forever to reach the saddlery. Curt stopped outside the door, which was propped open, and found himself examining everything from the white and yellow paint to the lettering in the window to the scuffed varnish on the hardwood floor just inside the door. His mind had whirled itself blank. He had no idea what he was going to say.

He drew a long, deep breath, filling his lungs to capacity, and stepped over the threshold. As always, his nostrils welcomed the smell of leather. He heard noises from the back room and walked through the empty store to the doorway. The preacher's back was to him, and he seemed hard at work on something.

Curt moved silently through the workbenches. He was a few feet from Bud before he spoke.

"Parson."

Bud's head turned in surprise. He set down his work and faced Curt, a pleased but uneasy look on his face. "Curt — hello."

Curt pointed at the partial side of leather on the bench where Bud had been working. The saddler had been drawing an odd-looking gauged tool along one edge, leaving a cut strip behind it. "What're you working on?"

Bud cast a relieved glance at his work. "Cutting straps," he answered. "I can buy them already cut, but it's cheaper this way. And I get more satisfaction from doing it myself."

Curt nodded, understanding. "What do you call that thing?"

"A draw gauge. Or a strap cutter."

Curt uttered a short, self-derisive chuckle. "Makes sense."

Curt couldn't miss the careful coolness in Bud's voice. "I thought about what you said. I decided you were right, that I oughta talk to Mary. Is she here?"

"She's running an errand for me. She should be back soon."

Curt took his eyes off Bud and looked around the shop. The older man's remoteness disturbed him. "I thought you'd be happy I came."

"You're only here to tell Mary good-bye. Why should I be happy about that?" Bud reached for his work, but his hand fell still and merely lay upon it.

Curt nearly let it pass then decided to say what came to his mind. Facing Bud again, he said, "I thought that was all right with you — you asked me not to leave her hanging. What do you want from me?"

For a second Bud did not even move, but then he answered, "I don't know. I suppose I want the Curt we came to love back with us."

Curt flinched when Bud said *love*. Stiffening, he swallowed. They cared about him enough to call it love?

Bud must have read the question in his eyes, for he said, "Yes. We care about you. Despite your early motives, we care."

Curt looked away again. Damn it, why did Bud have to tell him that? He could feel Bud's emotions reaching out for his, finding the kinship that had developed and wrapping around it, drawing Curt back to a common ground.

"Don't," he said.

"Why not?" Bud's hand was suddenly on his arm. "Why are you so afraid to have somebody care about you? Why are you so afraid to give real love in return?"

Bud's touch burned through Curt's sleeve. His first impulse was to jerk away, but he held himself stiffly, forcing himself to endure it so he wouldn't hurt Bud's feelings. He had an almost overpowering desire to please the man, and he didn't understand why.

"You don't have to change for us, Curt. We'd still like to see you as a friend."

Curt cocked an eyebrow at him. "What about your wife? I can't see her going along with that."

"Sarah will come around."

Curt doubted that. "I figured she'd be guarding the door with a shotgun." When she learned his true intentions, she must have been hell incarnate.

"I know what you're thinking," Bud said, shifting his hand to Curt's shoulder. "Yes, Sarah had her hysterics. Then Mary came home so upset after seeing you the last time that she put them aside. Sarah has her shortcomings like everyone else. But she is still a good woman, and she cares very deeply about her family."

Curt had to take Bud's word for that. Their heads turned simultaneously as Mary called her father from the front of the shop. A twinge of anxiety tightened Curt's stomach. Bud squeezed his shoulder and walked out ahead of him. Curt lagged behind, having to fight a case of nerves that had him scanning the shop for a back door.

"Hi, Dad. I found Mr. Harris and gave him his bridle. Here's the money he gave me for you." Mary sounded cheerful.

"Thank you, dear." There was a hesitancy in Bud's voice that told Curt he was looking behind for him.

"I brought you a roast beef sandwich today, with onions just like you like it."

"Thank you."

Curt heard the scrape of the stool as Bud pulled it back and sat down on it. *Damn it*, he thought. *Get a grip on yourself, Prescott.* Taking a deep breath, he straightened his spine and walked through the doorway into the store.

CHAPTER EIGHTEEN

He riveted his eyes on Mary's face to see her initial reaction to his presence. Her head turned in surprise, and he saw from her expression that she'd expected to see a customer. When she saw it was him, her face paled then flushed red, and she spun around to leave.

"Mary, don't go."

She froze, her back to him, and he saw her fold her arms across her chest. Bud picked up his lunch basket and walked past Curt into the shop. Curt stared at the back of Mary's head, allowing his eyes the pleasure of her long golden-brown hair falling down the middle of her back. She had on a white blouse and a black skirt. His fear began to drain away, replaced by a serene gladness that he was near her again.

"Mary ..."

She neither moved nor spoke.

"Mary, I ..."

"I'm not certain I want you to speak to me."

"I know." He fumbled around with words in his head, but none of them seemed capable of expressing what he wanted her to know. He took a couple of hesitant steps toward her. "I never meant to hurt you."

"Didn't you? I believe that was your intention from the beginning, now that I've had time to think about it. You were going to hurt me and my family to save yourself and your friends."

He stared toward the open windows along the south wall and pulled at his collar with his finger. It was suddenly hotter than he cared to stand.

"How could you?" she asked suddenly, the pitch of her voice strained. She turned her head just enough that he could see her pretty profile. "You planned to seduce me all along, didn't you? That is so — so despicable!"

The way she spat the word out made him cringe with self-loathing. "I thought it was the only way ... but, Mary, I could never hurt you."

"Then what do you call what you planned to do to me? Helping me?"

"I didn't do it, did I?" He spread his hands wide from his sides, as if she could see him appeal her.

Her shoulders lifted and dropped in a huff. "Don't ask me why not. You were so close you could have —."

"I could've ruined a nameless, faceless preacher's daughter, but I couldn't ruin you. Don't you understand?"

"No! No, I don't understand!" She spun around and faced him, her eyes vividly green and flashing with anger. "How could you plan to do that to someone — anyone?"

He dropped his hands to his sides. "I thought I had to discredit your family ... so people wouldn't follow your mother and her committee."

She regarded him with such contempt he shriveled inside. Shaking her head, she looked away from him.

"But I couldn't go through with it." He stepped a little closer to her. "I couldn't do it, Mary. I —."

"You what?" She met his eyes steadily.

A muscle twitched along the lean line of his jaw as he gritted his teeth. His hands clenched into fists at his sides, and he looked away again.

"Maybe you aren't the 'real man' Delores thought you were."

His eyes snapped back to hers, and his lip curled. Damn it, she could hurt him. He'd never wanted a woman, or anyone for that matter, close enough to hurt him like that. He turned and walked up between two rows of saddles, so he wouldn't have to face her. He stopped about half way to the windows and ran his hand over a saddle. It was smooth and supple — wouldn't take long to break in.

"My father says you don't act like you want our friendship anymore. Do you know how worthless and foolish that makes me feel?"

"I'm sorry." He heard her footsteps coming up behind him. She was in the aisle between the saddles, blocking his way back without coming too close.

"If I had any reason to believe that, I might forgive you."

A slight puff of air came in the window, cooling his face briefly but withdrawing before it did him any real good. The loss of it only made him feel hotter. He turned around to face her. "Please believe me. I am sorry."

"I can't believe you. I can hardly begin to sort out what was the truth and what were lies. I hate liars. And I hate myself for nearly letting you make me into one. And I hate that I hate —." She turned her face away, and he saw a tear trickle down her left cheek.

"Mary, you're not hateful. You're just angry. And you have every right to be. Please believe me, I never meant to do this to you."

"Yes, you did!" she cried, meeting his eyes again. "You did! You meant to corrupt me from the beginning! And I let you! I'm so ashamed!" Her hands flew to her cheeks, and she hid her face a moment then brushed away her tears. Then she folded her arms beneath her bosom once again.

He stared at her, feeling her anguish and seeing her fighting back more tears. He wanted to move to her, take her in his arms, and make all her hurt go away. "I didn't really understand the extent of what I was doing. Not at first. But once I did ..." Opening his palms to her, he asked, "What can I do to make things right? What do you want me to do?"

She looked into his eyes a long time, and he saw myriad emotions swelling and ebbing like waves within them. She looked away, wiped her face with her hand, and then tucked it back across her chest. For a second, he was afraid she would not answer him. Then she said:

"Show me what's in your heart. Show me the real Curt Prescott."

Involuntarily he took a step back. That was the hardest thing she could ask him to do.

"Let me see who you really are, so I can know if I love you or the man you were pretending to be." Her left hand dropped from her ribs and fingered the latigo strings of a saddle next to her. Her eyes followed her hand then lifted to his face and gazed at him steadily. "And don't try to fool me. I'll know now if you do."

Swallowing, he believed that she would. His throat was so parched he wondered if his voice would work. But what would he say if it did? If he told her the truth, she would want him to keep his promise of courtship. Perhaps the best thing he could do for both of them was lie. He opened his mouth.

"The truth, Curt."

He lost his track of thought and searched frantically for new words. She was smarter, more perceptive, and stronger than he had even suspected. Damn it, she had him by the balls, and they both knew it. He looked into her eyes and couldn't find the will to lie. As though he were taking a knife, cutting out his heart, and letting his lifeblood pour onto the floor, he opened his mouth and said, "I love you."

Mild surprise and a sort of knowing filled her eyes. She pulled her bottom lip in between her teeth. He stood there, enduring excruciating seconds before she spoke.

"I love you, too. What are we going to do about it?"

That wasn't exactly the response he'd anticipated. His head shook slightly back and forth. His right hand reached for the saddle next to him and gripped the near swell tightly.

"I don't know, Mary. It's too soon for me to even guess ..."

"At least that's an answer." She took a couple of steps toward him, and her manner softened. "Don't you see that's all I'm asking for — to know that we're truly friends, that we truly did share something genuine? Don't shut me out, Curt. Don't mourn her alone. You can lean on me if you need to. If you want to."

"That's never been a habit of mine, relying on someone else, burdening them with my problems."

"We all have problems, Curt. We all need help sometimes. All it takes is a little effort and a little faith in each other."

Leaning on the saddle, he shoved his left hand into his pants pocket. "I just need time ..." Even as he said it, he was overwhelmed with the need to hold her. Quickly he closed the distance between them and took her in his arms before she could object. To his astonishment, she allowed him and snuggled close to his chest.

"I'm sorry, Mary. Part of me wants to be what you want me to be."

She nodded, her eyes shutting against tears. "I know. I just wish —." She lifted her face and gazed up into his eyes.

Reflexively, he bent his head to kiss her but stopped himself. "I should go," he said. "Can I walk you home?"

She shook her head. "I promised to stay and help Dad tidy up."

"All right." He released her, but their hands trailed down each other's arms to fleetingly clasp together. With an effort of will, he tore his eyes from hers and let go of her hands. He stepped back and called to let Bud know he was leaving.

"Okay," Bud replied, appearing in the doorway and brushing sandwich crumbs from his hands on his apron. He approached Curt, and they shook hands. "Thank you for coming. And remember, if you ever get tired of cards, I could sure use a hand around here some days. Might work into something steady."

"Thanks, parson, but ..."

Mary interrupted. "Why don't you take him up on it? Try something new?"

"Because I don't know ... if I could stick with it. I might try it for a while, but I suspect it's not my calling. I'd just go back to poker."

"But at least you'd have tried. I thought gamblers were supposed to be good at taking chances?"

Her remark struck him speechless.

Bud reached and gripped his arm, breaking the sudden awkward silence. "Why don't you come by later and have dinner with us? That'll give you both some time to think."

Curt looked from Bud to Mary, whose eyes were sparkling with hope beneath the heartbreak. He shook his head. They might get the wrong idea if he took them up on it. And then there was still Sarah. "Sorry, parson, but I don't think I can handle an evening with your wife right now. I'll just take a walk."

Bud nodded. "I understand." He reached for Mary's elbow. "Come on, dear. I haven't finished my lunch yet. Keep me company."

Mary met his soft grey eyes then looked again for Curt's. Curt gazed back briefly then tipped his hat to them each in turn and walked out of the saddlery.

His feet carried him swiftly north, past the church and cemetery and through the field that bordered the ridge where the road rose into the forest. His boots swished through the tall late summer grass as he turned toward the creek.

Scrambling down the bank to the trail at the bottom, he almost hollered with relief at the peacefulness, the utter solitude he found there.

It was much cooler in the shade of the overhanging trees, and his nostrils welcomed the moisture in the air, the scent of the damp soil at the creek's edge. The path was soft and muffled his footsteps, so he himself hardly heard them. Above his head an occasional bird twittered and flitted through the leaves from branch to branch, never staying long on one but singing its little song and moving on to the next branch that looked inviting.

Maybe that's what he should do. Right then, packing it all in, and just taking off and leaving everything and everyone behind looked damned appealing to him. He had enough money stored away that he could live more than comfortably the rest of his life without ever lifting a finger again.

But he'd bore himself into an early grave; he knew it. He had to do something with his time. What he needed was something new, something different.

He could travel to the east, maybe, gamble in the big towns. Maybe he'd find the cards more of a challenge with fresh players. That was his problem — it was all too easy now. There wasn't a man in Victoria who could beat him. Even most passers-through hadn't any real skill with the pasteboards. Life had gotten dull. He needed a new challenge.

His feet nearly tripped him up, trying to turn on their own and climb the hill up behind Mary's house. He stopped and looked up to the top for a moment.

Who was he trying to kid? Life was far from dull, but he did need a change. More on target, he needed to make a decision. All he'd really done was maintain the status quo. And even though he was trying not to admit it to himself, that very lack of a real decision was eating him up inside.

He forced his feet to walk on down the path. He had to do something, but he didn't know what he really wanted to do. Grimacing at himself, he knew that wasn't quite true, either. He knew he wanted Mary.

His gut tightened as he allowed the thought into his conscious mind. What would he really gain from a move like that? She wanted marriage and children, and he wasn't sure about either one.

Del had never broached the subject of marriage. They had been committed to each other, and a ceremony had never seemed necessary. Del's ability to bear children had been ruined by a botched abortion long before he'd even met her, so it had never been an issue.

But commitment, above all, was an issue with Mary. She would not tolerate him looking for the pleasures of other women, even occasionally, whereas he suspected Del would have, as long as they were not local. And oddly, he suspected he would not be able to tolerate the guilt he would experience if he strayed from Mary were she his wife.

It didn't make a lot of sense to him, but he knew, somehow, that it was true. He wanted Mary differently than he'd wanted Del. Del had been a great bedpartner, and they had loved each other in their way, but theirs had been more a relationship of convenience. There was something in him she had never been able to satisfy, and he had never truly given her all of himself.

Glancing up at the sunlight breaking through the leaves above, he almost laughed aloud. If anyone had told him even a few months ago that he'd consider tossing everything away for true love, he'd have laughed himself silly. He'd never thought he needed it before, had always thought of it as a lot of romantic foolishness, but he'd never really experienced love before. It was a damned powerful force.

He turned back now, not ready to return to the Carlton. Something else was nudging at him from within, and he felt compelled to seek it out.

As he reached the meadow where he and Mary had often dallied, his feet stopped on the edge and held him there. He surveyed the meadow without hurry, enjoying the long, swaying grass, the sweet scent of it curing where it stood, the dragonflies whizzing through the air while butterflies winged lazily in the sunlight above the ripened seed heads. Wildflowers dotted the field with random spots of color. The leaves of the bigleaf maples were beginning to turn brown with the approach of autumn.

He picked a handful of wild flowers as he walked through the field. Back on the road, he retraced his path as far back as the cemetery. Stepping through the gate, he walked to the center of the enclosure and lowered himself to his haunches next to Lillian Prescott's grave. He placed half of the bunch of flowers before the weathered marker, paused a moment, and then turned and placed the other half at the foot of Del's new one. He sighed and studied the inscription:

Delores—The Loveliest of Wildflowers
With Us Until 3rd August 1877

He rubbed his hands over his face. Losing her, especially the way he had, still hurt. He knew it would ease in time, but for now it still hurt.

He stared at Lillian's marker once again. He still wished he could have changed things for her. His mind retraced everything he knew that had brought them each to their respective places in this life. "What would have been," he asked her softly, "if you'd had the courage to just go home?"

With all that she'd told him about her family, he was almost certain they'd have come round. Or was his a child's naïve fancy? He chuckled. If she had gone home, Curt himself might never have been born. Or, who would he have been if he had been born into her life with a different father, a man who loved her and married her and raised him properly? Would he still have been drawn to the sporting life, or would he have stepped up into his grandfather's flower and nursery business?

He sighed heavily. There was nothing that could be undone. There was only going forward from now.

He spent a few more minutes before the graves then rose to his feet. "Take care of each other," he said and left the cemetery.

The rays of the sun slanted in over the spiky treetops on the western hills as he walked back toward town. The saddlery would be closed now and Bud and Mary gone home. He paused at Pandora Avenue and gazed toward their street, considering, but still was not inclined to spar with Sarah tonight.

Movement caught his eye, and he noted a doe and twin fawns grazing on the overgrown lawn of the Sherman estate. The evening light cast a soft, warm glow on the wood and stone exterior. The terrace appeared burdened under the weight of the unruly Japanese wisteria. He scanned the rest of the gardens and, even from this distance, spotted the occasional ivy or fern, flower or shrub that still claimed its right to exist there. As much a mess as the gardens were, the property was certainly reclaimable. Mature pines, cedars, and Douglas fir supplied privacy and filled the air with their sweet, enchanting fragrances. Oaks, maples, and dogwoods offered a softened view amongst the sentinel-like evergreens and provided extra shade in summer.

If the house itself was salvageable, and he imagined it likely was, it was large enough to convert, say, the west wing into private quarters for himself and the rest of it into a residence, a home, for people in need. A place, perhaps, where, with help, women like his mother and Del could find themselves again.

With a start, Curt snapped his eyes back to the wisteria. That was it. Now he remembered.

Curt's blood began to run faster in his veins, his mind racing in search of ways and hows and possibilities. He was certain Mary would want to be involved, would be interested in running just such an operation. Maybe she could convince members of her mother's committee to take a more positive role in getting people off the streets.

He could provide the necessary funding. He didn't immediately see a role for himself beyond that, but the mansion occupied more than two acres. It would certainly keep him busy taking care of it. But what did he really know about gardens? In reality, nothing. He'd be better off to hire someone and perhaps learn from them as they went. He closed the distance between himself and the wrought iron fence, wrapping his fists around the arrow-like points of the post-tops. His imagination began to clear away the underbrush, replant the flowerbeds, and refinish the exterior of the house.

He'd never gotten inside, but he was certain it could be done. His first move would be to hire the appropriate tradesmen. The suite above the Carlton had become empty without Del, and he would be ready to leave it by the time the work was completed.

He spun round and strode downtown. The bank would be closed but he knew that Avery Watts, the manager, often worked late. Curt would give Watts the best reason he'd ever had to conduct business after hours. He had to get the ball rolling. Then he'd get the keys, and then he'd go get Mary.

Watts was stunned when Curt pounded on the bank's front door but, as Curt had suspected, was willing to start checking in to what it would take to purchase the estate. When they'd completed what they could, Curt took the keys from him, thanked him with an enthusiastic handshake, and headed back toward the mansion.

He made only one more stop, to make a purchase at the florist's shop. While there, he made the man an offer of employment, teaching Curt what he needed to know to look after things properly. The elderly florist promised to consider it and to send young, strong backs Curt's way for the heavy labor. Curt passed by the estate again only to bang on the Andrews' front door. Bud answered the door, and his mouth dropped at the sight of him.

"Curt! What a surprise!"

"I hope I haven't interrupted your dinner, parson, but I really need to borrow your daughter."

Bud's eyes popped with surprise just as Mary and her mother appeared behind him.

"Hello, Mary," Curt said, hardly able to contain a huge grin. "Evening, Mrs. Andrews."

Sarah merely replied, "Hello."

Bud stepped back from the door. "Would you like to come in? We've finished dinner, but I'm sure we could fix you a plate —."

"No, thank you, sir. I couldn't eat right now. I'd really appreciate you allowing me to borrow Mary for an hour or so — I've got something I need to show her, to discuss with her."

Bud turned and met Mary's curious green eyes. "It's up to you, my dear."

Curt held out his hand. "It's not far. But we need to catch the daylight."

"Can't this wait until tomorrow?" Sarah asked, peering outside.

"Please," Curt said to Mary.

She gave him her hand and smiled at her father.

"I expect you both back before dark for tea," Bud commanded with a grin. "And then I want to hear all about this emergency."

"You got it, parson," Curt said and led Mary out the door.

She began to giggle as she hustled up the slate path, trying to keep up with his long strides. "Curt, what is it? What's got you so excited?"

"You'll see," he replied as he closed the little white gate behind them.

He led her straight to the ornate wrought iron front gate of the estate and fumbled with the keys.

"This is where we're going? Why?"

The keys jangled, and the lock clicked and fell open in his hand. He lifted the chain clear and pushed open the gates. Then he took her hand again. "I'm buying it," he announced as he led her onto the grounds.

"What?" Even in her astonishment, Mary's eyes were looking beyond the run-down surface of the estate. Curt could tell she was imagining the lovely landscaping and the impressive home that it once had been.

"Yep. I'm taking your advice, turning over a new leaf, as they say."

"I don't understand," she said, so caught up in his energy she began to giggle again as they strode up the earthen road to the house. "But I think I like it." She halted suddenly, her hand coming to her mouth. "My goodness, that vine is amazing! And those flowers were beautiful when they were out! I thought they were some sort of lilac from the road, but they're not, are they?"

He followed her gaze to the dried, faded flowers draping from the arbors and trellises of the southwest terrace. "No, they're called wisteria, the Japanese variety, I believe."

She moved toward them as though drawn by an energy radiating from the flowers themselves. Mindless of the debris catching her shoes on the stone footing of the terrace, she gazed up at the hanging flowers, dangling seedpods, and twisting woody vines. Twirling slowly beneath them, she reached up and cupped a huge cluster of perfectly preserved blossoms, drawing it closer and burying her nose in it. "I can almost smell it," she declared.

Curt smiled, standing back, letting her enjoy herself. It seemed right, being here with her like this. He drew a deep breath of the fragrant evening air and allowed himself to feel the peace of the place, of the moment. Birds flitted in the branches above them, finding sanctuary for the coming night. The evening air was cooling, and the sun had slipped below the forested hills behind him.

"Oh, Curt, they must have something to say, these ... wisteria," Mary said. "Tell me."

He stepped closer and took her shoulders in his hands. Standing close behind her, he placed his mouth next to her ear.

"They signify cherished friendship and mutual trust. See how thick and strong the vines are ..." He pointed, and she looked up, nodding. "But they still need the support of the trellises to grow and flourish. Without it, they wouldn't survive. Even then, it takes years for the young vines to start flowering. But with the right soil and sun, the proper attention, they thrive and give us these amazing blossoms."

Mary covered his hands with hers and leaned back against him.

"Just imagine this place cleaned up and brought to life again," he said into her ear. "Imagine the gardens and the trees and the flowers all brilliant with life!" He fanned one hand in an arc over their view.

She tilted her head back to look up at him. "I don't think I've ever seen you this enthused!"

"I've decided to claim my birthright. Let's see if I've got the family gift for growing things."

"Curt, that's wonderful!"

"I figure I can build nurseries and greenhouses in the back and do everything right here. The possibilities are endless. I don't know what the house needs, but I'll find out."

"Can you do all that yourself?"

He chuckled. "I wouldn't know where to start. But I can hire the right people to do it, maybe get some folks work that need it."

She smiled up at him. Then, gazing at the mansion again, she said, "But it's so big. How could you live here all alone?"

"Well, I figure a portion of it can be converted to separate, self-contained living-quarters, and the rest can be allotted to something like a home, or whatever the correct term is, to house women who need help getting off the street. That's where you come in."

She turned around to face him. "Me?"

"Yeah." He shrugged. "I figured you've got all these great ideas, you'd want to be the one to run the place."

Mary's mouth opened, and she stared up at him with wide eyes. "You'd let me ...?"

"Let you? Hell, I'll be beggin' you if you don't say yes right away!"

"Oh, Curt!" She threw her arms around his neck and hugged him tight. "I will! You know I will!"

He held her tightly, his nose in her hair, breathing her sweet scent deeply into him. He could hold her like this forever.

"Perhaps we could call it 'Wisteria House'," Mary suggested.

"Whatever you like."

A faint breeze ruffled his shirt, and he became aware of the fading light. Loosening his grip on her, he kissed her forehead.

"I almost forgot." From inside his shirt pocket he brought out the small purchase he'd made at the florist's. "These are for you."

She held up her palms to accept the petite bouquet. "It's adorable," she murmured. "Thank you." Then she tilted her head sideways. "Does it come with a message?"

"Yes. The blue violets promise my faithfulness to you and the dogwood the durability of my love. Beyond that, right now, we'll have to wait and see."

She blinked back sudden moisture in her eyes and held the tiny bouquet to her bosom.

Curt dangled the keys in front of her. "Shall we go in?"

Smiling and gazing up into his eyes, she nodded. He took her hand, and together they walked toward the front door.

END

ABOUT THE AUTHOR

Photo by Debby Strong

A Canadian writer, Chad Strong has had the privilege of living in different parts of this vast and varied country: from Victoria, BC on the west coast, to the Manitoba prairie, to southern Ontario.
He grew up reading fiction and non-fiction of all sorts, from westerns to fantasies, from adventures to history. His writing has followed suit across multiple genres and his short stories have appeared in publications including *Bards & Sages Quarterly*, *Mysterical-E*, *Rawhide'n Roses - a Western Anthology*, and *Frontier Tales*.

High Stakes is his first novel.

Thank you for purchasing *High Stakes*. If you enjoyed reading this book, please consider leaving your review on Amazon or your favorite book-related site.

Visit Chad at:
Website: www.chadstrongswriting.weebly.com
Facebook: www.facebook.com/Chad.Strong.Writing
Amazon: www.amazon.com/author/chadstrong
Twitter: www.twitter.com/chadstrong5

Made in the USA
San Bernardino, CA
09 August 2017